KNOT ALL IT SEEMS

RAELYNN ROSE

TWISTED HEART PRESS LLC

KNOT ALL IT SEEMS

Raelynn Rose

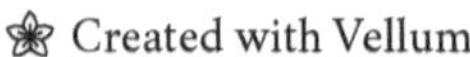 Created with Vellum

CONTENT AND TRIGGER WARNINGS

Before you start Maeve's story, I think I should offer a few warnings. While this book does contain a happily ever after, it is intended for mature audiences only. As an alternate universe story, there are mentions of knots, heats, breeding, and lots of detailed and spicy sex scenes that may contain more than two participants as well as MM and MFMM scenes. If that's not for you, turn back now.

Trigger warnings:

This book contains graphic sex, violence, cursing, mentions of past domestic violence, torture, and degradation (NOT by MCs). I tried to do my best to broach varying subjects with as much sensitivity, but please take care of yourself and stop reading if anything triggers a sense of anxiety or fear.

Wait! Have you joined the party yet? Oops...I meant the newsletter! Keep up to date on releases, cover reveals, and giveaways. You can join here!

CHAPTER 1

<u>Wilder</u>

The bar was packed per usual for a Friday night. But tonight, there were a lot more members of law enforcement, guards of Omega Change, and Omega Rescue and Extraction than usual. We'd all been working long ass shifts since the protestors came out against Omega Change – a company that aided in finding omegas housing, providing security, and helped them to attain education as well as suitable and safe jobs.

After six consecutive fourteen hour shifts, I finally got the night and the next two days off. And I planned to spend those either drunk or sleeping.

"That shit feels like it'll never end," Kai, my boss and friend, grumbled before tipping back his bottle and finishing off his drink. "I got to get home. See my mates. Get some rest, brother. I'll see you in a week."

"Two days," I said.

"Yeah. That."

I chuckled as he slapped a twenty on the bar top to cover his one beer and left, raising a hand over his shoulder before stepping through the door.

A week away from the screaming, threatening alphas and the counter protestors who were as loud – though not as violent – would have been a fucking vacation, even if I'd stayed home and done nothing but watch TV, eat junk, and polish my knob a few times.

But I could work with two days. I would wake up, eat, drink a few beers, then nap. Rinse and repeat.

As much as this current bullshit was stressing us all out, it was better than the missions I'd gone on in the past when I'd been a member of ORE. While I'd had to fire my weapon recently, even killed a couple of alphas who'd broken into Omega Change's headquarters and attacked the guards while trying to get to the omegas who lived upstairs, it wasn't a common occurrence. That had been the first and only time I'd had to discharge my firearm in my time with Omega Change.

A few fellow guards from Omega Change were scattered around the bar, seated at tables with their packs, or pulled up to the bar like me drinking beers or shots.

My plan was to tie one on and wander down the sidewalk to my apartment three blocks away. Then, if I was lucky, I could flop onto my bed and pass out cold for the next ten or twelve hours. Preferably twelve. Or more.

I swore I hadn't slept a full night since all this started, constantly struggling with the adrenaline or the nightmares that had plagued me since my first mission with ORE.

With my elbows resting on the bar top, my attention wavered from the game on the TV hung over the rows of liquor bottles to the mirror that hung just below.

I hated giving my back to any room, but there were enough of my former and current coworkers here I wasn't worried about anyone starting shit with me or attacking me from behind. Not that I'd earned the ire of anyone in particular recently, but those of us who fought against the douche canoes with the antiquated opinions about the rarest designation didn't exactly wear masks to hide our identities. All it would take was one asshole to spot one of us in public and decide to play Billy Badass.

"You want another?" the bartender asked, already reaching for a fresh beer before I could answer.

With a chuckle, I nodded. "Yeah. Thanks."

She set it on a fresh coaster and slid it toward me before moving down the bar to refresh drinks, take orders, and clear empties.

A flash of fire caught my attention in the mirror, jerking my gaze to the scene behind me. Not fire. Flaming red hair on a woman who couldn't stand more than a few inches over five feet tall. Omega. With her hair down, I couldn't see whether a bond mark decorated her neck or shoulder. And there were far too many scents in here to discern which was hers or whether she carried the scent of an alpha mate.

Bonded or not, I couldn't tear my eyes from her as she moved through the crowd as though she didn't have a care in the world, like she didn't give a fuck that she was surrounded by alphas and betas.

Her head turned as though she could feel my eyes on her, but I had a feeling I wasn't the only one watching her.

But when her eyes locked on mine in the mirror, my breath caught in my chest for half a heartbeat. Gold eyes. Not brown. Not green. Gold. Like the finest honey in sunshine.

She continued to push her way through the crowd, watching me as though leery of taking her eyes from me. I wasn't the threat. I would never be a threat to her or any of her designation.

She didn't know that. All she knew was a man was watching her closely.

When her eyes tore from my face, it felt like I'd been shaken awake from a dream and could finally take in a full breath of air.

I couldn't fucking help myself – I turned on my stool and watched her waist length red hair move through the crowd, noting all the sets of eyes on her.

What the hell was she doing here alone? I had zero problems with omegas doing whatever the fuck they wanted with their lives, but there were so many fuckwads who could hurt her. A podcast had come out within the year encouraging alphas and even betas to claim omegas against their will, to dark bond them. While none of us who worked to protect innocent men and women would stand by and let anyone hurt her, it was still risky for an omega to be out alone.

As though my thoughts conjured the scenario, someone approached her, wrapping a hand around her bicep and turning her a little too roughly.

When she tilted her head back to look into the alpha's face, there wasn't an ounce of fear or concern in those striking eyes. In fact, she looked pissed. And…was that a smile ghosting the corners of her full lips.

Before I could fully climb to my feet, the tiny omega raised a hand quickly and planted the palm of her hand directly into the alpha's nose before slamming her knee into his balls. The fucker's nose gushed blood as he cupped his junk and doubled over.

The crowd of guards cheered as she swung her left fist and punched the alpha in the face, knocking him to the ground.

Even now, she didn't look as though she was the least bit worried or even rattled.

Two alphas approached through the crowd, one with shoulder length wavy dark hair, the other a few inches taller, standing somewhere around six feet five or six inches tall. They ducked their heads, their backs to me. She was staring up into the faces, nodding as they spoke.

Then her shoulders rose and fell as though she'd sighed in frustration before stepping into the side of the giant alpha and letting him escort her from the room.

And yep, I followed her progress through the place as though my eyes were drawn to her like a fucking magnet. That was, by far, one of the sexiest fucking things I'd ever seen. That tiny omega put that alpha on his ass without so much as breaking a sweat.

Just before she stepped out, she turned her head and looked directly at me. And I could have sworn that one look seared itself into my very soul.

I had never been a big believer in love at first sight. But fuck me if that tiny redheaded badass omega hadn't changed my mind.

The door closed behind her and it felt like the air in the room became suffocating as noise finally filtered back into my brain.

Fuck. What was I doing? I couldn't let her simply walk away, not without at least hearing her voice, learning her name.

I assumed those two alphas were her packmates, and no fucking way would I ever try to come between an omega and her alphas, but I needed…

Fuck. I didn't know what I needed. All I knew was the moment our eyes had touched in that mirror it felt like some kind of invisible band had been connected between us and the further she moved away the tighter it stretched until I felt as though something inside me was about to crack.

The stool wobbled as I shoved to my feet and practically plowed through the crowd in an attempt to catch up with the mystery woman. Ideas of what to say to her rushed through my mind. I would simply tell her I was concerned about her, maybe flash my badge and tell her I wanted to see if she'd injured her hand.

Cool air rushed across my skin as I pushed through the door and hurried across the lot, swinging my head left to right in search of bright red hair and two towering alphas.

"You're bringing too much attention to yourself," a male said.

"He put his hands on me," the woman said. Her voice was soft, sweet, with a touch of rasp.

"There was no reason for you to be here in the first place," the other male said.

"You came out for one reason only. How far would you have taken it if we hadn't found you?" the first male said.

I didn't bother slowing my steps nor hiding my approach. She didn't sound as though she'd been forced to leave, but she didn't sound overly happy that she'd been discovered at the bar.

"One more arrest and we might not be able to keep the feds off your ass."

That one statement drew me up short as I rounded a row of vehicles to find the trio speaking.

"I wouldn't have gotten arrested. There were plenty of witnesses who would have spoken up. I was minding my business. *He* touched *me*. I defended myself."

Hell, I was one of those witnesses and would have made that exact statement.

"That wouldn't have gone so smoothly if you'd killed him."

Shit. What? Killed him? She was half the alpha's size and had merely kicked his ass a little. I'd never heard of anyone dying from bruised balls.

"You have to be more careful, Maeve. You're under the microscope more than ever. The world is watching every fucking omega."

The wind picked up and three heads whipped in my direction as my scent carried to them on the breeze.

"Didn't mean to scare you. I'm Wilder Bratton. I'm a guard with Omega Change. Just wanted to make sure you were okay. Do you need to have your hand looked at?" In my head, my reason for being out here had sounded like a solid excuse.

But the way the three were looking at me made me feel as though I'd just made a bit of a fool of myself.

"She's fine," one of the alphas said.

My eyes darted to his face. "I was asking her. I need *her* to answer."

"*Her* has a name. Maeve. And I'm fine," she said, holding out her hand and wiggling her fingers as though she hadn't just cracked a dude across the face less than ten minutes before. "Thanks for your help, officer, but I'm fine."

Shaking my head, I offered what I hoped was a disarming – and charming – smile. "Not an officer. Just a guard. Former ORE, though."

"Great. Awesome. Like I said, I'm fine."

Maeve glanced up at one of her alphas and nodded. Then, as though they'd rehearsed it, they climbed into the SUV they'd stood beside talking. Maeve slid into the back, swinging the door shut after one last glance in my direction.

And then they pulled away, leaving me watching them go.

That...had not gone the way I'd hoped. I had a name, I'd heard her voice, but...nope. Not the scenario I'd conjured in my mind.

One more arrest...

The feds...

That wouldn't have gone so smoothly if you'd killed him...

That was a whole lot in such a short conversation. The two had spoken as though she was a seasoned criminal, as though she were on some kind of watch list rather than an at-risk omega alone in public.

She'd been right – had someone called the police or had she accidentally killed the man, any one of the more than two dozen people in the bar would have declared it a justified killing. Self-defense.

But...fuck, I might have been imagining shit, but it sure as shit sounded as though the alphas were warning her against repeating a prior behavior, as though she'd killed someone before. And, obviously, she'd been arrested in the past. For what?

The alphas were right – omegas were under a microscope more than ever because of the podcast and the subsequent protests that had involved violence, resulting in deaths and millions of dollars in property destruction.

Who was that woman? And had I just let a possible threat drive away?

With a shake of my head, I stepped back inside, paid my tab, and headed home, the memory of that sexy redhead clocking the alpha playing on loop in my mind.

CHAPTER 2

<u>Maeve</u>

"What the fuck were you thinking?" Owen growled from the passenger seat as Beckett aimed the vehicle for home.

"She wasn't. That's the problem," Beckett said.

I sat with my arms crossed, watching through the windshield and ignoring the glances in the rearview mirror from Beckett.

"Do you realize how many fucking cops were in that bar? Of all places–"

"I just needed to get out of the house."

"You could have asked one of us to take you out. Instead, you snuck away and almost got your ass in trouble again because, what, you had to release some pent-up energy?" Owen growled.

A smile bloomed unbidden on my face at the memory of that douche doubling over, of the crunch from his nose when I'd slammed the heel of my hand against it, the groans of pain as he'd hit the floor.

He'd deserved it. They always did.

And yep. Owen was right. I'd had too much energy boiling under the surface. It had to come out one way or another. And since my little pack refused to spar with me, I had to take it out on someone. What better way than teaching an asshole alpha the world didn't belong to him?

"You have to be more careful," Beckett said. He turned and frowned at me. "There's only so much we can do if the feds take notice of your...extracurricular activities."

"I am careful," I protested, jutting my chin in defiance.

"Really? Need I remind you again of how many fucking cops and ORE members were in that fucking place?" Owen said, his voice growing louder with each word.

"Hey. That...guard or whatever came out to check on *me*. Not arrest me. Not question me. It was self-defense. I'm just an omega. A victim, right? And that alpha grabbed *me*, not the other way around."

"And if that asshole's friends had decided to jump in to help him?" Beckett said, turning in his seat to raise a brow at me.

"Like Owen said – *there were so many fucking cops in that place.*" I lowered my voice in my best impersonation of the grouchy alpha.

My grouchy alpha.

We weren't...conventional. Yeah. My alphas loved me. I loved them. But instead of showering me with gifts or doting on me, they'd ensured I'd been well trained in hand-to-hand combat and every possible weapon known to the free world. At least the ones they could legally get their hands on.

And we often shared a bed, but to...well, sleep. I had a hard time allowing anyone access to my body outside of my heat. Even with my cycle, my alphas had procured suppressants so I could put it off as long as possible. I knew they hated that I took them, but only because there was very little research as to the effects of long-term usage of the pills.

What did it say about me that I was more concerned with perfuming around alphas than the possibility of infertility?

A giggle bubbled in my chest, but I swallowed it down. My alphas wanted a family. I knew that. But they knew I was...broken. They'd found me that way and knew it would take a lot more than a soft, pretty nest to convince me I was safe enough to give my heart, mind, and body to anyone freely.

It wasn't that I didn't trust Owen and Beckett. They'd done everything in their power to convince me of that since the day we'd met. Or rather the day they'd saved me from hell.

I wasn't sure I trusted myself. I didn't want to risk giving birth to a child that might one day present as omega or alpha. What if I didn't love them because of that? What if I wasn't able to look at my alpha son and see the child I birthed instead of another monster?

But Owen and Beckett weren't monsters. It had taken over a year for them to prove that to me, for me to be comfortable sleeping in the pack bed with them without fear they would touch me against my will.

"We just don't want you to get hurt," Beckett said after a long stretch of silence.

Owen pulled the vehicle into the garage, waiting for the door to rumble closed behind us before killing the engine and pushing open his door.

He pulled my door open and waited, his eyes boring holes into my head.

Shaking my head, I crossed my arms over my chest like a petulant child. "I'm not getting out if you're going to lecture me for the rest of the night."

"We're not lecturing you. We're your alphas. It's our job to protect you. And we can't do that if you intentionally seek out trouble every night."

My lips twitched at the corners as I reluctantly slid from my seat, hopping down from the backseat. "It's not *every* night."

"How the hell did you even get an uber all the way out here?" Beckett asked as they both followed me inside.

The house was entirely too big for the three of us. I assumed the two had hoped to add to the pack someday, whether through packmates or kids.

Tugging my jacket off, I hung it in the mudroom then kicked off my shoes, lining them up beside the boots I wore when we trained out back.

"I want to know how the fuck we didn't know she'd left. How the hell did the systems not alert us to the arrival of a car?" Owen said.

Easy. I'd disarmed the motion sensors, snuck out of the house, and waited to be picked up at the end of the driveway, out of range of the security system surrounding the property and house. But if I voiced that out loud, there was a good chance one of my alphas would change the security code. Not that I was a prisoner. But both of them always worried I would end up hurt or captured...again.

Before I could make a beeline for my bedroom to shower and change, Owen stepped into my path. They both knew better than making a grab for me, especially if I didn't see it coming.

"We need to talk about this, Maeve. We can't protect you if you keep sneaking off. We...I can't..." He inhaled through his nose and blew it out through his mouth in a rush of air. "I can't lose you, Maeve. You're my omega. You're my best friend."

I don't know whether either of my alphas loved me past the bonds of being packmates. But even that was enough for me. And I hated that I had caused the look in his eyes. I hated that I was a constant source of stress for them.

"I'm sorry," I said after a few minutes of looking from one of them to the other. They both wore matching expressions of fear and concern. They weren't mad at me for wandering off alone and intentionally looking for an alpha to punish.

They feared they wouldn't find me one day. They feared the government would grow tired of arresting me and list me as feral. They feared an alpha would get the best of me one day and either hurt me, dark bond me regardless of the marks on my shoulder, or worse, kill me.

Two years ago, death would have been welcomed. But in the time I'd spent with Beckett and Owen, I had learned to find an outlet for the anger that burned through my veins every day. I'd found love, even if it wasn't the romantic kind. I'd found a family, even if they were more like my best friends than lovers.

Stepping forward, I wrapped my arms around Owen's waist and pressed my cheek against his chest. "I'm sorry. You're right."

His big strong arms wrapped around me, his cheek resting on top of my head. "We love you, baby girl. We need you to be safe."

"I know. It was stupid."

After a few seconds, I stepped away and turned my head when Beckett bent to press a kiss to my cheek. "Go shower. You smell like an ash tray. Pack bed tonight. You scared the shit out of us."

"Pack bed. I'll meet you there," I promised before hurrying off to my personal bedroom.

I had my own area, a seating room, bedroom, and nest. But I rarely segregated myself anymore, not since growing closer to my two alphas. We often shared the pack bed, especially after nights like tonight when their alpha sides needed reassurance that their omega was still in one piece and home safe and sound.

As I stripped and tossed my clothes into the hamper, a new face played through my mind. Wilder. Wilder who was formerly with Omega Rescue and Extraction but now played guard for Omega Change.

I'd noticed him watching me through the mirror when I'd stepped into the bar. I'd seen him climb to his feet when that alpha grabbed me. Then he'd followed us outside to check on me.

For the first time in a long damn time, a man had caught my attention and it had nothing to do with the urge to punish anyone for my past.

It didn't hurt that his light oranges and sweet cream scent told me he was a beta. *Safe.* He was safe. He wasn't an alpha.

Though he was sure big enough to pass as one.

While he wasn't as tall as Beckett or as broad through the chest and shoulders as Owen, he was bigger than the average betas I'd met through my life.

And he was part of law enforcement. Meaning he was the last person I needed to think about when I was naked in the shower.

But...there had been something about him, something that made me almost feel guilty about causing a scene in the bar.

When I'd first spotted him watching me, there had been something in his eyes, a weariness. Not just like he'd had a hard day, but like life had beat him down for far too long. And then something had entered them, a lightness, and a part of me liked the thought that maybe *I* had caused him to perk up a little.

After washing my hair and scrubbing the cigarette smoke and sweat from my skin, I rinsed and dried off, wrapping another towel around my hair. Even as I applied my skin care for the night, Wilder's stormy gray eyes flashed through my mind. Why had he looked so sad, so tightly wound?

And what had made him follow me outside to check on me when I obviously had a pack? Well, two alphas. Still a pack, though.

Could...could he have hoped for more than the attitude I'd given him when he'd asked whether I was injured, if I'd needed medical attention? Could he have been attracted to me?

More importantly...did I want the attraction of another man? I knew my alphas were physically attracted to me, that they would love more from me than the nightly cuddles in the pack bed or the offered cheek when they bent to kiss me.

But even though they'd proven they would never hurt me, I still feared what would happen to my mostly splintered mind and fractured heart if I were to give myself wholly to my alphas or anyone else for that matter.

It didn't matter. None of that mattered. I would never see Wilder again because I didn't plan on returning to that bar again.

After pulling on a pair of panties and some pajamas, I brushed out my long, red curls, then headed toward the pack room where Beckett and Owen waited, their backs against the headboard, the television playing on low.

No silence. I couldn't sleep with silence. I couldn't sleep in pitch dark, either.

And my alphas took care of me the best way they could. There were times where I felt like a failure of an omega. I didn't beg for their attention, didn't strip and spread my legs any time either of them got a boner. Yet they still accepted me, broken pieces and all. They loved me.

I loved *them*…in my own way. Or at least to the best of my ability. There was always the fear if I let them get too close, I would lose them. They owned the last slivers of my heart, and their loss would completely destroy me.

Maybe I should tell them. Maybe I should tell them exactly how much they meant to me in case there came a day when I no longer had the voice, no longer had the chance to tell them what their support had meant to me.

Not tonight.

Even as I thought about uttering those words while their eyes watched me move across the room, anxiety burned through my veins and increased my heart rate.

Owen's brows puckered as I neared. He'd caught the change in my scent but didn't ask. They never asked. They never pushed. They were simply there for more.

Damn it.

"I love you," I blurted out as I climbed up the end of the bed to settle between them.

There was a sharp intake of breath but that was the only reaction. The fact neither of them reacted helped me settle, helped ease the painful thumping of my heart behind my ribs. Had either of them made a big deal of it, I might have reverted to the beginning of our life together and clambered out of the bed to hide away for the rest of the night. Or the rest of the week.

I'd said it. Even as I'd tried to talk myself out of it, I'd told them how I felt. And the world had yet to crumble around me.

At least for the moment.

CHAPTER 3

<u>Wilder</u>

Two days wasn't nearly enough to rest. It didn't help that I'd spent nearly every waking moment fixated on that redhead.

For some reason, she'd stuck with me to the point of obsession. Not like she was the first beautiful omega I'd met in my life. Hell, Violet was a gorgeous omega and she was one of my best friends. More like a sister.

But Maeve...there was something about her, like a mystery I needed to solve. The things her alphas had said to her before they'd realized I was approaching made me wonder what kind of trouble she'd been in in the past. But without a last name, it would be more difficult to find her in the system.

How many omegas named Maeve could there be in the area, though?

Maybe after my shift, I'd run through the database and see if I couldn't find a little more information. I didn't want to get her flagged by snooping, but I had to know more about her, even if I never saw her again.

Although…if I found enough information, if I learned more about her, I might be able to accidentally bump into her, get her number, and see if I couldn't woo her.

She had a pack. She had alphas. That didn't mean she wouldn't be open to a beta in her life. Did it?

"What crawled up your ass?" Kai asked as he shouldered his way through the guards to take a post beside me.

"Nothing."

"You're scowling like you smell dog shit."

I huffed a surprised laugh. "Just lost in thought." About a gorgeous redhead with a hell of an upper cut. "How's little Lara doing?"

"Growing like a weed. She's officially walking and trying to talk."

Kai and his mate, Sophie – the omega who'd opened Omega Change – had given birth to a sweet little baby girl just over a year ago. They'd also added a beta to their pack while Sophie was still pregnant. Kai had said many times through the years that he didn't want a pack, yet Sophie had worn him down. Now, they had their tiny pack of three…four if you counted the baby girl all three of them adored.

Maybe my obsession with the redhead was because I'd grown lonely. Over and over, I'd watched as my friends and coworkers found their mates, found their packs, and fell in love.

And here I was, still single, still living alone.

Movement across the parking lot caught my attention. The protestors reorganized day after day, even after they'd been tear gassed last year while attacking one of Omega Change's employees while leaving a news interview.

Day after day, they congregated outside the now empty Omega Change office building, as though the office complex itself was a symbol to fight against. These assholes wanted the laws changed. They wanted omegas to be required to register with the government.

They wanted laws against omegas in the workplace, citing the possibility of violence if they happened to perfume in public, as though they had any control over the actions of alphas.

Out of the dozens of alphas chanting and cursing, what had drawn my attention?

There. A shock of bright red moving through the crowd, there and then gone just as quickly.

Someone moving through the crowd wouldn't normally be of any concern, but the height was too low. Omega. There was an omega swimming in the sea of sharks. And something about that fiery red color let me know exactly who was currently infiltrating the enemy.

What the fuck was she doing?

Darting across the parking lot, keeping a tight hold on my rifle, I ignored Kai's questions and searched the crowd for that red hair again. How the hell had no one noticed her? Surely, her scent would give her away. Although she could very well have been using scent blockers.

But she was tiny. Perhaps the men thought she was a beta. Still, she was a lone woman in a crowd of violent, misogynistic men.

I had to get to her and drag her ass out of there before someone caught on. Where the fuck were her alphas? Why the fuck would they let her wander out here like this all alone?

"Wilder!" Kai yelled at my back as I ran closer.

Some of the protestors might see this as an attack. But I didn't give a fuck. I needed to find Maeve and get her out of the lion's den before the mob noticed her and attacked.

There. The shock of red was moving along the back now, away from the crowd. Her head lifted and her eyes locked on mine for a brief second before doing a double take. And the fear and confusion lit up her beautiful honey gold eyes.

"Hey!" I yelled, chasing after her.

What the hell had she been up to? For a moment, I'd thought she was trying to rile up the crowd, maybe pick a fight. But she was moving toward an alleyway now.

Boom!

The explosion shook the ground as smoke tickled my nose. Screams of panic erupted. Feet thundered against the pavement as everyone dispersed, running from the unknown threat.

It wasn't unknown to me. Everything I'd heard last night began to come into focus.

The tiny omega was a bit of a domestic terrorist, a vigilante. And, unfortunately, both were crimes in this state.

"Maeve!" I bellowed, my longer legs eating up the space between us quickly.

Others were running behind me and I could only hope it was other members of law enforcement and not alphas wanting revenge for whatever damage she'd just caused.

"Stop!" I yelled as I reached for her.

But since I'd seen how quickly she reacted to being touched, I was able to duck as her fist swung toward my face.

"Maeve. Stop," I said, lowering my voice and ducking another swing. "I'm Wilder. We met a few nights ago. I need you to stop."

Her nostrils flared as she sucked in gulps of air.

Kai and another guard, Keaton, flanked her on each side.

"What did you do?" Kai asked. "What was that?"

"Nothing. They needed to leave. I made them leave."

"By setting off a bomb?" I asked, my brows pulling low.

The omega was beautiful and smelled like absolute bliss, a combination of spring rain and something citrusy like lemons, but I couldn't let my newfound obsession with her negate the fact she'd endangered lives.

"It wasn't a bomb," she said with a roll of her eyes. She yanked her arm from my grasp and turned in a slow circle as though making sure she was able to see the men surrounding her. Two alphas and me.

She couldn't have been too afraid of alphas if she'd willingly inserted herself smack dab in the middle of them to set off what she claimed was nothing more than a diversion tactic. Perhaps she didn't understand the risks of those who might have been close to the benign grenade. Had anyone been too close, they could have endured burns. There could have been debris that might have hit someone in the head.

If anyone had been injured due to her actions, she would be charged and there wasn't a fucking thing I could do about it.

CHAPTER 4

<u>Maeve</u>

I sat in an office with cuffs locked around my wrists. Not the first time I'd been handcuffed. Although, no one had bothered frisking me too thoroughly. As far as any of the men currently looking in my direction and whispering about me knew, I was hiding some kind of weapon under my bra or underwear.

Not that I was. I'd left my one and only weapon for the assholes back in the parking lot.

"She has a pack," Wilder said, his voice rising over the others. "Just call her alphas."

"She's lucky there were no injuries, Wilder," the big dark-haired alpha, Kai, said before shooting me a glare. I assumed he was in charge. Or at least over Wilder since he was the one who'd demanded I be detained for questioning.

"Well, there weren't. She just scared the shit out of a bunch of assholes." Wilder smirked in my direction and I fought the urge to smile at him.

Both Kai and Wilder looked at me with something that sure looked a lot like respect. Even if Kai was still angry over the fact I'd caused so much chaos. But I'd known what I was doing. I'd known the concussion grenade wouldn't cause any major damage as long as I didn't leave it too close to any of the protestors. *More like assholes.*

"No one got hurt," I muttered, pulling my eyes from them and lifting my chin defiantly. "I knew they wouldn't get hurt. I'm not an idiot." I'd learned my lesson about what I should or shouldn't use in those kinds of situations. Owen was right; eventually, they wouldn't be able to get me out of trouble.

"That you know of. There's always a chance someone could have gotten hurt when they trampled over each other to get away from what they thought was a fucking bomb," Kai said.

"Hey, they shouldn't have been there to begin with," I said.

"She has a point," Wilder muttered under his breath as he fought a smile.

I sucked my lips into my mouth to hide my own at his words. He was trying to defend me. But this could be over his head. It would be up to Kai or even the local police if any charges were filed against me.

"Why don't we call her alphas and have her picked up?" Wilder offered.

Yeah. They should do that. Because it wasn't like my alphas would lock me in a tower.

Although there was a real good chance the security code would absolutely be changed this time. There would be no way for me to leave the house without alerting Owen and Beckett.

So...I guessed that meant I *would* be locked up, just without the tower.

Shit.

"You don't need to call my pack. I'm sure they're busy." Which wasn't a lie. They would be on the clock. The two ran a small private security company, installing systems for at risk or wealthy people.

Kai raised one brow. "Call her pack," he said while looking right in my eye.

They didn't have either Owen's or Beckett's numbers.

Wilder lifted the phone they'd taken during the short pat down they'd done when they'd first taken me into custody and brought it to life. Then he carried it over, stepped behind me, and used my fingerprint to open it.

Well, damn. I should have used a code instead of my print.

There were only two numbers saved in my phone, three if you counted my favorite take out place, so it wouldn't be hard for Wilder or Kai to figure out who to call.

The beta's soft gray eyes were on me as he touched a number and put the phone to his ear.

"This is Wilder Bratton, guard with Omega Change. We met a few nights ago...yeah. In the parking lot. I currently have your omega here at the Omega Rescue and Extraction headquarters...yes, sir."

Yes, sir? I nearly barked out a laugh at his formality.

"There was...an incident at the rally today. We'll need you to pick up your omega."

"Maeve. My fucking name is Maeve," I said as irritation over constantly being referred to as someone's property caused my emotions to override all logical thought.

"Do you need the address?...Great. We'll see you then."

Wilder ended the call then set my phone on the desk beside me.

"Let me guess...they're on their way?" I asked when he looked down into my face.

Kai snorted a sound that was part frustration, part amusement. "And I thought Sophie was a handful."

He left the room, leaving Wilder and I alone.

"This isn't your first rodeo," he said, rolling a chair from a desk and parking it across from me before lowering into it. "How long is your record?"

"Look it up. You have all those fancy computers. I'm sure I'm in your database."

"I *would* except you've refused to give us anything more than your first name. You realize the only reason I was able to get you released is because of your designation."

"Right. Because we poor little omegas must be protected at all times." I batted my lashes and put on my best show of submission.

"Yes. You must. At all times," he said, his head nodding in an exaggerated motion. "Because had a single one of those fuckers noticed you sneaking around beside them..." He didn't finish his sentence. He didn't need to. The disgust and horror in his eyes said it all.

"I didn't hurt anyone..." *This time.* I left those words off. No reason to let him know it wasn't my first incident and probably wouldn't be my last.

"You've got to be more careful." He rolled his chair closer until our knees were almost touching and I realized it suddenly grew harder to breathe as the taste of a creamcicle melted on my tongue.

The strangest desire for this beta to reach forward and touch me flitted through me until I consciously willed myself to sit back as far as my cuffed wrists would allow. I winced as the metal bit into my skin, but refused to take my eyes off the man who was officially in my personal space.

"Here. Turn around," Wilder said, reaching for me.

I moved back against the chair as far as possible, ignoring the pain. "Why?" I didn't even bother to hide the suspicion.

"So I can take off the cuffs. You look like they're hurting you."

"Oh...yeah. They are."

Scooting forward, I gasped when his knees bumped against mine, his body heat radiating through our clothes, and turned enough to reveal my wrists without putting myself at risk by fully giving him my back.

Keys jangled a second before first one cuff was released then the other.

Quickly turning back in my seat, I rubbed at the tender skin around my wrists, frowning at him.

Wilder tossed the keys onto the desk beside my phone and leaned back in his seat, the springs squeaking with the movement.

"So what's your story?" he asked after studying me a few seconds.

"What do you mean?"

"I've never met an omega who...attacks alphas. I've never met a single omega who would have been willing to barge right into the middle of that insane mob."

"They didn't know I was an omega."

"Scent blockers," he said with a nod as though he'd come to some conclusion. "But why? Are you a member of some counter-protest?"

"*Ha!*" I burst out before lifting my hand to cover my mouth. "No. I'm not a member of any organization."

He leaned forward, resting his elbows on his knees, and watched me. And something about Wilder was both calming and disarming while anxiety inducing. I had a feeling the anxiety had everything to do with the fact I found myself wanting him to move even closer, that I still had the urge to touch him, or for him to touch me.

Before I could make a fool of myself, the front door opened and two extremely angry alphas stormed in, their eyes moving around the room until they settled on me.

"Are you fucking kidding me?!" Owen boomed over the noise of the office.

Wilder lunged to his feet and moved until he was blocking me from my pack. Ballsy being as they were both bigger than him. And they were *my* alphas which would make them more possessive of me.

"I need you both to calm down," Wilder said, holding his hands out in front of him as Owen and Beckett approached.

"What happened this time?" Beckett asked, but his eyes were on me, not Wilder.

"She set off a concussion grenade at the rally downtown—"

"Protest. It was a protest. They were protesting omega freedom," I bit out, slowly unfolding myself to stand.

Stepping around Wilder, I inhaled deeply, sucking in his sweet scent before closing the space between me and my pack.

"Any injuries or property damage?" Beckett asked.

"None that have been reported," Wilder said. "For now, we're choosing not to charge her with anything. But if one of the protestors decides to pursue charges…"

"You could always lie and say you didn't know who was responsible," I muttered under my breath.

"Except my boss and others witnessed you fleeing the scene and being detained," Wilder said with a smirk.

Was it me or was he entertained by what I'd done? Kai seemed pissed. Wilder...he didn't seem like the kind of guy who was rattled by much. Or at least he hadn't exactly been upset that I'd chosen to disrupt the assholes' little party outside of a building that was supposed to be helping those of my designation.

And he'd stepped in front me when my alphas arrived as though to protect me from my own pack.

"Can I get a guarantee from you that you'll stay away from any future *protests*," he said with a smile, "and alpha filled bars? At least for a few days?"

"She'll stay away," Owen said, glaring down at me.

Wilder's brows dropped and he pushed a hand through his light brown hair. Turning his back to my alphas, he lowered his voice and bent at the waist until we were almost eye to eye. "Are you safe to return home with them?"

A snort came out as I tried to hold back the giggle. "Them? Yes. I'm absolutely safe."

In fact, they were the only alphas in my entire life that I trusted. They'd spent a long time earning that trust and proving that not everyone of their designation was the same.

His gaze bounced back and forth between my eyes before he lifted my phone that was still on after he'd called my pack and dialed a number. A second later, a phone chirped in his back pocket.

"My number is in your phone. If you have any issues or need anything..."

What if I just want to have phone sex?

I swallowed back the burst of laughter that threatened to explode from me at that thought. Phone sex would not only ensure I could get off without anyone touching me, but a stranger wouldn't get a glimpse of what I hid from the world. Only my alphas had seen the permanent scars littering my body and that was only during my cycle when I had no choice but allow them to help me through the fever and pain.

They'd gasped the first time they'd seen them, had questioned me, had been enraged and determined to hunt down the culprit.

And I'd reminded them the culprit had been more than punished and would never have the opportunity to leave another mark on my body.

Taking my phone from his outstretched hand, I glanced at his number and quickly saved it with his name. "Thanks."

"Is there any paperwork we need to sign?" Owen asked, his brows pinched together so tightly I worried his handsome face would be permanently marred with creases.

"Not at the moment. As long as she stays out of trouble," Wilder said, cocking a brow at me as he smirked, "and stays under the radar, I'm sure we can make this go away."

I snorted. Honestly, the only thing that scared me was if the government registered me as feral. That would mean being taken away from my pack and locked up. That would mean returning to a life far too similar to the one I'd escaped almost two years before. I would take myself out before I ever let that happen.

But...I couldn't seem to stop myself. I couldn't seem to stop myself when these thoughts arose, when the plans began to build in my head. *Punish them. Make them pay.* It was as though part of my brain was so broken that it saw every alpha as the enemy.

Not *every* alpha. Not *my* alphas. And Wilder's boss didn't appear to be a monster. But what did I know? Anyone could put on an act in public. I was more than aware of how beautiful someone could appear before they struck like a fucking viper.

"See you later," I said as I slipped my phone into my back pocket and smiled wide at my alphas.

"Let's hope in a better setting," Wilder called after me. "Please stay away from the protests."

I waved over my shoulder but didn't bother promising a damn thing. My alphas constantly made me promise. And more often than not, I broke those promises.

It wasn't like I *wanted* to put myself in harm's way. Nor did I want to get in trouble. But I swore there was a second voice in my head that demanded I seek retribution for the time in hell I'd endured. That voice wanted blood. She wanted her ounce of flesh. And she didn't care whether it was from a complete stranger or not.

Punish them. Punish them all.

But all alphas weren't like those from my past nor were they all like the dickheads causing chaos all over the country. My alphas were nothing like them. Obviously. Otherwise, they would have either locked me up in the house or voluntarily turned me over to the government.

Instead, they struggled to help me find some kind of balance, helped me find outlets for my violent tendencies, and held me when I woke up screaming from night terrors.

For once, Owen was quiet as we left the building and made our way to the SUV. I'd been taken to ORE headquarters since the building of Omega Change had been damaged by those same assholes I'd scared off. Well, scared off for the time.

They would rally again. I had no doubt about that.

But if the look Owen gave me as I climbed into the backseat was anything to go by, I wouldn't be leaving the house unescorted for a while. And there wasn't a doubt in my mind that not only would the codes be changed immediately, but one or both of my alphas would make damn sure there were even more security measures put into place to keep me from sneaking out to cause more trouble.

"It's not like I planned it," I blurted out as both alphas climbed into their seats.

They hadn't asked me a single thing since we'd left the building, but I still felt like I needed to defend myself.

"You absolutely planned it," Owen growled out. "You waited until we left. You, I assume, called another fucking uber. Which, by the way, gives complete strangers our address. You intentionally chose some-thing that would cause enough panic without injury. All fucking planned, Maeve."

His eyes met mine briefly in the rearview, and I actually shrunk a little under his glare.

My alphas would never hurt me. But they were angry. Irate. And, of course, worried.

"All it takes is the right person to catch wind of your bullshit, Maeve. Then there's nothing we can do. Once you're registered as feral, you will forever be out of our reach," Beckett said. My gentle giant kept his voice low and even, but I could hear the hint of a growl rumbling from his chest as well as the anger and fear in his tone.

Feral. Locked up by the government. From the research I'd done after my alphas warned me about what could happen, I'd learned that no one really knew what happened to the omega after. They weren't allowed visits, the omega's family or pack never saw or heard from them again.

"Shit changes *now*, Maeve. We've tried…you either trust us or you don't," Owen said.

My brows slammed together. "I told you I trust you. What does that have to do with…anything?"

"We're trying to keep you safe. Yet you have this bone deep desire to put yourself in the middle of every fucked up situation you can find. And you rarely tell us where you're going. How the fuck are we supposed to find you if someone gets their hands on you?" Owen said.

"Oh please–"

"No!" Owen barked out, and my omega had no choice but to listen. The asshole knew how I felt about the use of the alpha bark, but apparently, I'd gone too far this time. "I don't want to hear any bullshit about how you can take care of yourself. I can only assume you're not carrying any weapons. What if that crowd had noticed your presence? What if they'd turned on you? What if they'd rutted you right there on the fucking parking lot? Or dragged you away where we would never find you? Do you ever think about any of that shit?"

I opened my mouth, so many retorts on my tongue, but snapped it shut when Owen shot an anger filled glare at me in the rearview, as though warning me to keep my excuses to myself.

"Shit changes now. Do you understand me?"

"Are you pulling alpha on me?"

Owen pulled the SUV into the garage and waited until the door lowered before putting the vehicle in park, removing his seatbelt, and turning in his seat to level a look on me. "If that's what it takes to keep you safe, then fuck yes, I'm pulling alpha on you."

He shoved from his seat and stomped into the house, swinging the door shut hard behind him.

Beckett sighed loudly. "You know he's just worried about you."

"I know," I said, suddenly feeling like a complete and total asshole.

"We love you, Maeve. You have to know that by now. You're literally the center of our pack. You're…well, fuck. You're everything to us. Do you have any idea what would happen to the two of us if something happened to you? If you were killed? Or if they were to drag you away from us forever? The bond would snap. We would be left with a fucking hole in our hearts and souls."

He pushed from his own seat then pulled my door open, resting one arm on the roof, the other on the top of the door as he partially hovered over me. "I promise you the codes will be changed. I know you're going to be pissed at us. And I'm willing to accept that. I am *not* willing to accept your loss."

He stepped out of the way, walking toward the door as though his legs were struggling to hold him up, only glancing back at me to make sure I was coming inside and not attempting to run off again before they'd had a chance to put more security measures in place.

When Beckett hesitated in the door, raising his brows at me as though silently ordering me into the house, I huffed a breath and hopped down from the backseat.

I could hear Owen stomping around upstairs as I stepped into the mudroom, lining my shoes up with the others before hanging my jacket on the hook. I didn't carry a purse. Didn't carry an ID or money.

Hell, I didn't even have a birth certificate. The only people who knew more than simply my first name lived under the same roof with me. I hadn't even given Wilder and his buddies my full name. I was surprised they'd been so willing to overlook the fact they had no idea who I was.

My designation. Perhaps there *was* a perk to being an omega. They'd simply seen a tiny female who must be protected at all times.

Where had people like Owen, Beckett, and Wilder been the first twenty-four years of my life. Perhaps had my alphas or even Wilder found me earlier, I wouldn't have been so fucked in the head.

Beckett grabbed a beer from the fridge then dropped heavily onto one of the chairs at the kitchen table. He looked so tired. Lavender crescents underlined his pretty hazel eyes, and the perma-smile I swore he usually wore was nowhere to be seen.

"I'm sorry," I muttered, stepping behind him to wrap my arms around his neck and shoulders, nuzzling against his throat to inhale his scent deep into my lungs.

Moving to the side, I grasped his face in both hands and lowered my head, feathering a kiss across his lips.

When I pulled back, his brows were raised and his eyes were a little wide.

"I love you guys, too. And thank you for not making a big deal when I said it. Or this time. I'm sorry I keep...I'm sorry I'm like this. You both deserve...shit. You deserve a better omega. One who will actually..." I shrugged as my cheeks practically burst into flames. "It's not that I don't want to, you know. I just..."

The scars. As much as I had the same bone deep physical needs as any other omega, I hated the thought of anyone seeing my past permanently etched into my flesh.

Beckett slowly wrapped his arms around my waist and pulled me closer until I was settled between his knees. I knew neither of them sought any sexual gratification with anyone else. They simply suffered the abstinence. Because of me. Because they loved me.

"We're here whenever you're ready, Maeve. We told you from the get-go – you're fully in charge of your life and our lives together. Except–" he said, holding up a finger when I opened my mouth to speak. "When it comes to putting your life and safety at risk. That is not up to you." He chuckled. "That's literally the only freedom we won't give you. When you're ready to share more of yourself with us, we're here. But, fuck, Maeve. You have to stop. You have to stop sneaking out of the house and putting yourself in the direct line of fire."

His eyes were glassy, and I felt like the biggest fucking asshole in the world.

Lowering onto one of his knees, I let him hold me as I rested my cheek on his shoulder, simply breathing in his warm scent, the hints of fresh ink and old book pages soothing some of the sharper edges of my constant anxiety that had become both a hindrance and a companion over the years, one of the few things I knew I could count on being present.

"How long do you think Owen is going to pout?" I asked against Beckett's neck.

"He's not pouting. He's panicking," he said, his deep voice rumbling against me.

My alphas were panicking. Because I'd once again caused a mess they would have to clean up and hope that no one sought to press charges against me.

I was the worst kind of omega.

CHAPTER 5

I was going to end up blind. I had jerked off so many fucking times since Maeve had left the building and my life that I was sure I would end up blind or with hairy palms.

It wasn't enough. Fucking my own hand to fantasies of the beautiful redhead wasn't even close to enough. I was sure I wouldn't get the fiery omega out of my mind until I was buried balls deep in her tight heat.

Hell. It would take more than that. I couldn't explain it, but I wanted her in my life. I wanted to be in her life.

And that spelled fucking disaster.

Maeve was a force all her own. She obviously had no fear of alphas or consequences. And I was part of law enforcement, even if I no longer worked directly for Omega Rescue and Extraction.

There was definitely something more to her than her violent tendencies. And yep. I wanted to know everything. I wanted to know what urged her to sneak right into the middle of a bunch of screaming alphas to leave a concussion grenade of all things. And where the hell did she even get the fucking thing? Not like they sold them at big box stores or over the counter anywhere.

She'd said her alphas were busy when Kai and I decided to call them to pick her up. What did they do for work? And did she not work? They didn't come across as the kind of alphas who demanded she stay home and wait for them to return, nor did she come across as the kind of omega who would agree to such.

It had been a week since she'd set off the flash bang, and I was tempted to find her address to send her flowers. The crowd hadn't gathered since, giving those of us who'd been working twelve to fourteen hours shifts a much needed break.

The tear gas hadn't worked, but the threat of a bomb apparently had been all it took to give the protestors a big enough scare to give up for a while. Although I had no delusions the break would last.

Reaching for the towel on the side of my bed, I cleaned off my hand and stomach from my latest jerk off session, then tossed the nasty thing toward the hamper. Close enough. I'd pick it up in the morning when I got up for the day.

Now that my balls were no longer full of baby batter, my mind returned to the fact that my house was too quiet, my bed cold and empty. For a while, I'd sated my baser needs with one-night-stands, but those had begun to make me feel even lonelier.

Rolling my head on the pillow, I glanced at my phone. I hadn't heard from Maeve again. I wasn't sure that was good news or bad.

Who the fuck was I kidding? Bad news. But only because I'd hoped she would want to talk to me, to see me again. Yeah, she had alphas, but it wasn't uncommon for betas to be a part of a pack, regardless of how small that pack might be.

Lifting the phone, I brought it to life and checked the time. Not quite eleven. Was it too late?

Fuck it.

Before I had time to talk myself out of it, I shot off a quick text, phrasing it so I didn't look desperate, but instead looked as though I was simply checking in to make sure she was doing okay and staying out of trouble.

Setting the phone on my chest, I hooked my hands behind my head and stared up at the ceiling. There was a chance I wouldn't hear from her until tomorrow. Or I might never hear from her again.

When my phone vibrated on my chest, I nearly threw it across the room as I tried to bring it to life to see the reply.

> Maeve: I'm on house arrest. Lol Sorry about causing a problem for you guys.

I SMILED at the text and wondered if she was in the pack bed with her alphas or in her own room. And what was she wearing? Was she a comfort girl who wore oversized t-shirts and sweats? A nighty girl? Or did she go fully nude and snuggle into the warmth of her alphas?

Honestly, any of those options would be sexy as fuck on her. I had a feeling Maeve would look amazing in a fucking potato sack.

> Me: Need me to break you out of your prison?

THE BUBBLES APPEARED on my screen and my heart began to race as excitement skittered through my veins.

> Maeve: Are you offering to be my white knight and save me from my tower?

> Me: As long as you don't try to blow anything else up.

Maeve: Hey. I knew what I was doing. Don't underestimate the skill of a pissed off omega.

Me: Never. I've seen what you're capable of.

THE BUBBLES DIDN'T APPEAR for a few minutes, and I realized how boring our conversation had started. As much as I wanted to flirt with her, I also didn't want to push her or come off as one of those fuckers who used their position of power to coerce her into anything.

When the conversation bubbles started again, my stomach flipped.

Maeve: Do you have a pack?

THAT WAS GOOD, right? If she was curious, did that mean she was interested in me? Or was she simply making small talk?

No. Maeve didn't come across as the kind of woman who would waste words simply to fill the silence.

Me: No. Is that a deal breaker? Can't be friends if I don't have a pack?

I SENT A CRYING gif to accompany my text in hopes of keeping the tone light.

Maeve: Nope. Not a deal breaker. But why don't you have a pack yet?

. . .

How the hell was I supposed to answer that? It wasn't like I was ugly or a jerk. It just...hadn't happened.

When I'd been a part of a major extraction mission and had met Violet, I had hoped to find the same attraction and connection she'd found with the alphas who'd claimed her. But all I'd felt was affection, the kind I felt for my friends or siblings. Not that she wasn't a stunner or that she didn't have a body to make any red blooded human hot. She just...wasn't my omega.

> Me: Just never happened. I want one someday, tho.

And preferably with an omega with flaming red hair, a violent streak, and tits and ass that could bring me to my knees. Of course, I left all that out of the text.

> Maeve: How come you're still up?

> Me: Couldn't sleep. You?

The bubbles appeared, then a picture came through and my heart did a weird flip in my chest. It was Maeve smiling sweetly, the two alphas on either side, their lips pressed against her bare shoulders.

> Maeve: They snore.

. . .

I BARKED out a laugh in the quiet of my room. They were right next to her ears. And if they really did snore, I could only imagine how hard it would be to sleep.

Since she sent a picture, I felt the need to return the favor. Holding the phone up high, I made sure to keep the image from my waist up. No reason to scare her off by sending her a pic of my rock-hard dick.

Maeve: Nice tats. How many?

Me: Lost count. You have any?

THE CONVERSATION WENT silent for so long I wondered if she'd ended up falling asleep.

Maeve: No.

Me: Piercings?

Maeve: Just my ears. Used to want more but don't like needles.

Me: Then you'll definitely hate getting a tattoo. Lol

Maeve: Can I see more?

MY DICK TWITCHED. More? More tattoos...or more of me?

Me: Could u be more specific?

BECAUSE I DIDN'T WANT this to end when I sent her an eyeful of something she had no desire to see.

Maeve: Your tattoos, perv.

A WINKY FACE emoji accompanied her text.

I HUFFED a laugh at her response and craned my neck to see which tattoos I wanted to send her. My arms were safe enough. I took pics of each of my arms and sent them.

Maeve: Those are really pretty. Where else?

HMM. Taking a chance, I pulled the blanket up until my cock was covered but the curls at the top were visible to showcase one of my bigger pieces that covered me from sternum to pube line.

A few seconds passed before a picture came through from Maeve.

She'd pulled the blanket down more to reveal her cleavage and what I could see of her face. She was biting her lip.

My dick bumped against the blanket as though demanding to be released.

Throwing the blanket off my leg while keeping my dick and balls covered, I sent her a shot of my thigh piece.

And then she sent a pic of her torso down to her belly button, nothing but her arms covering her tits. Or rather, covering her nipples, because I saw more than enough of the swells that I wanted to bury my face in until my lungs burned from depriving them of oxygen.

Fuuuck. We hadn't actually shown each other anything directly, but this was by far the most erotic text conversation I'd ever had. Precum wept from the head of my cock and my balls ached again.

My hand wouldn't be enough. It hadn't been enough in the week since I'd laid eyes on Maeve.

Taking a chance, I threw off the blanket and covered my cock the best I could behind my hands and snapped a pic.

The next pic was a scowling alpha squinting at the phone screen.

I threw the blanket back over my lap as though he could see through the phone. It was like we were two teenagers caught sexting by our parents.

A few seconds later, my phone chirped with an incoming Face-Time call.

"Shit," I muttered before answering.

"If you two are going to flirt and send dirty pics, could you do it during normal business hours?" Beckett grumbled, his voice hoarse with sleep.

Not the response I was expecting. I'd half anticipated being cursed out for flirting with their omega, for flashing her all but my twig and berries.

"Sorry about that," I said, struggling to hold back my chuckle.

"Hey, I tried to sleep in my own bed. The flash wouldn't have woken you," Maeve said just off camera.

Beckett muttered something under his breath and handed the phone back to Maeve as he settled his head back on the pillow, his lips once more pressed to her shoulder.

"Say goodnight," Owen grumbled. "Call him tomorrow."

Both alphas were aware we'd been chatting and sending pics and neither were pissed? Maybe they were too tired or half asleep and weren't aware what we'd been up to.

"Goodnight, Wilder," she said. And just before she ended the call, she grinned wide and pulled the blanket down completely, giving me the perfect view of her freckle covered tits with dusky pink nipples.

"Fuck me," I muttered as I tossed my dark phone back onto the nightstand.

I had to have Maeve. I needed her like I needed my next fucking breath. And I would do whatever it took to make that happen. I would send her gifts, flowers, poems, and anything else I could think of that appealed to omegas.

Although...Maeve wasn't like other omegas, not any I'd met, anyway. While she was strong like Violet, Sophie, and Joy, there was a darkness to her, something that apparently thrived on violence, or maybe the darkness was what caused her to commit violence.

I wanted to know what caused that darkness. I wanted to know if I could help bring light to her life.

I wanted to feel her in my arms, in my bed, and under my hands, my tongue, and writhing beneath my body.

CHAPTER 6

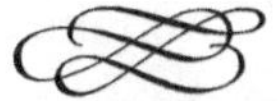

This was probably a bad idea, but I needed to know whether we should be anticipating a new pack member, whether Maeve was making plans for Wilder to sneak her out of the house, or whether she was simply flirting with the beta.

After all, betas didn't pose a threat to her. Not in her mind, anyway.

As Maeve slept curled up on her side, the blankets creating a little burrito out of our omega, I flipped through the conversation she'd had last night, the same one that had woken both Owen and I when she began taking pictures, the flash glowing behind my closed lids.

The conversation started off benign enough. Wilder was checking in, making sure she was staying out of trouble. Then, little by little, the conversation turned until a picture of Maeve sleeping between her alphas filled the screen. We both looked content – happy even – nestled against her. There was the softest, sweetest smile on her face. *They snore*, she'd said as to the reason she couldn't sleep.

That wasn't fully the truth. Maeve had had problems sleeping from the first day we'd met her. Owen and I had had to grow accustomed to sleeping with the television on, the sound low. It had taken a while, but now neither of us noticed the flickering light or low hum of whatever program was playing on loop.

She'd come to bed last night in pajamas. At what point had she removed them? In the picture, it was obvious she wasn't wearing a top. Had she actually removed it to take the picture?

As jealous as I should have been over that thought, I was…well, shit. I was hopeful. A little excited. That meant she was dropping her guard a little more. She knew we would never grope at her or force her to do anything she didn't want to do. And this beta put her at ease enough she'd sent him teasing pictures of her stomach, only her pale, freckled arm covering her nipples.

I'd seen her perky tits on a few occasions but had only felt them in my hands or on my tongue a handful of times. Only during the heats when she didn't use suppressants to avoid her cycle.

I wasn't lying to her when I'd told her that I'd loved her, that she was my best friend. What I had never told her was how deeply in love with her I'd been from the beginning. But, sometimes loving someone so deeply meant giving them the time and space they needed to feel safe.

And then the pic of my glower appeared in the text thread. I chuckled softly at the look on his face when I'd video called him. And the look of surprise on his face when I'd told him to wait until morning to chat with her.

Of course I would urge them to spend more time together if she wanted him. I wanted her happy. And if that happened to be with Wilder, so be it.

I knew Owen felt as deeply for our omega as I did. Except his possessive, protective urges tended to push to the surface more often than not. He wanted her safe. And every time she snuck out of the house without telling either of us where she was going or what she was up to, she was putting herself at risk. It was driving Owen insane.

Hell, it wasn't sitting right with me, either. But I'd always been the more even keeled of the two of us.

"Are you going through my phone?" Maeve's sleepy voice startled me.

Only one eye peeked up at me as I smiled sheepishly and set the phone on the nightstand.

"I was. Sorry."

"Did you think I sent naked pictures?"

"You kind of did," I teased.

She pulled the blanket down until I could see the mischievous smile on her face. "Are you jealous?"

"I've seen your boobs."

The smile faltered. "Are you jealous that I was flirting with Wilder?"

Lowering onto the side of the bed, I brushed my fingers through her hair. "Do you want him in your life?"

Maeve rolled onto her back, gripping my hand and tugging until I laid beside her.

"I'm not sure," she said, turning her head to look into my eyes, my hand hugged to her chest and nestled between her tits.

"I think you do. But you're scared."

It was like a flip switched. The smile was gone. The twinkle in her eyes died out. And then she released my hand.

Nope. We weren't doing this again.

Lifting until I could plant a hand on either side of her head, I caged her in. "Do you want him, Maeve? You could invite him here. Owen and I would never let anyone hurt you. If you decided you wanted him to leave, we'll toss him out on his ass."

The corners of her lips quirked the slightest bit, but there was still that darkness in her honey gold eyes as she stared into my face. When that gaze dipped to my lips briefly, my heart kicked up a notch. When was the last time I'd tasted her kiss? More than the gentle, chaste brush of her lips when she was trying to reassure me, but the deep, passionate kisses we'd shared…damn. That had been months ago. Maybe even longer.

Her chest rose and fell as she took a deep breath. "You really think either of you would be happy if I decided to fuck the beta when all we do is share a bed?"

"If it made *you* happy…yeah, we would."

Tears welled in her eyes. Damn it. That was not what I'd intended.

But then…she wrapped her hands around my neck and tugged me down until she could raise her head and press her lips to mine. It was deeper than the sweet press of her lips the night she'd let me hold her in the kitchen. But she didn't slip her tongue into my mouth, simply held me there, my shirt covered chest pressing against her bare breasts.

"I do love you, Beckett," she whispered when she broke the kiss.

"I know."

"I'll be better. I'll try harder to be…I want to deserve you. I want to be the kind of omega who deserves you both."

And now the backs of my eyes burned with unshed tears. "I don't know how many fucking times the two of us can tell you this, but we love you exactly the way you are. Crazy, *broken*," I said, raising my brows and using the word she'd used far too many times. "We love every single sharp edge and soft corner of your heart and mind. You're our omega. And you're fucking perfect."

Her bottom lip quivered. A tear trailed down her temple to soak into her hair.

"We love you exactly the way you are. If you want the beta, you have our blessing. If you want us for nothing more than friendship, that's what we'll give you. But if you'll let us in, if you'll let us show you how perfect you are…" I wasn't even sure how to end my thought.

We had tried to show her she could trust us. And I was pretty sure we'd proven that time and time again. But without trying to speak for Owen, I wanted in her heart even more than I wanted in her body.

Not that I would turn that down. I craved the physical connection with her, craved making love to an omega in the way only an alpha could, to fill her with my knot, my seed, and, hopefully someday, my child.

She blinked back her tears and released her hands around my

neck. When I moved to roll off the side of the bed, she tugged the blanket down her body until she was revealed to me like a gift, nothing keeping us apart but her thin cotton panties and my clothes.

"Are you sure?" I whispered. "I don't…that's not why I said what I said, Maeve."

"I'm sure," she said, reaching for me.

Her hands shook slightly as she tugged at my shirt until she worked it over my head. Instead of immediately shucking my slacks, I lowered until I could claim her mouth again, then kissed and nipped down her jaw, her throat, kissing the mark she'd allowed me to leave only a few months ago, before kissing the swells of her full breasts. Her nipples pebbled under my attention and begged for my lips. And who the hell was I to deny them or Maeve of any pleasure?

Her back arched off the bed as I licked and sucked each of her nipples, softly grazing them with my teeth before lowering further, pressing soft kisses and nips to her stomach, causing her to squirm as I tickled her.

"Beck," she moaned when my fingers hooked into the sides of her panties and slowly slid them over her hips, giving her plenty of time to stop me.

I planned to feast on her, to bring her to release with my mouth and tongue. And if that was all she wanted from me, I would leave the house with the worst case of blue balls, but I would do just that – leave her glowing in our pack bed.

Her thighs parted as I settled between them, and she sucked in a deep breath when I pressed a kiss to her thigh. "If you need me to stop, tell me," I said before lowering my head and licking her slicked pussy with a long swipe of my tongue.

Fuck. She tasted like absolute bliss, like paradise, sweet and warm and heady.

Her fingers tangled in my hair and her hips began to move as though she was fucking herself with my mouth. My cock was painfully hard. I was tempted to rub myself against the bed to ease some of the tension, but I would wait. This was the first time Maeve had opened her arms to me, welcomed me not just into her bed, but into her body, and I planned to take my time and memorize every moan and sigh that left her lips.

And fuck, I hoped this wasn't the one and only time she allowed me to taste her, to feel her.

Her breathing grew heavier until she was nearly panting. With one arm under her thigh, I smoothed the other up her stomach until I could cup and fondle her breast, rolling her hard nipple between my thumb and finger.

Her body tensed and she cried out, her slick coating my tongue with sweetness until I felt drunk. I continued to work her clit with my tongue, lapping up every drop in the hopes of keeping her scent and flavor for the rest of the day. I had a fleeting thought of how Owen would react when he scented her on me, but...yeah. That thought was fleeting.

"More," she breathed out, tugging my hair as though trying to drag me up her body.

After pressing gentle kisses to her folds, then each thigh, dampening her skin with her release, I sat back onto my haunches and struggled to undo my pants and free my cock.

The sweetest – and somewhat foreign – giggle erupted from her lips as she watched me fumble with the button and zipper of my pants and then finally shove them down my hips.

I'd made her laugh like that. I'd made her moan. I'd made her fall apart. I had made her smile.

And fuck yes, I wanted to do all of those things every day for the rest of my life. And if Wilder made her happy, if my omega wanted to spend time with him, or wanted him to join our pack, I'd beat his ass to make that very thing happen if necessary.

Maeve was still smiling when I finally kicked my slacks off, then held her arms out as though to invite me down. My heart swelled and softened at the open affection on her face.

There wasn't an ounce of doubt in her pretty eyes as I lowered between her parted thighs and let my cock nudge against her opening.

"Same thing, sweetheart. If you need me to stop–"

She hooked her feet around my back and pulled me forward until I was fully sheathed inside of her. We moaned in unison as she stretched around me. Her hands were soft as they brushed over my shoulders, my chest, then finally up to cup my face.

"I'm sorry," she whispered, her voice raspy with emotion. "I'm sorry for…I'll be who you deserve. I'll try harder."

Instead of arguing with her or reminding her what I'd told her moments ago, I leaned down and pressed my lips to her forehead, each of her cheeks, the tip of her nose, before slanting my mouth over hers.

"I love you, Maeve," I whispered against her lips as I slowly pumped my hips, sliding in and out of her core.

She was so tight. So warm. So fucking wet. And so damn responsive to my touch.

Her feet stayed locked around my waist and her inner walls began to flutter around me as another release built.

Hell yes. I wanted to feel her clenching around me, to feel her coming on my dick.

I wanted to knot her.

But I knew Owen was downstairs waiting for me. If I knotted her, we would be locked together for a while and would end up being even later for the job we had lined up for the morning.

"Beck," she moaned against my mouth, her arms wrapping around my shoulders and tugging me until my chest was pressed against hers. I struggled to keep my weight off her, resting on my elbows as I licked and kissed her shoulder, her throat, dipping my tongue into her mouth for a wet, claiming kiss.

Her walls clenched around me as she moaned into my mouth, her nails scoring my back with a sting. But nothing could keep me from pounding into her as her cunt milked my cock until I felt as though I would pass out. Tingles worked up my spine, my balls tightened, and I came with a grunt, pulling my mouth from hers and throwing my head back as pulse after pulse filled my omega.

The few times she'd allowed Owen and I to help her through her heat, we'd worn condoms to ensure we wouldn't get her pregnant. But this wasn't one of those times we needed to be concerned. There were a few more weeks before she would be fertile again, a few more weeks before she would either request suppressants or, hopefully, would let us knot her through her heat while wearing protection. As much as I wanted a child – or more than one – it was completely up to her whether she carried a baby for us.

As the aftershocks faded, I drew my head back so I could look her in the eye, to make sure she was okay, to check for any regret in her golden eyes.

There was nothing but lust, love, and affection. That and a touch of humor.

"I can't believe I went so long without…that," she said with a huff of laughter. Her soft laughter turned into full blown giggles and turned contagious.

My cock still in her, I squirmed as her giggles made her squeeze me deliciously. "You're killing me, sweetheart," I said, carefully pulling from her as we both struggled to stop laughing.

Her laughter followed me into the bathroom as I grabbed a towel and wet it, carrying it back to the bedroom to clean her up before allowing myself to get dressed and head out for our first appointment.

There was still a smile on her face, but there was…something else in her eyes.

"Do you think Owen will be pissed?"

I frowned as I wiped away my cum and her slick. "Why would he be pissed? You're our omega."

"Okay. Will he be hurt? Because I had sex with you and not him?"

I shrugged up my shoulders. "I don't think so. I would have been a little jealous if you'd been with him and not me, but we've told you from day one – everything is on your time. If you had wanted nothing physical from us, we would have accepted it."

"Even if I had sex with Wilder?"

I snorted when I tried to hold back the laugh at her mischievous smile. Apparently, our omega had already contemplated getting naked with the beta.

"Even if you had sex with Wilder. We want you happy. And safe," I said, raising one brow before standing and pulling my clothes back into place. "Being safe means keeping your ass at home or at least letting us know when you're leaving and where you're going so we'll know how to find you if you need help."

She rolled onto her side and watched me tug my shirt over my head. And my heart and dick were at war when I realized she was watching me with what I could only describe as want, lust, need.

"Promise me you'll stay home until we get back. Maybe...invite Wilder over. If he's not working. The two of you can flirt in person instead of waking up your alphas." I gave a faux glare and forced a fake growl, eliciting another giggle.

When was the last time I'd heard her laugh so much in one damn day. Not even a whole day, an hour. Had meeting Wilder loosened something inside of her? Was it our acceptance of her seeking another packmate?

Or had she finally accepted the fact we wanted her the way she was and didn't expect her to change nor heal from her past trauma overnight?

Whatever the cause of her smiles and happiness, I hoped it would linger longer than this morning.

Bending over the side of the bed, I pressed my lips to her forehead and leveled a look at her. "Promise me, Maeve," I said. We were always careful to use her name rather than her designation. We had learned early on that was a major trigger for her outbursts.

With a roll of her eyes, she flopped onto her back. "Well, being as I heard Owen changing the alarm last night, I guess I promise." And then she winked at me.

She actually winked at me. It was so flirty and sweet, and now I hated that I had to leave her here for the day. I wanted to strip off my clothes, climb back into bed, and feel her pressed against my body for the rest of the day, just enjoying the warmth of her skin and the sweetness of her scent.

And maybe sink into her pussy a few more times.

"I love you, sweetheart," I said.

"I love you, my big ol' teddy bear." Her teddy bear. Usually, she called me her gentle giant. I'd take teddy bear. It was uber affectionate and meant I was one step closer after such a long time together.

With my heart melting in my chest, I left her alone in the bed and found Owen on the couch, fully dressed and shoes on his feet. His brows rose nearly to his hairline when he caught sight of me, but I lifted a finger to my lips. I didn't want to chance her leaving the room and hearing our conversation then retreating back into her shell again.

Once we were in the car, with Owen behind the wheel and pulling down the driveway, I nearly fist pumped the air.

"I can smell her all over you. And I heard...a lot," Owen said.

I turned to look at him to find him grinning. I'd claimed Maeve, but only as a protective measure, a layer to keep others from trying to force a claim on her. She'd yet to allow Owen to mark her. So we didn't have the bond that would let us feel each other's emotions. Hell, even with Maeve, she kept the bond locked down so tightly I rarely felt anything from her.

"First of all, we got to get that beta over here. She definitely wants him," I said.

"You okay with adding a member to the pack?"

I raised a brow. "Dude, if it makes her happy, I'll add ten more fucking members to the pack. You should have seen her face when I mentioned that we were okay with her talking to him."

"And then she just...opened her legs? How the hell did all that transpire?"

I told him everything from Maeve catching me snooping to her calling me her teddy bear.

"That's better than her giant," Owen said.

"*Gentle* giant," I corrected with a grin that refused to fall from my face. I swore my cheeks would be sore by the end of the day. "And yeah. I'll take teddy bear. Especially if that means more cuddling and more–"

"Yeah. You can stop rubbing salt in the wound." Owen glanced at me before returning his attention to the road. "Well? Any idea how to get the beta to the house?"

"I made her promise not to leave until we get home–"

"I changed the codes. She can't leave without us knowing."

"Yep. She apparently heard you plugging in the new code," I said with a huff of a laughter. "I suggested she invite the beta over to keep her company. No idea whether he's working, but…"

"But you hope he'll jump on the chance to hang out with her."

It was my turn to look at Owen. "Aren't you?"

Owen scratched at the stubble coating his cheeks. "I mean, I won't lie and say the thought of you and now the beta being intimate with our omega doesn't make me a little jealous. But you're right – I'd bring anyone she wanted into the house if it made her happy."

"You should have seen her smile. And heard her fucking giggles." I sounded like a lovesick teenager as I sighed and rested my head against my seat.

"She was giggling?" he asked, an incredulous look crossing over his face. "Yeah. We definitely need to find out whether this beta is the cause of her newfound lightness."

If Maeve didn't text or call the dude today, I had every intention of contacting ORE or Omega Change to get his information myself and forcing the beta to hang out with our omega. It might have sounded twisted to an outsider, but…Owen and I would give anything, sacrifice anything for the woman we'd found bloodied and bruised, the woman who'd hidden in the nest for the first few weeks.

The woman who'd wiggled her way into our hearts one smile at a time.

CHAPTER 7

Maeve

Why had I been so scared to share my body with my alphas? After the absolute pleasure Beckett had shown me, I was tempted to kick my own ass. Almost two years and I'd been missing out on that?

All because of my stupid past, my memories…

My scars. Which was stupid. Even if we didn't make love, my alphas had seen me naked numerous times. We'd even lounged together in the oversized bathtub on occasions. And the two had always kept their distance, only rubbing my feet or letting me rest my back against their chests.

Now that I'd allowed Beckett to fuck me, I was tempted to ask Owen for the same type of attention. I wasn't even near my heat, but now that I'd felt that level of release, I wanted more.

It would be hours before my pack returned home. And not only had I promised Beckett I would keep my ass at home, but there was no way for me to leave without them knowing. I'd assumed correctly when I'd heard the buttons beeping – Owen had changed the code. Meaning there was no way for me to disarm it without setting it off.

I still couldn't believe Beckett was more or less trying to convince me to invite Wilder over, even knowing I was attracted to him. Being as my alpha had seen the flirty texts containing pictures, there was no point in denying it. Not that I'd ever been the best at lying, especially to my packmates. They'd never given me a reason to become good at lying to them.

Like Beckett said, they accepted me.

That didn't mean I accepted myself. I wanted to be better, be the kind of omega who enjoyed gifts and soft stuff. Instead, I found myself behaving awkwardly anytime my alphas tried to shower me with attention.

Until this morning.

I couldn't help but dwell on the fact I'd gone so long without experiencing the kind of pleasure I had with Beckett and, honestly, was counting down the hours until he was home so we could do it again. Maybe I would invite Owen to join us.

Was I ready for that, though? I wasn't lost to my hormones, so it was possible all my past trauma would rear its ugly head and ruin the moment. They didn't deserve that. My alphas...they were fucking amazing. And extremely attractive.

And now I could add amazing in bed. At least for Beckett.

Something else hit me – I'd not only deprived myself but my alphas. For almost two years they had patiently been by my side, never pushing, never demanding anything from me other than, well, my safety. Anything and everything they'd done since the day they'd brought me to the pack house had been to keep me safe, to protect me from both the outside world *and* myself. Because, let's face it, I was just as much a danger to myself as any alpha.

After such a beautiful morning, I was back to beating myself up. They deserved so much better than what I had given them. They deserved an omega who welcomed them into her life, into her heart, into her body with open arms.

And all I'd given them was legal fees and heartache.

Tossing the blankets away, I sulked to the bathroom and started the shower. Still naked, I stood in front of the mirror as I waited for the water to heat up and studied my body in the mirror.

I had sent a teasing picture to Wilder, barely covering my nipples. But what would he think if he saw the back side of me?

Turning as far as I could and still see the mirror, I grimaced at the patchwork of flesh. From my neck down to the top of my butt, even the backs of my legs, there were raised, pink scars that crisscrossed each other and, for a moment, brought me back to the time before Beck and Owen had found me cowering in the basement while they'd installed a security system.

They'd had no idea at the time they were installing alarms to keep me in, not to keep bad people out.

And then…

Inhaling deeply, I swiped the steam away from the mirror as the room grew humid. I wasn't that woman anymore. I wasn't there anymore. But that didn't stop the rush of anger that burned through my veins and demanded an outlet.

Except, I couldn't fucking leave. I was once again locked in a house. Only this time, it was for my own safety.

I supposed I should have worried each time I snuck away to punish an alpha, each time I inserted myself into a large group of alphas with the intent of punishing the men from my past. One of whom no longer had a beating heart.

Apparently, that little fact didn't seem to matter to my omega or my nightmares. And now that I was home alone with no way to leave, everything came rushing back until my lungs felt as though they couldn't draw in a full breath.

Shower. I would shower, then eat. One step at a time. That was how my alphas had pulled me out of the darkness in the beginning. One step at a time. Shower. Dress. Eat.

Focusing on the feeling of my bare feet on the tile, I took my time in the shower, conditioning my hair and shaving my legs. One step. All I would focus on was pampering myself in the shower.

Once all that was done and I'd slathered my body in lotion, I brushed through my tangle of red curls and sprayed it with leave in conditioner, leaving it to dry on its own. I rarely did much more with my hair than brush it or pull it away from my face in a scrunchie.

Next step. Get dressed. Even as I repeated the steps as we had done in the beginning, the anger continued to fester.

"Focus, damn it," I muttered under my breath as I stepped into my walk-in closet. The space was far too big for the meager selection of clothing I owned.

Not that my alphas hadn't tried to drown me in gifts. But I was a comfort girl. Jeans, sweats, leggings. T-shirts, sweaters, and hoodies. Much more than that and I began to feel constricted. At least during the summer, I could simply wander the house in shorts and tanks.

After pulling on a pair of panties, I tugged on some leggings and a long-sleeved t-shirt before sliding my feet into a comfy pair of boot-style house shoes, one of the few gifts I'd actually accepted from my alphas without feeling...weird. Or like they were trying to buy my loyalty.

Which was stupid. Omegas were supposed to love gifts. They were supposed to adore soft things, silky things. They were supposed to be...different. Sweet and obedient. Not possess violent tendencies.

"Nope. One step at a time."

I'd enjoyed such a beautiful moment with Beck this morning, and now it was as though I was trying to punish myself.

But why? It was stupid. Logically, I knew it was stupid. Yet I couldn't seem to stop myself from wondering why the hell either of my alphas would want anything to do with such a broken, poor excuse for an omega.

Pushing all the thoughts and doubts away, I chose to focus on Beckett's words from this morning as I made my way downstairs for coffee and breakfast.

But if you'll let us in, if you'll let us show you how perfect you are...

They had rescued me from hell. And all they'd done from that first day was treat me as though I was the most important person in their lives. They had done everything in their power to prove I could trust them. And all I'd done was bring chaos into their lives.

Not that I wanted to be a source of pain for them. But sometimes, it was as though something took over my thoughts, like I was possessed and another entity claimed my body and acted upon the impulsive and intrusive thoughts I refused to voice to anyone.

I didn't have to voice them. I was pretty sure my alphas knew exactly what went through my head every minute of every day.

And yet...I kept them at arm's length, weaponizing my affection. Not that I consciously used their love against them. It was just...

Well, how could anyone love something so broken and ugly inside?

Yanking the fridge open with more force than was necessary, I stared unseeing at its contents. I wasn't actually hungry. But it had always been the next step on the list.

Fuck it. I would get a cup of coffee and...then what? I couldn't leave. My pack was gone for the next few hours.

Glancing at the phone in my hand, I wondered if Wilder was working today. Only one way to find out.

Pulling up his name, I sent a simple text of *good morning*, then set it on the counter while I dumped sugar and creamer into my mug of steaming coffee. Owen often teased me that I was a fan of the sweetness and caffeine, not that actual coffee itself. Whatever. Not everyone liked the bitterness of drinking it black and plain.

As the spoon clinked against the inside of the mug, my phone dinged with an incoming message. That was quick.

Wilder: Good morning.

I BIT BACK A SQUEAL of excitement at such a simple text. How silly. I didn't squeal. And I didn't giggle.

But I'd giggled this morning. In fact, I'd smiled and laughed more this morning than I had...in as long as I could remember. At least long before I'd met my alphas, before I'd been taken, before...

Nope. I wasn't going to let the memories ruin what could be a good day. For once, I wanted to enjoy simply existing. Enjoy the tingling that brought a glow to my skin caused by Beckett's attention this morning.

Me: Working today?

WILDER REPLIED IMMEDIATELY.

Wilder: Off today. Someone scared away the protestors.

HIS MESSAGE WAS ACCOMPANIED by a winking emoji with its tongue hanging out.

ANOTHER OF THOSE giggles that I'd released this morning bubbled up my chest. Carrying the phone into the living room and setting my mug on the side table, I considered what Beckett said, that I should invite Wilder over. He'd said he wouldn't be jealous, but I had no idea how Owen would feel. No matter what Beck said, I needed to know from Owen's lips that he was okay with me possibly courting a beta when I already had my little pack.

Me: Guess you should be thankful for that someone.

Wilder: That someone definitely deserves a gift or two. Or at least a nice dinner.

Pulling my feet onto the couch and under my butt, I rested against the arm of the couch and smiled down at my phone, letting Beckett's words flow through me.

Screw it.

> Me: You could thank that someone by hanging out with her while she's on house arrest.

> Wilder: Address?

Oh my gosh. This was really happening. He hadn't asked what time, hadn't asked whether I was sure, hadn't said he needed to check his plans for the day. He'd simply asked for my address within seconds of receiving my text.

I sent the address and then looked around the house, my attention stopping on the alarm system. Shit. How the hell was I supposed to let him in when the alarm would blare the moment I opened the door?

> Wilder: Be there in an hour.

Shit. Shit shit shit. Pulling up Beckett's number, I hit it and held the phone to my ear, chewing on my bottom lip as it rang over and over again.

When Beckett finally answered, his voice was deep. "What's wrong?"

"Nothing. You said to invite Wilder over. But Owen changed the code so I can't let him in. He's going to be here in an hour."

A deep chuckle rumbled over the line and my body went tight at the sound. I'd always found both my alphas appealing. But meeting

Wilder had awakened something in me. Making love to my alpha this morning seemed to seal the deal and reminded me that I was safe in this house, with this pack, with my guys.

Even if I was alone with Wilder, I was fully aware there were cameras in every room. If the beta turned out to not be such a nice guy, my pack would see and either rush home or send someone to intervene.

"Oh shit." The cameras. There were literally cameras in every room. Had Owen watched as Beckett took me this morning? Or had he given us privacy?

And why didn't the idea of Owen watching as I finally gave myself to one of my alphas send heat flooding through me until slick dampened my panties?

Could I be closer to my cycle than I'd estimated? I needed to ask one of my guys to procure some more suppressants for me.

Or…I could let them help me through my heat. I could let them do as their biology demanded and allow myself to be cared for the way an omega needed.

"What?" Beckett asked at my soft outburst.

"Nothing." I was not bringing up my concern about the cameras. That might remind them to keep a closer eye and I wanted at least a modicum of privacy while spending time with Wilder today.

"Hold on," Beck said.

There was a shuffling sound over the line as the phone was passed to Owen.

"If I give you the code, are you going to sneak away and commit another felony?"

"I have never committed a felony," I protested.

"No. You've never been *charged* with a felony. You've committed more than one." There was humor and a warning in my grumpy alpha's voice.

"I promise not to take advantage of your charity and rob a bank while you're at work."

A soft growl rattled through the phone and I could almost picture him rubbing his forehead as he often did when I stressed him out.

He rattled off a series of four numbers. "Do not disarm it until Wilder is at that door. And don't you dare disarm anything else. You hear me, Maeve?"

"Yes, alpha," I teased.

Another growl rattled through the phone, but this one held something more than his usual frustration. If I wasn't wrong, Owen liked my use of his designation. It was something else we never did, never referring to each other's place in society.

Just because I had an issue with it didn't mean I should deprive my alphas.

Man. In the course of a few days, I'd begun to question everything about my place in this house and about the way I'd treated my alphas.

"If there are any issues, call us immediately. We'll keep an eye on the cameras as much as possible, but we have a pretty full day," Owen said.

"You know I can take care of myself." They'd both spent countless hours training me to be a bad ass. So, technically, I supposed I wasn't fully at fault for some of the assaults and destruction.

"I do. But be safe. Try to get the beta to stick around so we can properly meet him."

"You met him."

"No. We picked you up from ORE headquarters and received a report from him. I want to make sure this dude deserves time with my – with you."

"With your omega," I said, saving him from having to say it.

"Yeah."

Damn it. Because of my inner demons, I'd forced two of the best men I'd ever met to feel as though they had to change their lives to tiptoe around me.

"Hey, Owen?"

"Yeah, baby girl?"

"I love you."

And then I ended the call as heat rushed my cheeks. I'd said it. There. I'd told them before, but I wanted to make sure I said it to each of them independently. I wanted them to know how much I appreciated them, appreciated everything they'd done for me, the way they'd bent over backward to help me heal.

I did love them. As I spent some time looking inward, I realized I'd loved them for a while. And more than simply because they were my pack, or because they were my alphas. I loved them deeply.

There had to be a way for me to prove to them, to prove that I deserved them, regardless of their insistence that they wanted me just the way I was.

I had less than an hour before Wilder arrived at the front door. I didn't need to jump up and tidy the house. Owen and Beckett had a weekly housekeeper who kept up on all that since I was so reluctant to behave in a domestic manner. Yet something else that had made me feel like a failure. A good omega took care of her alphas and her home.

A good omega didn't reject her alphas, didn't force them to feel as though they were nothing more than roommates.

But we weren't a typical pack. Why couldn't I simply accept that they didn't expect anything from me that society deemed normal? Besides, I'd heard once that normal was nothing more than a setting on a dryer.

I chuckled at the trajectory of my thoughts and realized I was doing anything I could to distract my brain from the fact I was about to be alone with the first man to not only catch my attention but who also didn't send a rush of anger and fear coursing through my veins.

Nope. From the moment I'd spotted him sitting on the stool at the bar, he'd felt as though he was a missing piece in my life. Then he'd detained me after I'd set off the concussion grenade and had argued on my behalf. In fact, he'd seemed mildly amused at my antics. And had been more than ready to protect me when my alphas came barging through ORE headquarters doors, rage obvious all over Owen's face and in his voice.

Butterflies took flight in my belly as I watched the time and tried to think of what we could do today. Something that didn't require the removal of our clothes…

Or Wilder witnessing my scars, whether visible or emotional.

CHAPTER 8

<u>Wilder</u>

*H*oly shit! She'd invited me over. After the texting last night, I'd worried I might have gone too far. Especially when one of her alphas video called me and asked that we finish our conversation in the morning.

They didn't come across as domineering or controlling, but I had seen the best and worst of society through my years in law enforcement. As much as it had hurt me, I'd feared her pack would have demanded she stop talking to me.

And I would have stepped back if my presence made her life difficult. Or I would have led the charge to extract her if she was in a dangerous situation. After all, that was my job.

But she'd texted me this morning, had invited me to her house. Did that mean her alphas were on board with me possibly courting her? And did that mean I was courting them, as well?

Fuck. I wasn't sure who I could ask about this. Kai and his mate, Sophie, had courted their beta, not the other way around. They'd been the ones to initiate a relationship with Devyn. And Kai had fallen as hard for the beta as his omega.

Honestly, I hadn't paid much attention to Owen or Beckett when they'd picked Maeve up after her little incident at the protest. From what I remembered, they were attractive, one of them was a few inches over six feet, and the other looked as though he wanted to throttle Maeve for getting picked up by the police once again.

Except I wasn't the police. While I was still in law enforcement and carried a badge, I'd been hired as private security by Omega Change. The worst I could have done was turn her over to the local police department. Not that I'd had any intention of doing anything of the sort. I could have kissed her for finding a non-lethal way of dispersing the assholes who'd congregated every day for the past few months.

Like she'd said, I should definitely thank her. Hence the reason I'd told her an hour instead of rushing to her house the second I had her address.

Stepping into the omega marketed store, *Nesters*, I stopped a few feet inside and looked around with wide eyes. I'd never been here and had no idea where to start.

"Hi. Can I help you find something?" a pretty omega asked as she approached. Her hair was pulled off her neck, showcasing the marks that indicated to anyone who might have any sick ideas she was claimed by a pack.

Not that some sick fucks cared about such a thing.

"I…where are the gifts? I mean, I'm meeting an omega today. And I wanted to thank her for something. And it's kind of an inside joke. She doesn't seem like the frilly kind of woman. I just…I have no idea where to look or what to get."

I sure as hell hoped I'd guessed right when I'd assumed Maeve wasn't the frilly kind of omega. The two times I'd seen her, she hadn't been dressed in expensive clothing and hadn't looked as though she wore makeup or jewelry. Although that might as well have been because she'd been on a mission of destruction. Why would she bother getting dolled up when she'd planned on blowing shit up?

"Does she like jewelry? Do you know her favorite color? Does she have a pack or do you know her signature?"

She smelled like the sweetest spring rain and lemons. But I wasn't sure how that would translate into a gift.

"Or we have products where you can add your own pheromones so that she'll have access to your scent whenever she wants."

"I'm a beta," I said.

"The scent can still be transferred. It just won't be as strong as an alpha's."

"This is…I guess you could call it a first date."

"Okay," she said with a smile, leading me further into the store.

Too much time was passing. I'd told Maeve I would be there in an hour, and I'd already wasted twenty minutes looking through blankets, pillows, lotions, and the like.

And then my eyes caught on something. "That. Can I get two of those, both colors?"

The pretty omega's brows pinched together as she looked at my choice then turned her attention to me as though I'd lost my mind.

"Are you sure? For a first date?"

"One hundred percent." A grin split my face as she grabbed two of the gift I'd chosen in the size I guessed Maeve wore, then carried it to the register.

She spent a little too much time folding and wrapping the items in tissue paper before setting them in the bag and handing me the receipt.

"Everything here can be returned or exchanged," she said as though giving me an out. Obviously, because she thought my omega would hate what I'd picked out.

Not *my* omega.

Not yet anyway.

"Thank you. Have a great day."

I grabbed the bag and hurried out to my truck. The address Maeve had given me was twenty minutes away. Either I would be late, or I had to speed and risk a ticket.

Fuck it. I'd risk the ticket. I hated to think of her watching for me and thinking I'd bailed when too much time passed and I'd yet to pull into the driveway.

Gift bag on the passenger seat, I plugged the address into my GPS and pulled into traffic. I should have worn a t-shirt instead of the sweater I'd pulled on. My nerves were making me sweat and the last thing I wanted was to show up a soggy, stinky mess the first time I got to hang out with the sexy omega without so many eyes on us.

Or the threat of legal repercussions.

With my foot pressing hard on the gas pedal, I used talk-to-text to let Maeve know I might be a few minutes late. Hopefully, the warning was unnecessary. Especially since I was more than ready to be face to face with her again, to hear her voice again, to look into her whiskey golden eyes again.

Glancing at the gift bag, I hoped I'd read her right after our super short encounters. Otherwise, I would return to that damn omega store and buy a crap load more. I'd buy a bunch of fuzzy blankets and soft pajamas and anything else I could think of that might make her smile.

There were no other vehicles in the driveway when I pulled up and the garage door was closed. Would her alphas be here, as well? Would I be spending time getting to know the entire pack at once?

It shouldn't be overwhelming being as there were only three of them, but I'd wanted a pack of my own for so long I found myself worried I would ruin it before I had a chance to win anyone over.

Truck parked, I killed the engine and grabbed the gift bag, checking my reflection to make sure my hair wasn't sticking up all over the place from as many times as I'd raked my fingers through it since Maeve invited me over.

I probably should have taken a little more time getting ready. I'd merely showered, tugged on some jeans and a sweater while still damp, and finger combed my hair. I didn't bother with any scent blockers in hopes that she would be as attracted to my signature as I was to hers.

The front door opened as I stepped onto the porch and the

redhead who'd possessed my every waking thought, my fantasies, even my dreams stood there with an unsure smile on her full lips.

"Hey," I said and winced. *Smooth, asshole.*

"Hey," she said, stepping back to make room for me to pass before swinging the door shut behind me.

"I got you something. It's silly. But you were right – I owe you a thanks for the extra day off."

Her cheeks flushed the prettiest pink as she reached for the bag I offered. She looked…well, she looked uncomfortable receiving the gift. Until she ruffled through the tissue paper and pulled out two camouflage hoodies in the softest material. I'd chosen the traditional green, tan, and black, and another in dark blue, gray, and black.

A smile stretched across her face as she shook out first one then the other. "Are you serious?"

"Hey, if you're going to be doing covert missions and infiltrating mobs of alphas, you should probably try to blend in better."

Her laughter was so sweet and feminine as she hugged the hoodies to her chest. "These are great. Thank you so much."

A grin pulled up my lips as she did the cutest wiggle when she unfolded the hoodies again and held them up.

"Owen's going to kick your ass when he finds out you're aiding and abetting a not-yet-known felon."

I threw my head back and laughed at that. I would gladly take an ass kicking over anything that made her smile like that.

"Are you hungry? I haven't made breakfast yet. I can…I'm not great at cooking, but the guys tend to leave things in the fridge for me."

"I'm good. But definitely eat if you're hungry." She was a bit on the thinner side, and I'd always been a sucker for a thick woman. Not that I wanted her to change anything about herself for me. But a fat ass never hurt anyone.

She shoved the hoodies into the bag, then held it by the handles in front of her, her eyes lifting to my face before darting away.

"I…what do you want to do?" she asked, looking up at me again.

"Honestly? I hadn't thought any further than seeing you again," I admitted.

A cloud of sweetness lifted on the air and I instantly hardened. Fuck. The last thing I wanted was to make her uncomfortable by walking around with a chubby when we were merely trying to get to know each other. But the memories of last night's text did nothing to quell the need rushing through me.

As I stared into her face, her pupils dilated, her lips parted, and her chest rose and fell with heavy breaths.

Fuck.

Before I'd had a moment to think about my next move, I was closing the space between us, catching her when she launched herself at me, her arms wrapping around my neck while her legs hooked behind my back.

With both hands cupping her ass, I slanted my mouth over hers, groaning when she began to grind against my hard cock while her tongue plunged into my mouth, tasting, teasing, dualling with my own.

Her sweet rain and lemon scent wrapped around me, soaking into my pours, and sending every drop of blood rushing to my cock. All logical thought escaped me, especially when one of her hands tangled in my hair and tugged.

Her other hand trailed along my face, cupping my jaw, before raking her nails across the back of my neck.

I needed to be inside of her. I needed to feel her skin against mine. I needed to feel her falling apart around me, beneath me, her inner walls clenching me as she came on my dick.

"Wait," I said, pulling my mouth from hers and chuckling when she tightened her hold and tried to pull my lips closer. "Maeve, wait."

Her lids fluttered open and she looked at me with lust filled eyes. Her pupils were completely blown, the scent of her slick warred with the thick perfume rolling from her, and she was still rolling her hips and grinding her core against my cock.

"We...shit. I can't believe I'm going to say this, but we need to slow down."

It wasn't that I was opposed to fucking her on our first date, but I needed to make sure she was fully aware of what she was doing. She almost acted as though she was in heat, and that was a boundary I wouldn't cross without the presence of her pack.

With her still wrapped around me, I carried her across the living room and lowered onto the couch, groaning when she shifted against my raging boner. If she kept that up, I'd end up blowing my load in my jeans and making a complete fool of myself.

"Let's talk," I said, pulling my hands from her ass and cupping her face to keep her for diving for my mouth again.

"Talk?" she repeated, her voice sounding as though she was drunk.

"Yeah. Talk. Like...are you in heat?"

Her smile was shaky as she slowly climbed from my lap. I would rather have had her close, but if she needed space, I would allow her that without complaint.

"No. I'm not in heat. Yet," she said, adding the last part under her breath. "Why?" Now she looked and sounded suspicious.

Holding my hands out, I turned my body more toward her so I could face her straight on. "I just didn't want you to regret any time you spent with me. And I don't want to step on your alphas' toes."

She huffed a laugh, opened her mouth, then snapped it shut. "You wouldn't be stepping on toes. But no, I'm not in heat."

Her phone chirped from the side table. Glancing at it, she huffed an exasperated sigh with a roll of her eyes and lifted it to type out a quick reply before setting it back on the table.

"Everything alright?" I asked her when she sat back, crossed her arms, and glared off into the corner of the room.

She huffed out another of those sighs. "Yeah. Just dandy."

Frowning at her phone sitting on the table, I turned my attention back to her. Had her alphas texted her? Did they know I was here and weren't too happy about that?

"Should I go?" I asked. *Please say no. Pleeease say no.*

"Hell no," she blurted out, then sucked her lips into her mouth as though she hadn't meant to say that out loud. "I mean...they're not mad." Her cheeks flamed bright and elicited a smile from me.

"So...what did they say?"

If possible, her cheeks flushed even brighter. And now I *really* needed to know what was in that text.

"For fuck's sake," she muttered under her breath when her phone dinged again. "They asked me why we stopped." She threw her hands in the air then went right back to crossing her arms under her perky tits and highlighting the fact she wasn't wearing a bra.

"Blame it on me."

Her russet brows drew together. "What?"

"Blame it on me. Tell them I was worried about moving too fast."

"You're not...it's not weird that they're watching us?"

I looked around the room, finally noting the various cameras aimed at the room. "Well, I hadn't really thought about the fact we'd have an audience." Shit. Anything Maeve and I did would be on camera. Did that mean her pack were voyeurs? Or had they simply checked in when they'd received an alert to my arrival?

"I don't know that I love the fact we would have an audience, but as long as it's not a big deal to you. Or them. I don't want to come between your pack."

"You're not. It was, um...it was their idea. Well, Beckett's idea. Since I'm technically under house arrest–" She raised a hand and flipped off the camera and I wondered if there was sound along with the video. "Beckett suggested inviting you over after seeing our text conversation last night."

Now it was my turn to blush as heat burned my cheeks. If he'd gone through her phone, he would have seen the pics of my tattoos along with the suggestive one when I'd shown all but my dick and balls.

"I just...before we...I'm not normal. Or...whatever. I'm not a good omega."

It took a few seconds for her words to sink in. "What the hell does that mean?"

"It means I highly doubt there will be a day when I'll be content sitting around the house waiting for my pack to come home. Or that I'll ever stop doing shit that pisses my alphas off."

"Like setting off concussion grenades in a crowd of protestors?"

Her smile was slow but stretched across her pretty face. "Yeah. Like setting off concussion grenades in a crowd of protestors."

Something I'd heard them say in the parking lot tickled my mind. Her alphas had made it sound as though she'd killed someone in the past, as though they feared the government would one day label her as feral. It was rare, but it happened. And those with that label were never able to find a pack again. They weren't allowed to wander through society without an armed chaperone. It was fucked up and terrifying to think of Maeve locked up like that.

"You realize there is no such thing as a perfect omega, right? Just like there's no such thing as a perfect beta or a perfect alpha. The world would be pretty fucking boring if we all acted like cyborgs."

She chuckled softly. Her fingers toyed with the ends of her hair, tugging it over her shoulder. "I guess."

"There's no guessing to it, Maeve. I don't know your alphas, but they seem to care about you."

"They do." Her voice held something that sounded like a mixture of whimsy and doubt. How could she doubt the way anyone would feel about her?

"I'm pretty sure they would have voiced their opinion or chosen a different omega if they'd wanted a spoiled prince or princess or if they wanted one who fit into a particular mold."

Her text dinged a few seconds later. She glanced at it and groaned.

"They agreed, didn't they?" I chuckled, but it was growing a little uncomfortable that they were watching our first full interaction so closely. Finding one of the cameras, I looked at it and said, "Any chance we can get some privacy, alphas?"

Half a second later, the red light below it went dark. I hadn't meant for them to turn off the cameras, only that it would be more comfortable if they weren't hanging on every word spoken between the two of us.

"How the hell did you do that? I've been trying to get some privacy for a while."

I barked a laugh before I could stop myself. "I'm pretty sure they knew you wanted privacy so you could head out to commit a few misdemeanors."

She rolled her eyes, but her body shook with laughter. "Good point."

"All I'm trying to say is I don't expect you to behave in any certain way. And...if your alphas are okay with it, I would really like to court you."

"I didn't know betas courted omegas." Her eyes dipped to my lips and I wanted nothing more than to tug her back onto my lap so I could go back to kissing her.

"I don't care what we are or aren't supposed to do. I want us to get to know each other, I want your alphas to learn they can trust me with their omega, and then..."

"Then you'll join our pack," she said as though it was the obvious conclusion.

And fuck if that wasn't exactly what I wanted. Almost as much as I wanted to have her wrapped around my body the way she had been when I'd first arrived.

CHAPTER 9

<u>Owen</u>

So many conflicting emotions warred in my heart. The biggest one was jealousy, which was so fucking stupid.

I was jealous of my packmate because he'd finally broken through our omega's walls enough to feel her beneath him, to actually have a deep, heartfelt conversation. She'd told him she loved him the night that we'd brought her back home after she'd played vigilante in the middle of a group of angry, asshole alphas.

Now, she was at the house with a beta. I'd watched as they'd crashed together as though they'd been drawn together by some unseen force. It was a collision of want and lust.

And then Wilder had stopped her before they could do anything more than make out.

No, I didn't exactly want to share my beautiful Maeve, nor did I want to see her fucking someone else. But if the beta could break past the barriers she'd erected from day one, I would throw him a mother fucking ticker-tape parade.

That would also mean sharing her with yet another person. But... she wasn't really mine. She'd allowed Beck to mark her a few months ago, and that was only after he'd explained it was merely to protect her, to show others that she was claimed in hopes of deterring any overzealous alphas.

But she didn't carry my mark. I couldn't feel her through a bond. While I loved her more than I knew was possible, she was more a best friend than anything. Of course, she would stay my best friend regardless, but every day was a struggle to refrain from pulling her against me and slanting my mouth over hers. She was so damn beautiful. So strong. Stronger than even she realized.

I couldn't imagine going through what my sweet omega went through and not hating the entire world.

Well, she wasn't exactly fond of alphas. Beckett and I were the only alphas she could stomach being around without her violent tendencies rearing their head. And, while she would sleep between us in the pack bed, this morning was the first time she'd allowed either of us to touch her in a romantic gesture outside of her heat.

Hell...the last time she'd actually ridden out a heat with our help had been almost a year ago. Since then, we'd procured suppressants at her request.

"What are you doing?" I asked as Beckett stood outside the SUV, tapping away on his phone screen.

"Asking her why they stopped," he said with a smirk.

"You're going to piss her off."

I pulled up the screen and watched as she checked her message, glared at the camera, then sat back with her arms crossed.

But there was a ghost of a smile. The sounds of the house increased as Beckett turned up the volume and then the two of us become fucking voyeurs, listening in as our omega chatted with a beta she was obviously attracted to.

They were both on the couch, but there was space between them now. And they were both fully clothed, although even through the screen on my phone, I could tell Maeve hadn't bothered with a bra after the shower that left her pretty red curls damp.

"I just...before we...I'm not normal. Or...whatever. I'm not a good omega."

What the fuck? She was the perfect omega. At least she was perfect for us.

Wilder frowned at her. "What the hell does that mean?"

"It means I highly doubt there will be a day when I'll be content sitting around the house waiting for my pack to come home. Or that I'll ever stop doing shit that pisses my alphas off."

"Like setting off concussion grenades in a crowd of protestors?"

She smiled and shook lightly with a chuckle. "Yeah. Like setting off concussion grenades in a crowd of protestors."

"You realize there is no such thing as a perfect omega, right? Just like there's no such thing as a perfect beta or a perfect alpha. The world would be pretty fucking boring if we all acted like cyborgs."

Was she playing with her hair? It almost looked flirtatious, but maybe she was growing anxious over the subject matter.

"I guess."

"There's no guessing to it, Maeve. I don't know your alphas, but they seem to care about you."

"They do." Their voices were tinny through the phone speakers, but that sure as hell sounded like doubt in her sweet voice.

"I'm pretty sure they would have voiced their opinion or chosen a different omega if they'd wanted a spoiled prince or princess or if they wanted one who fit into a particular mold."

Beckett's fingers flew across his screen again. A second later, I heard the ding of her phone through the speakers.

"They agreed, didn't they?" He looked up at the camera on the west side of the house. "Any chance we can get some privacy, alphas?"

Looking up at Beckett, I watched as he smiled down at the phone, then hit a button. A second later, my feed went dark. I could easily switch to a different camera, and we could still listen in, although the words would be harder to make out.

But if they wanted privacy, we would give it to them. I wasn't worried about Maeve with the beta – she was right, she was perfectly capable of taking care of herself against one male.

It was only when she went into public where there were dozens or even hundreds of alphas that I grew worried about her. Especially since my omega would never back down from a fight even if she was far outnumbered.

"Well?" Beck asked me.

"Well, what?"

We needed to get to work. We'd been standing here too long watching the cameras instead of finishing up installing the system for our newest client.

"You think…" He let his words trail off.

"Honestly? I don't want to think about someone else fucking our omega." Especially since it had been far too long since I'd felt her wrapped around me, since she'd let me do anything more than hold her while we slept.

But she'd let Beck closer. I had to find a way to break through the wall of ice around her heart. She trusted me. She trusted both of us. It had taken months to get to that point, to get her to avoid hiding in her nest day in and day out.

Sleeping beside us was all fine and dandy, but more and more, it felt as though we were living as roommates. And fuck me, I was so crazy in love with the fiery omega.

As I carried equipment to the side of the house where we'd be installing cameras, I came to a startling realization – I would gladly step aside if she only wanted Wilder and Beck in a romantic sense. I was willing to sacrifice my own heart if it meant she would feel whole.

"Stop," I said as I spotted Beck pulling his phone out and checking on Maeve and Wilder again. "They're fine."

"They're still sitting there talking."

"Let them talk. Wilder seems like a standup guy." And probably feared he was rushing her when they'd launched themselves at each other after he'd given her the gift bag. I hadn't quite been able to make out what she was holding up, but it had looked like a couple camouflage hoodies.

The beta had picked up on the fact my omega wasn't into pretty stuff, the shiny baubles or pastel blankets that were sold at stores marketed to omegas. I'd tried just about everything through the almost two years since she'd joined our family. While she liked things that were soft like any omega, she gravitated toward more neutral colors and wasn't hip on jewelry or fancy clothes.

I huffed a silent laugh over the thousands of dollars I'd spent on fancy, designer brand clothes for her only for her to wear jeans or leggings every single day. My omega was more into comfort than appearance.

Honestly, I wasn't sure I wanted a spoiled omega, the kind who wanted to be pampered and doted on. I liked that Maeve had risen from the ashes like a fucking phoenix and became a warrior. I liked that she preferred to play with firearms or throwing knives over wrapping herself in blankets and curling up on the couch all day.

The leggings and thin t-shirts probably did more for me than the fanciest fucking dress I'd ever bought her. The stretchy material clung to her slight curves. The thin t-shirts showcased her perky tits.

Fuck. Just thinking about Maeve was giving me a chubby. And we had a few more hours of work before I could lock myself in my bedroom and rub one off.

If she'd finally slept with Beck, what were the odds she would finally sleep with me?

Ugh. I felt like an asshole even contemplating ways to get into her pants. But…I was an alpha and she was an incredibly sexy omega. My fucking hormones couldn't exactly be controlled. Only my actions.

After a quick glance around to make sure the homeowners and neighbors weren't watching, I reached down and adjusted myself to keep my dick from getting crushed when I climbed up the ladder.

Yeah. I would willingly sacrifice my heart to make Maeve happy. But I was pretty sure I would end up dying from the worst case of blue balls known to mankind.

CHAPTER 10

<u>Maeve</u>

ilder had pushed a little further than I liked, but he'd apparently caught on to my body language and had changed subjects to more benign topics like favorite foods and other minor crap like that.

This, I could do. I wasn't overly fond of small talk, per se, but it was far better than telling Wilder why I found the need to lash out at alphas. Especially since I didn't see him as a threat, therefore, he would never suffer my wrath.

I almost laughed at my own thoughts. *My wrath.* Like I was some big, strong, uncontrollable beast that all should fear. I was barely a quarter inch over five-foot-three and recently got up to a whopping hundred and ten pounds. Not exactly a beast of a person.

But my alphas had made sure I felt safe, and that meant I could handle any weapon handed to me with perfect accuracy. They'd hired a beta to teach me hand to hand combat, they'd purchased several firearms and set up targets in the back for practice, and had even installed a pretty cool gym in the basement complete with a hanging punching bag for when the angry energy demanded an outlet.

Although, I preferred to punish people rather than the damn bag.

Turning my head to glance at Wilder, I realized that for the first time in a long damn time...I didn't feel that violent urge, didn't hear the voice that demanded I find someone to punish, that I take my past out on an alpha who behaved as though my designation was nothing more than property or an adornment to their life.

Wilder looked in my direction, back at the movie playing, then did a quick double take.

His lips quirked at the corners when he caught me staring, even when I tried to avert my attention and pretend I was focused on the movie.

"What?" he asked, humor in his words.

"Nothing." My attempt at blasé and unbothered was belied by the tremble in my voice.

Shit.

"Maeve? Did I...should I go? I don't want to make you uncomfortable or wear out my welcome."

"No," I blurted too quickly. I definitely did not want him to leave. As much as I adored my alphas, and even though I trusted them implicitly, even they couldn't bring me the peace I felt with Wilder's oranges and sweet cream scent easing the rougher parts of my mind and heart.

Finally facing him, my heart stuttered at the openly concerned look in his pretty gray eyes. When he'd stopped us before we could end up a naked, sweaty tangle of arms and legs, his eyes had been closer to blue. Now, they were back to that storm cloud gray, and I wondered if they changed with his emotions. How cool would that be to gauge his emotions solely by the shade of his irises?

Of course, if he were to become pack, if one of my alphas were to mark him, I could feel him through our bond. But that would also mean opening the connection to Beckett, something I had been reluctant to do since his teeth had sunk into my shoulder for fear he would learn how ugly and dark my heart really was. My giant alpha was so sweet and gentle. Surely, he would throw me out on my ass if he realized he'd taken in someone as broken and scary as me.

"I'm not uncomfortable. You haven't worn out your welcome. And I definitely don't want you to leave," I said, my voice shaky and a touch breathy.

This was way too close to admitting true feelings, something that scared the shit out of me. Even my alphas weren't privy to the innermost shit that churned deep inside of me.

At least not until this morning. The realization that I actually felt a little lighter after not only sharing my body with Beckett, but my fears that I would never be enough, never be good enough, never be the kind of omega who deserved such amazing people...it felt good.

He hadn't judged me. My alpha had merely done exactly as Wilder had done earlier and reminded me that nothing was expected of me. No one expected me to fit into a specific mold.

After all, Beck and Owen knew they were in for a hell of a ride when they'd first found me. They knew life with me wouldn't be easy when I attacked them any time they came close enough the first month or so in their house. They knew I would never be the submissive, dutiful omega when I screamed and threw shit at them during my first heat in their house, choosing instead to suffer through it alone while they'd damned near lost their minds as they listened to my wails of pain and endured the heady clouds of perfume that permeated every square inch of my nest and living quarters.

While that time was barely a blur of a memory, the image of the way they'd looked when I'd finally stumbled out for a shower was permanently burned in my brain. I'd let them help me through a few after that but had relied on suppressants more often than not.

But what if...

What if I allowed my body to experience its natural cycle and allowed my pack to get me through it? What if, instead of fighting biology, instead of fighting my feelings and assuming I wasn't worthy, I allowed my pack to care for me?

And...what would my alphas think if I asked that Wilder was present, too? Would he even be open to something like that?

I had a few weeks to worry about that little tidbit. And that gave him time to get to know me better and decide whether I was a train-wreck he had no desire to witness any further than a few dates spent on the couch.

Wait. There was no way my alphas would demand I spend every minute of every day in the house, not if there was at least someone there to keep me out of trouble. And what better person than someone who worked so closely with the ORE?

"You still look as though you would rather be anywhere but here," he said, raising a brow at me.

With a heavy sigh, I turned my body more so I was facing him. "I'm just…thinking."

"About?" His other brow joined the first.

"You. Me. My pack."

"Any chance you can tell me a little more? Because the last thing I want is to get in the way of you and your alphas or for you to think I'm trying to force anything with you. I mean…I want you. In a way that I'm reluctant to voice just yet. But I never want you to feel as though you don't have a choice in whether or not I court you. Or date you. Or you know, whatever."

He looked like there was a lot more he wanted to say, but snapped his mouth shut when he began to ramble, his words starting to run together.

Staring into his eyes, my body grew warmer by the second. There was a distinct chance he would run away screaming if he were to get to know me, if he were to see the grotesque display that permanently decorated my back and legs.

Or not. Even as a beta, he appeared strong, and not just physically. I couldn't imagine being weak minded and dealing with alphas screaming, cursing, threatening, or throwing things at me. It would take a heart and mind of steel to deal with that kind of shit day in and day out without snapping and attacking someone.

So…maybe he wouldn't run away. Maybe he wouldn't be disgusted by the deep, dark secrets only my alphas were privy to. Maybe he wouldn't find my scars hideous.

But I sure as hell didn't want his pity, either. I'd survived, something so many omegas couldn't say. I'd survived the pits of hell, torture, and attempted rape, and was leading a somewhat stable life, even if I tended toward crime and vigilantism from time to time.

"Have you ever worked with an omega?" I asked as my thoughts ping ponged in my brain.

I'd gone from wondering whether Wilder would be interested in a long-term deal with me to wondering if someone like me could be hired to…well, to keep alphas away from omegas.

He huffed a laugh then pushed a hand through his light brown hair. "You mean as a guard or ORE member?" I nodded. "No. Tons of alphas and some betas. But no omegas."

I cocked a brow at him, ready to lambast him about how we were just as capable of manning a firearm as he or any other man, but he held up his hands to stop me.

"I've worked with female alphas and betas. It's just…omegas tend to be smaller. And their scents…the fuckers – sorry, the jerks we deal with on a regular basis wouldn't bother controlling their instincts if they caught even a hint of an omega's presence. And we try to refrain from firing unless absolutely necessary." Something crossed through his eyes, a shadow of regret or maybe sorrow. But it was gone just as quickly as he forced a smile. "You thinking about applying?"

It was a tease, but yeah, that had actually crossed my mind. Not that my alphas would be on board with me intentionally crawling into the lion's den. And not just crawling in – more like dangling raw meat in front of the rabid beasts.

"I'm just…I hate that I don't have a role. I wasn't joking when I said I was on house arrest." She turned and glared at the camera, then seemed to remember they were no longer watching us. "I would love to get a job, but shit seems like it's getting worse for my designation instead of better."

"You know who I work for, right?"

"Yeah. Omega Change. But the office is closed." And had been completely destroyed by the same assholes who I'd seen scattering a week ago.

"But Sophie and the others are still working. They're still helping. I could...do you want me to put you in contact with Sophie or her assistant, Joy? They could help you find a job, one that's safe. For both you *and* alphas," he said, adding the last part with a mischievous grin.

When he smiled like that, I had to fight the urge to climb onto his lap and kiss him until we were both breathless.

So...what the hell was I waiting for? Why did I find the need to constantly ignore my instincts? I'd done it with my alphas and look what that got me – almost two years of zero intimacy.

His mouth opened as though he would say something, but I launched myself across the couch and kissed him, our teeth bumping together with the force.

"Oh! Shit. Sorry," I muttered, pressing my fingers to my tender lips before touching his mouth.

Apparently, I hadn't hurt him as much as surprised him.

He cupped the back of my neck and pulled me closer until our mouths collided with so much force and passion I swore my toes curled in my fluffy socks.

His hands gripped my thighs and urged me onto his lap until I was straddling his hips, my core resting directly over his rapidly growing erection. Holy hell. There were two layers of clothing separating us, but already I felt as though I would fall apart from the mere touch.

My panties grew damp with slick and my pussy clenched around air as the need grew in me until my skin felt warm and my heart pounded behind my ribs.

When was the last time I felt such unbridled, raw need? I couldn't help but wonder if Beckett hadn't opened some floodgate, and not just the physical kind. For the first time in a long time, I felt less...hollow. I felt as though I could be myself, as though I was being seen for the woman I was and not the omega I was supposed to be, the omega so many in society thought I should be.

Wilder cupped my face and pulled me away, ducking his head so we were perfectly eye to eye.

"Tell me if you need to stop."

"Don't stop," I said with a whimper, dragging him back to my mouth.

I felt fucking alive. I felt safe. I felt…fuck, I felt *whole*.

My alphas treated me wonderfully. They loved me. But the moment I was in Wilder's arms, it felt as though my life was finally complete. It would have been even better if Beck and Owen were here, if we could form a bond together, if we could…

If we could complete our pack.

That was a conversation for another time, not our first official date, not when I was so close to ripping his clothes away and riding him right there on the couch.

Wilder's hand roamed up my sides until they cupped my breasts. I moaned into his mouth as he fondled my nipples through the thin cotton of my long-sleeved t-shirt, causing his dick to twitch beneath me.

And then his hands roamed under my shirt and around my back. It was like someone had thrown ice water over my head.

Pulling away with a gasp, I grabbed his hands and held them in mine, staring into his lust hazed eyes.

"Wait," I breathed out.

"Shit, I'm sorry. Too fast."

"What? No. Not too fast. It's just…" If I wanted Wilder to even contemplate joining my pack, if I wanted him to be open to being my beta, if I wanted to be with him in a more intimate matter, he needed to know what he would see the moment I was naked. Because I sure as hell didn't want to see pity or disgust on his face when we were in the throes of passion.

He reached forward and pushed my hair away from my face. "I'm not expecting anything from you, Maeve. I'm just as content watching movies with you for a few hours. Or we can talk. Or whatever."

With a smirk, I wiggled my hips. "Doesn't feel that way to me."

He groaned then chuckled. "I didn't say it would feel great. Just that I would be fine if you didn't want to—"

I kissed him, just a quick peck of my lips before pulling away to look at him. "I definitely want to do more than watch the boob tube. But I need to show you…there's something…damn it."

How did I tell him without telling him every minute detail? I had no desire to relive the nightmare that was my life for almost four years. And in that time, I had endured more than I would have ever thought I could survive. I carried the reminders with me every day of my life, both inside and out.

"I don't want you to freak out," I said, leaning back a little so I could fully gauge his reaction to my words. "But my back…I have scars."

His dark brows drew together as his eyes lowered to my torso. "I saw you. In that text."

"Not there," I said, waving toward my chest and stomach. "My back. And legs. They're…the scars are kind of ugly."

"Nothing that is a part of you could ever be ugly," he said with so much conviction I almost believed him. He could say that now, but what would happen if we did bond, if he and my alphas finally felt what was deep inside my heart and soul? If they finally felt the hate and anger that still festered so long after I'd been rescued from that basement?

Tears burned the backs of my eyes as he searched my gaze. He looked so genuine, his words so sweet. And as much as I wanted us to start out on the right foot, I was terrified he would reject me if he learned too much.

But I refused to lie. I refused to hide. Not anymore. Beck had proven this morning that I wasn't nearly as defective or broken as I'd believed for far too long.

"I was held and tortured for eleven months, sixteen days, and twenty-two hours. Beckett and Owen were hired to install cameras and alarms to keep me in when I tried to escape too many times. He tried to beat me into submission but failed. The security system was his last-ditch effort. But he didn't expect two amazing alphas to find me and get me out. But not before – fuck. Wilder, I killed the first alpha who tried to bond me. He tried to make me his little slave. And I killed him the moment Owen got me out while Beck held him at bay. I grabbed a butcher knife and shoved it right into his heart. He was dead before he hit the ground."

Wilder didn't say anything for so long I questioned my sanity for revealing so much to someone who could easily turn me over to the authorities.

"He tortured you?" he asked, his voice deep, a growl wrapping around the words.

I nodded.

"Did he…did anyone…"

"Rape me? No. Not for lack of trying. But that was where the beatings came in. He thought he could train me, turn me into a mindless sex slave."

With a deep breath, I climbed from Wilder's lap, turned, grabbed the bottom hem of my shirt and tugged it over my head so he could get the full picture. But that wasn't enough. I wanted him to know it all so he wouldn't be surprised or repulsed when he tried to smooth his hands down my body and came across the raised edges of the scars.

Tossing my shirt to the ground, I slid my hands into the sides of my leggings and shoved them to my ankles, straightening and pulling my hair over my shoulder. There was no more hiding. Either Wilder would accept all of me the way Beck and Owen had, or he would decide I wasn't worth the energy it would take to earn my trust and respect.

Who was I kidding? One day spent with him and I trusted him. I felt as safe with him as I did with my alphas, and it had taken them months to earn that.

A growl unlike any I'd heard from a beta rattled behind me. His fingers were so gentle as he ran them across the raised ridges. His breath was warm as he leaned close and pressed the sweetest kisses to various places along my back, between my shoulder blades, the top of my ass, even the backs of my thighs as though he could kiss away the ghost pain or even the memories.

"There is absolutely nothing ugly about these or about you. The only ugly part is that I can't take away the memories left behind from your time with that mother fucker. If he weren't dead, trust me when I say I would make it my life's mission to track him down and remove his balls with the rustiest blade I could find."

A sad smile pulled up my lips. And then amusement washed away the sadness as his words settled around me. He wasn't disgusted. He wasn't showing me pity. He was angry on my behalf.

Without bothering to cover myself, I turned slowly, my body fully on display. He was still leaned forward after showing my marks such loving attention.

Wilder reached forward and pulled me closer by my hips until I stood directly between his spread knees. His attention stayed on my face instead of ogling my breasts that were bared for him or lowering his gaze to the apex of my thighs.

"You are not your past. You're not what happened to you. I've seen…fuck, you have got to be the strongest woman I've ever met. You think you're not the perfect omega? You're right. You're the perfect person. Your designation has nothing to do with that. Honestly, it's just a perk." He winked. "What part of all of this did you think would scare me off?"

I barked out a laugh. "I literally just told you I killed someone. And my backside looks like a freaking…well, I don't know. A roadmap?"

"The fucker deserved to die. And even if someone had called it in, one look at your back would have proven it was self-defense."

"He was restrained by Beckett."

"You really think either of those alphas wouldn't have lied for you? I barely know them, but it's obvious how much you mean to them, Maeve. How do you know they wouldn't have killed him if you hadn't?"

I blinked at him. Then blinked again. We had never had that conversation. Not once had I ever broached that subject, not once had I bothered asking them what they would have done with Clay had I not shoved the long butcher knife into his heart.

Tears burned my eyes again, but for a different reason. For so long, I'd thought I was broken, that I had this ugly monster in my heart because of what I'd done to Clay, because I wished I could punish any and every alpha who'd ever committed anything like what Clay had done to me.

But…it *was* self-defense. Maybe it hadn't been in the middle of one of my beatings, but I'd prevented him from doing the same thing or worse to another omega once he no longer had me chained up in his basement.

"You should probably know I still plan to cause more chaos. I will take every opportunity to punish any alpha who mistreats an omega."

"How about you don't tell me about it beforehand? That way, it won't be seen as premeditated."

Another surprised huff of laughter escaped me. He didn't order me to refrain from hurting anyone. He didn't tell me he would alert the authorities or even my alphas of my future plans. He simply wanted to remain oblivious. Plausible deniability and all that.

"How are you so…amazing? More importantly, how have you not been scooped up by a pack?"

His smile was so sweet as he pressed a hand to my back, guiding me down so he could claim my lips. I didn't need much urging. Moving closer, I straddled his lap again, sighing as his tongue swiped into my mouth, the sweet citrus flavor sending slick gathering between my thighs again.

If he kept his pants on, they would end up soaked, especially since I couldn't stop myself from grinding against the hard length restrained behind his jeans.

"Clothes off. Naked. Now, please," I muttered against his lips before reclaiming his mouth.

We separated only long enough for him to pull his shirt over his head. I helped pop the button and rip down the zipper on his jeans, then giggled as he lifted his hips – and me with them – so he could push them down his hips until they pooled around his ankles.

"Tell me if you need me to stop," he said against my lips then trailed them down my throat and nuzzled my shoulder directly over Beckett's mark, sending ripples of pleasure through my limbs.

"Don't stop," I said, reaching between us to grip his cock and hold him steady as I lowered onto him, slowly taking him inside of me until I was fully seated on his lap and he was fully buried inside of me.

We moaned in unison and my body began to tighten at the first contact. For the first time in too long, I felt as though I was fully in control. And not just of my body, but my heart and mind, as well.

Beckett had done that for me. And now Wilder was confirming that I wasn't a mistake, that I wasn't broken, that I deserved to be loved and cherished.

CHAPTER 11

Beckett

I had checked the cameras a few more times between jobs. The last time I'd checked, I'd smiled as I watched Maeve slowly riding Wilder.

Fuck. Finally.

Why the hell I was cheering my omega on when she was fucking someone other than me or Owen was a bit of a mystery. Maybe it was because a twinkle had been present in her eyes both times she'd run into Wilder, regardless of the situation. And then, after seeing the way she was obviously flirting with him while sleeping between her alphas, it was more than obvious she was sexually attracted to him.

She was completely naked, meaning he was aware of her scars. Had she divulged how she'd attained those scars? I really hoped she had. Because that meant she was opening herself up to the beta, similar to how she'd reluctantly opened her chest for me this morning for me to see straight to her beautifully broken heart.

My sweet Maeve didn't believe she was worthy of me, worthy of

Owen. She didn't believe she was worthy of love, no matter how hard we'd tried to prove otherwise.

Perhaps the beta could finally help us break down the impossibly strong walls and hold a mirror up to her face so she could see what we saw in her.

Now Owen and I were heading home. I couldn't seem to wipe the damn smile from my lips, even knowing Owen would more than likely feel a tad hurt or at least jealous that he'd yet to break through her walls.

It wasn't for lack of trying.

The two of us had spent what felt like an eternity proving to her that not all alphas were complete douche canoes. Problem was, there were enough of my designation who were the exact same as the fucker who'd kept her locked up and tried to train her through torture including physical beatings and food restrictions. She'd been skin and bones when we'd brought her home. Not that her weak state had stopped her from trying to attack us any time we came near her or so much as stepped foot into her nest.

Since then, she'd become comfortable enough with us to sleep in the same bed. And this morning...

Fuck. This morning was everything. It felt monumental, as though she finally accepted me as pack, as though she accepted that we loved her.

And she'd told us both she loved us.

After almost two years, she saw us, truly saw us and was no longer attempting to hide herself from us.

I couldn't help but wonder if the beta had a lot to do with that. If so, the dude deserved a fucking trophy. Or a car. Hell, I'd buy him a fucking island if his presence meant Maeve would no longer keep us at arm's length.

Owen was quiet, his hand wrapped so tightly around the wheel his knuckles were white. He knew as well as I did what we were about to walk in on when we got home. The last time I checked the camera, the two hadn't moved. Meaning, they would be out cold and butt ass naked on the couch. There had been a blanket draped over them, but that would do nothing about the scents and pheromones that surely filled the house.

"You going to freak out when we get home?" I asked without looking in his direction.

We'd been friends our entire lives but hadn't become pack until we'd found Maeve on a job. The two of us had never been romantically involved, nor did we share a bond through our omega, but I could read Owen like a fucking book.

"Why would I freak out?" he asked. A muscle jumped in his cheek and his eyes were focused straight ahead.

"Because there's a beta in our house lying naked on the couch with our omega."

Finally turning to look at my packmate and friend, I waited for an answer.

The softest growl rattled up his chest and he raised a hand to scratch at the stubble peppering his cheeks. "I don't know."

It wasn't much of an answer but at least it was an honest one. He couldn't quite say how he'd feel until we'd walked through the door, until he saw our omega with his own two eyes, until he scented their signatures mixing in the air.

"You realize a beta in the mix could be good for her?" I asked as Owen drove the SUV down the driveway and waited for the garage door to rumble up. "He's neutral. She's attracted to him. She feels safe with him."

"I noticed," Owen bit out through clenched teeth.

"Is this...are you mad she had sex with me this morning?"

He put the vehicle in park and frowned at me. "Why the fuck would I be mad that she had sex with you? You're her alpha as much as I am."

"Let me rephrase it: Are you mad she had sex with me this morning and then with Wilder this afternoon but hasn't been with you for—"

"Almost a year," he muttered.

Damn. Had it really been that long since she'd let us help her through a heat? Since neither of us had sought relief from anyone outside the pack, that meant we had both been on a long ass drought. No wonder Owen had grown more and more surly. He was horny as hell.

Until this morning, I totally knew the feeling. Now? Now, I was on cloud nine. Fucking floating.

We both sat in our seats for over ten minutes. Stalling. We were stalling for fear of how Owen – or both of us – would react to seeing our omega with someone who wasn't pack.

Yet.

"We can't sit out here all day," I muttered, pushing my door open and stepping into the garage.

Owen's door clunked shut a second after mine and a heavy, dramatic sigh escaped his lips as he followed me up the two stairs that led into the mud room.

Maeve's shoes were lined up in a perfect row, her jackets hanging on hooks arranged by color.

No sound filtered through the house, but the pheromones went straight to my dick, all the blood rushing from my brain until I felt like I'd pass out right there in the entryway to the kitchen.

A sound that was part growl, part purr rattled from Owen's chest as he slowly made his way through the kitchen and came to a stop behind the couch. I moved to stand beside him and we both stared down at the sleeping couple.

Our omega looked so peaceful. At ease. There was even a ghost of a smile on her pretty pink lips. And now it was my turn to feel a twinge of jealousy. What was it about Wilder that brought her that sense of peace? Was it simply because he was a beta? Because she didn't see him or his designation as a threat?

Or had it been as I'd assumed this morning and I had finally gotten it through her thick skull that she was absolutely perfect for us, perfect exactly as she was. At no point had either Owen or I voiced our desire for anything or anyone different. We didn't need a spoiled, pampered princess.

And, as much as I wished she would let us follow our natural instincts to take care of her, we didn't begrudge the fact she craved independence. Hell, she more than craved it. She downright demanded it.

Turning to glance at Owen, I did a double take. His pupils were blown, his scent was stronger, and his eyes were zeroed in on the couple. He didn't look hurt. He didn't look pissed.

He looked turned on.

Perhaps our omega wasn't the only one attracted to the beta.

As quietly as possible, I guided Owen away from Maeve and Wilder and rummaged through the fridge until I found a beer. I held it up and raised my brows, grabbing a second when my packmate nodded.

Then we took our beers to the screened patio to hang out while we waited for the two to wake. Although I had a suspicion Owen would have much rather dove in the middle of the two, though I wasn't sure whether it was to hold them both or to feel their flesh against his.

"They look good together," I said, cocking a brow at Owen as he lowered onto one of the wicker chairs situated in a semi-circle.

Owen popped the top of his beer and tossed the cap onto the table before nodding. "Yeah."

"Yeah?" I teased, turning my body more toward his. "Just admit it – you think he's hot."

The frown my friend and packmate shot me was lacking any venom. He could pretend all he wanted, but I'd caught the same whiff of oranges and cream that he had. Wilder smelled delicious. And yeah, he was an attractive beta. But I hadn't reacted the way Owen had.

Whether it was because he was merely horny or because he was fighting the realization he wanted the beta in a romantic sense, I wasn't sure. And, while I would have loved to push him further until he admitted it, Owen looked too close to snapping.

"We should invite him to stay here for a while. Give them more time alone together." Hey, just because I wasn't going to push Owen to admit to anything didn't mean I wouldn't find a way to keep the beta closer in hopes of both enticing him to join the pack for Maeve's sake, and maybe even give Owen a chance to decide whether what he'd felt was genuine attraction or simply a lack of intimacy.

"He's got a job. I'm sure he doesn't have time to hang out with our omega all day every day."

"I didn't say anything about all day," I said, hiding my smile behind my beer bottle.

"He has a home of his own. A life. Why the fuck would he uproot everything…"

But he didn't finish the sentence. His eyes had darted toward the glass door leading into the kitchen.

Wilder stood in front of the open fridge, his jeans open and hanging low on his hips.

Damn. I wasn't into the beta but even I could admit he made a sexy as fuck picture in our kitchen.

"Holy shit," I breathed out.

The beta didn't notice us watching him at first. The setting sun cast a warm glow on his toned body, his light brown hair was mussed, and there was definitely a ghost of a smile on his lips like someone who'd enjoyed the warmth of an omega.

When he found a can of soda and turned as he swung the door shut, he caught us staring. No reason to try to act as though we hadn't noticed him.

Raising my beer, I smiled and jerked my head for him to join us.

Owen shifted in his seat and I did everything I could to pretend I didn't notice the way he adjusted the bulge in his work pants.

"Hey," Wilder said as he stepped out. "When did you get home?"

"A few minutes ago. We didn't want to wake you two up," I said, shoving a chair closer to him with my booted foot.

He lowered onto the chair and cracked the top of the can before taking a long pull. Depending on how many times they'd made love, he might need more than a soda to replenish. I had to clear my throat to prevent the chuckle at that thought from bursting from my mouth.

"So uh…" Wilder glanced from one of us to the other. "This is awkward," he muttered.

"Nothing awkward about it," I said with a grin.

Owen groaned and shifted in his seat again. Yep. My packmate was absolutely attracted to the beta and not just the combined scents that now coated every inch of our couch. Although, he did still carry Maeve's sweet spring rain and lemon pie that had always made my mouth water.

"You're uh...Maeve...shit," Wilder said, pushing his hand through his hair and making it even more charmingly disheveled. "Is this weird? Me being here?"

"Not at all," I said, kicking my feet up onto the table. "You two had fun?"

Wilder's cheeks flamed a bright red.

"Fuck, Beck," Owen growled. "We're not pissed if that's what you're worried about. We just want her happy. You make her happy."

Was it my imagination, or were Wilder's pupils as dilated as Owen's? I supposed it could have been the aftereffects of fucking Maeve, but I hadn't noticed it when we'd been speaking, only when he turned his attention to Owen.

Interesting.

It was like after emptying my balls for the first time in almost a year, I was determined to play matchmaker with my pack. I had zero problem with either of them enjoying the beta if he made them happy. And Wilder was obviously a good dude. He could have easily turned Maeve over to the authorities instead of calling us. What she'd done that day could have been labeled as domestic terrorism. And we already feared the government growing tired of her antics and registering our girl as feral.

"Your omega...Maeve is amazing," he said, his words almost huffed out as a smile bloomed wide on his handsome face.

"She is," I said, tipping my bottle back to take another pull. "Owen and I were chatting," I said, glancing at my packmate and earning a glare. "I know you have a job and shit, but would you be amenable to hanging around a while? Not, like, babysitting her. But...she likes you. You've done something to heal a part of her we haven't been able to reach. We'd be honored if you allowed us to court you."

"For fuck's sake," Owen muttered under his breath.

"I thought *I* was supposed to court *her.*"

Owen chuckled a deep sound. "Good luck with that."

"She isn't into being courted. Gifts...you got her a pretty good one. But I wouldn't make a habit of it. At least not the traditional omega gifts."

"I assumed that. I mean, I'd only met her twice, but she didn't come off as the kind of woman who would be into sparkly shit," Wilder said.

Little by little, he was beginning to relax, sitting back in the chair and propping his feet on the table next to mine.

"I don't need to be courted. Or whatever. I just...I wouldn't mind spending more time with her. A lot more time," he said, adding the last part almost under his breath. "As long as it doesn't interfere with your relationship with her."

"Nope. Not at all. Like I said, you make her happy. And that's all we want for her." I took a chance and sat forward. "You saw her back?"

"Yeah. She told me...well, the basics of her past before you two. And I know about the alpha."

"Fucking prick," Owen grumbled.

"Just know it'll be a little more difficult to connect to her on an emotional level. If you're willing to be patient with her–"

"She's worth it," Owen and Wilder said at the same time.

And then they stared at each other long enough I wondered if they'd forgotten I was still sitting here.

"If the two of you are about to make out, I'm going inside."

"Beck," Owen warned. "You don't have to say every single thought that pops in your head."

Ah, but neither denied the thought had crossed their minds.

CHAPTER 12

<u>Maeve</u>

The most delicious sensations tingled through my body as I pulled my arms over my head, pointed my toes, and stretched. Orange creamsicle tickled my nose and memories of earlier came crashing back.

Wilder.

Wait. Why was I alone on the couch? His shirt sat on the floor beside my clothes, his signature still clung to the fabric of the couch and lingered in the air as though he was still here.

Low rumblings of male voices came from the direction of the kitchen. My cheeks flamed hot at the realization that my pack had returned home while I was out cold on the couch. And not just asleep but completely naked. Had Wilder still been wrapped around me when they'd come home? And were the low voices possibly my pack reading him the riot act?

Nah. Beck had texted when Wilder pulled away asking why we'd stopped. *Freaking perv*. Had Wilder not asked them for some privacy, I would have wondered if my alphas had crowded around their phones to watch every minute Wilder and I had spent touching and pleasing each other, if they'd watched as I'd straddled the beta's lap and ridden his cock like it was the only thing keeping me tethered to the planet.

I was both turned on and embarrassed at the thought.

Tugging my clothes on, I shoved my feet back into my fuzzy socks and padded through the house, following the low drone of conversation to find them on the patio, sipping beers.

Well, my pack were sipping on beers. Wilder had a can of soda clutched in his hand.

My stomach fluttered and my heart clenched at the sight of the three men conversing so easily. There were smiles, chuckles, Beck even threw his head back and laughed at one point.

It looked so natural. The three of them looked as though they were meant to be there, to be here, to be in my life.

Yet I'd only known Wilder for, what, a whole day? Not even. The first two encounters had been fleeting moments. And he'd only spent a few hours with me today, and most of that had been either naked or sleeping.

Beck muttered something and jerked his head toward me. Owen glanced in my direction and Wilder turned in his seat. His face softened at my appearance and a sweet smile graced that deliriously handsome face. Seriously. How the hell could a man look so damn good? It should be illegal.

After a steadying breath, I schooled my face and wandered outside, taking a seat between Beckett and Owen.

"You boys gossiping?" I teased.

Beck leaned over and I offered my cheek. "About you," he said without bothering to pretend.

And just like that, my walls slammed back into place.

"What about me?"

Were they warning Wilder about my issues? That I could be more than a handful for even an alpha?

"We were asking Wilder if he'd be interested in moving into one of the spare rooms so we can court him," Beck offered.

My brows pulled together in confusion as I turned my attention to Owen. He shrugged and shook his head. "Don't look at me. Beck's idea."

"Betas aren't courted," I said, looking to each man in turn.

"Well, we're changing the rules. Especially since you never let us court you. I need to spoil someone."

"I'm spoiled. How many weapons have you bought me through the years?"

Wilder huffed out a surprised laugh that bordered on a choke as he tried to take a drink of his soda.

"Knives and firearms aren't the usual courting gifts," Owen said.

"And we're not the usual pack," I fired back.

"Hence the reason I suggested courting Wilder. If we're going to make our own rules, I vote for spoiling the beta and buying his affections in hopes of coercing him into joining our pack," Beck said. He leaned back in his seat, his long legs stretched out, feet propped beside Wilder's on the deck table.

I'd had a similar thought already. In fact, it sure as hell seemed like Beckett had been trying to push me in that direction since he and Owen had been awakened by the flash of my phone when I'd sent Wilder suggestive pictures. We hadn't technically sexted, but pretty damn close.

"Wait...is this some way to make sure I have a babysitter twenty-four hours a day?"

Wilder choked out another laugh and coughed hard.

"It doesn't hurt to have another set of eyes on you," Owen muttered under his breath, but I'd heard him just fine.

Lifting my hand, I saluted him with my middle finger. Then added my other hand so he had a double salute.

Wilder and Beck chuckled. Owen shook his head with a smirk.

"If that's what this is, if you're hoping that I'll become the dutiful omega who waits around with an apron wrapped around my waist..."

It was Owen's turn to bark out a laugh. "I don't think anyone who has ever met you would expect that from you. No. That's not what this is."

I glanced from Owen to Wilder and realized their scents were stronger as they eyed each other before their gazes darted away.

What the hell was that? Their scents weren't sour or burnt smelling. So, no anger, no fear, no anxiety.

Holy shit...was my alpha crushing on the beta? And why the hell did slick dampen my panties at the thought? Shouldn't I have felt a tad more possessive?

Although that would be mildly – if not severely – hypocritical. If my alphas were expected to share me not only with each other but with a newcomer, why shouldn't I be just as charitable?

Charitable. As though any of these men were mine to gift to another.

But weren't they? Not once had they returned home carrying the scent of anyone else. They weren't going to clubs or bars in hopes of a one-night stand while their omega rejected them at every turn.

That wasn't completely true. I wasn't rejecting *them*, I'd just been terrified of growing too close, of letting them too far in for fear of them realizing I wasn't worth all the headaches I'd given them.

And wasn't that the stupidest shit I'd ever done?

Okay. Maybe not *the* stupidest, but pretty damn close.

My alphas were amazing. They'd found me in a broken state, had given me plenty of time and space when I'd screeched like a banshee any time they entered my nest or living space. Then, after I'd allowed them to help me through a couple heats, they had willingly procured suppressants and kept their distance sexually. While we might snuggle in the pack bed each time I scared them, they kept their hands to themselves...sexually. They still held me tight, squeezing me into their bodies even when they were dead asleep.

Who was I kidding? I snuggled into them, too.

After my conversation – and time – with Beckett this morning, then with Wilder, I'd made a decision to make more of an effort. I would never be the kind of omega who sat around and waited for gifts. I would never be submissive or subservient. But I could stop being so damn...prickly.

Beckett suggested courting Wilder. And, honestly, after they guaranteed me this wasn't a ploy to keep my ass locked at home every day, I was having a hard time finding a downside to it. I liked Wilder. I wanted him. I wanted him in a way I hadn't let myself want another human since…

Since before. Before I'd thought I could trust an alpha. Before I had been treated as though I was property. Before I had been beaten to within an inch of my life and starved to the point of being weak enough I could no longer fight.

Wait…

"You asked him to move in here so we…so you could court him? Why would he need to move in?"

Beckett glanced in Owen's direction then shrugged. "Because you like him. He makes you happy. I want you to be happy."

My heart squeezed and tears burned the backs of my eyes, though I wasn't sure whether it was from the rush of love and appreciation or shame. Shame and guilt that I'd made my pack feel as though they weren't enough for me.

"Um, Wilder? Could you give us a second?"

His brows twitched up and then he nodded. "Sure. Of course."

He pushed to his feet, fastening the top button and pulling the zipper up on his pants, then headed through the door into the kitchen. And yep, I watched that tight ass the entire time.

When I turned back to my alphas, I realized I wasn't the only one watching Wilder's every move. Perhaps Beck hadn't invited the beta to stay with us solely for my benefit, not if the longing on Owen's face or the heat in his eyes were anything to go by.

Once the door was closed and Wilder rounded the corner and left our view, I turned to my alphas.

"If I've made either of you feel as though I don't appreciate you, or like…I don't know, like you're not enough for me, I promise you that's not the truth. I…I love you both. I should have said it a lot more and I'm sorry. But I do. And, uh, I'm going to be better. I mean, I still won't act like a princess or whatever, but I promise to be nicer. Or whatever."

Beckett's lips quirked as he tried to hold back his smile at my rambling words.

"Maeve–" Owen started, but I held up a hand.

"I swear if you tell me you love me the way I am I might throat punch you. Or junk punch you. Or both."

He slowly lowered his hand to cover said junk as though afraid I would do as I promised.

"I know you love me. You two have done nothing but show me for almost two fucking years. And I've been an asshole–"

"You have–"

"Last warning," I said, glaring at Owen. "I totally *have* been an asshole. I might not be the stereotypical omega, but I've also been a terrible friend, a terrible packmate, and a terrible mate. Period. It's…I can't promise anything will happen overnight, but I'm going to try harder. Beckett…he said this morning…" But I couldn't finish the sentence. The looks on their faces warmed *and* broke my heart.

"I told him everything," Beckett said. "He knows about our conversation."

"And we are still interested in courting Wilder if he makes you happy. And you can stop grinning, asshole," Owen said, raising a middle finger at Beck without turning to look at him.

"Only if you'll admit you want him," Beck said, that grin still in place.

"He's hot. And he smells—"

"Amazing," Owen and I said at the same time.

"Yeah," Owen said as pink washed over his cheeks.

When I smiled at him, then that smile turned into a wide grin, Owen went almost tomato red and ducked his gaze, shifting and trying his best to hide the fact he was adjusting his boner.

"You two swear this isn't a bodyguard thing or a *we're not enough for our omega* thing?"

"I don't think the second is actually a thing," Beck said. "But I think he'll be good for all of us. He's a beta, so there will be no posturing. And he's obviously a good dude if his job is anything to go by."

I didn't bother telling my alphas I'd felt something shift in my chest that first night I'd caught him watching me in the bar. Or that the moment his lips had touched mine I'd felt as though my world had tilted on its axis, or like everything finally made sense in my life.

Who would have thought adding a packmate would have made my world make more sense?

"Okay. If the two of you are on board and Wilder is in, I'm in for courting Wilder. But don't be surprised if he doesn't want to move in here. He has a job, and a home, and a life of his own."

Beckett snorted and glanced at Owen, who smirked.

"What?"

"I mean, we can't speak for Wilder, but I can speak for Owen when I say the moment we met you...you became our whole world. And from the look on his face when you were riding him–"

"You were watching?" I barked out.

"You became his world today, too."

My mouth opened, then closed. I tried to find words, an argument, anything that would make sense of Beckett's words, or even a retort or protest. But nothing came out.

Probably because as of this morning, I realized my entire world revolved around my alphas. And now, it revolved around a beta, as well.

CHAPTER 13

<u>Wilder</u>

Clay. Clay Soren. That was the name of the alpha Maeve had killed. I'd gotten it out of her the fourth night since I'd agreed to move into the pack house. So they could court me.

Such a strange concept no matter how many times I tried to convince myself that their pack was anything but typical. The last thing I needed was to be courted, to be convinced that I wanted to be with Maeve, to be packed with Beckett or Owen.

The latter had taken me by surprise. Of course I'd noticed him when Maeve's alphas had retrieved her the two times I'd witnessed her rebellious streak. But it wasn't until I'd noted his scent when I found the alphas watching me from the patio that I realized I was attracted to him. I'd had relationships with betas and omegas but had never found myself fantasizing about a fucking alpha.

Nonchalantly glancing around to make sure no one was paying me any attention, I typed Clay Soren into the database and frowned when nothing came up. No arrest record. No death certificate. No pack registration.

How the hell had they avoided the authorities discovering his murder? And more importantly, did I really want details if Maeve's alphas had disposed of his body after she'd killed him?

I couldn't think of his death as murder. The fucker deserved it. He'd deserved far more than an easy death after everything I'd learned about my omega's time with him.

Shit. One week and already I was thinking of Maeve as mine. Hell, I was thinking of the pack as mine, too.

Weren't they, though? I was pretty sure my heart had claimed Maeve from the moment I'd seen her walk through the bar, from the moment we'd locked eyes in the mirror. And especially after watching the petite woman put the handsy alpha on his ass with a few well-placed hits.

Beckett was exactly as Maeve described, a gentle giant. For as tall and broad as the alpha was, he was gentle and sweet when it came to his omega. And the dude was funny as hell.

Owen...fuck. The alpha was broody and serious and sexy as fuck with shoulder length, wavy hair that was so dark it was almost black. He constantly had stubble on his cheeks as though he only shaved a couple times a week, and there was the faintest accent to his words. His skin was a deep tan, hinting at a Hispanic or Latino ethnicity.

But the two of us hadn't spent a single moment alone since I'd packed a bag and moved into the spare room while the four of us decided whether I was a good fit for their pack.

Well, the three of them. Because I already knew exactly where I belonged – and that was anywhere Maeve happened to be.

Kai crossed my periphery, so I quickly deleted the search bar before questions were raised. The big alpha dropped into his chair and turned on his computer before huffing out a sigh.

"I appreciate the break, but I didn't think your little omega would affectively scare the protestors away permanently," he said.

I huffed a laugh. "I doubt it's permanent. They're either recouping and coming up with some stupid ass plan or they're going to move the protests somewhere else. No fucking way are they going to give up."

A bunch of politicians recently began to come out in support of the protests, agreeing with the sentiment that unchaperoned omegas were a danger to society. They spouted bullshit about their scents and pheromones causing violence when alphas went into rut.

Amazing how many alphas I knew and not a single one of them had turned into mindless monsters around an omega, whether she was in heat or not, whether she'd perfumed in public or not.

Your little omega. Kai had referred to Maeve as mine. And nope. I didn't bother correcting him. Because I would do everything I could to make sure the pack accepted me and bonded me into their family.

The thought of feeling Maeve in my heart and soul sent a thrill through my body, and blood straight to my cock. I would also feel Owen. And Beckett, of course. A pack. Finally. After so long, after watching all my friends find their families, I would have one of my own.

We hadn't gotten to the point where we'd discussed whether or not Maeve was interested in children, but I sure as fuck hoped she was interested in motherhood. I'd always wanted to be a father. I had always wanted a house full of kids. And I had never given a fuck what designation they presented as during puberty.

"Who's Clay Soren?" Kai asked, tapping on his keyboard before leaning back in his chair to look at me over the top of his monitor.

Well, shit. Apparently, I hadn't been nearly fast enough to erase the evidence of my private investigation.

"Nothing. No one. Just looking into something. How's Sophie?" I asked, hoping bringing up his mate would distract him.

He inhaled deeply through his nose and groaned. "Pissed. Frustrated. Antsy. She wants to return to the office but knows it's too dangerous. Although, if those fuckers stay away much longer, I don't know if I'll be able to restrain her from rebuilding the offices."

I shook my head. "Still too dangerous."

There had been tempered glass and secured doors and the mob had still been able to breach the building and destroy everything inside. They'd almost succeeded in burning the place down before those of us who worked as armed security for Omega Change had resorted to opening fire. There had been no choice, not when there were omegas still living upstairs at the time.

Since then, they'd been moved to secret and secure locations with private guards and top of the line systems and cameras to alert several sects of law enforcement should anyone discover the locations and attempt to harass or assault the terrified and traumatized men and women.

"I agree. But you've met my omega – I'm pretty sure she would give your little Maeve a medal if she knew about the concussion grenade."

"You didn't tell her?"

He leaned back in his chair with a squeak of the springs and shook his head. "She knows there was some kind of explosion caused by a counter protestor, but I didn't give her the details. I figured the less people who know who was responsible..." He let his words trail off with a shrug.

"I appreciate that," I said.

The less people who knew who was behind the chaos, the less chance of Maeve being brought before a judge. And the less chance of my beautiful, fiery omega being labelled a terrorist or feral.

"So..." Kai said.

I glanced up from my computer to find him smirking.

"What?"

"You're living with the pack?"

With a frown, I stifled a groan. "They're, uh...they want to court me. Or whatever."

Kai's brows shot up his forehead. "What does that consist of? Are they buying you pretty shit and showering you with gifts?"

"Asshole," I muttered. "No. I think...it seems more like it's for Maeve's benefit. Like, I don't know...they're giving her the chance to change her mind."

"She won't. I saw the way she looked at you."

"When we were questioning her?"

He nodded. "Even in trouble, she looked at you like she wished you two were alone. Like she wanted to bury her face in your neck and cover herself in your scent."

I grunted a soft sound and looked through the front windows, thinking back to that day, to the way she tried to convince us to let her go, tried to convince us her alphas were too busy to be bothered.

"There's…she has two alphas."

"And?"

My cheeks burned hot as I contemplated confessing that I found myself fantasizing about Owen almost as much as I did about Maeve.

"It's not uncommon for a pack to add a beta," Kai said. And then his eyes raised to my face, and he must have caught the blush burning my cheeks. "Shit. You're into one of them."

"Shh," I said, looking around. Not that any of my friends would judge me, but I almost felt like the pack could hear every word. And since I was having a hard enough time admitting it to myself, I wasn't sure I was ready to admit it to anyone else just yet.

Leaning forward, Kai rested his forearms on his desk. "You better have this conversation with them before y'all go any further. The last thing you want to do is lie to yourself or anyone else. Hell, I was resistant to having an omega or a pack and *I* was the one who fell for Devyn first."

A wistful smile tugged at his lips as he dropped his gaze to his desk and I wondered if he was picturing his pack.

"Maeve…I have to take things slow with her. Let her lead."

"You realize you're covered in her scent, right? I know you're either sleeping with her or *sleeping* with her," he said with a shit-eating grin.

I couldn't help myself. I grinned, too. "Both," I admitted.

"And the alphas?"

"They've been giving us time and space."

Not that I expected that. Hell, I would have loved to have Owen snuggled in her bed with us but I sure as hell wouldn't make the first move. Just because it appeared he was attracted to me, too, didn't mean he wanted to pursue anything romantic or sexual. They'd simply invited me to entertain the possibility of joining the pack for Maeve's sake.

"Talk to them. Or at least talk to the one you're attracted to. Be honest with him and yourself. And if the two of you decide you'd rather focus your energy on Maeve, so be it. But why dance around the subject if you could be happy together?"

"I hate when you're all philosophical and shit."

He chuckled as his phone vibrated on his desk.

"This is Kai," he answered, and leaned back in his chair as the person on the other line spoke.

I hated that he was right. And I hated that I had been a fucking coward. I just couldn't see myself walking up to Owen and saying *hey, I think you're hot and want to see if this is merely sexual or if there's more between us.*

My phone dinged and I glanced at it. Beckett had started a group chat.

> Beckett: Date night tonight. Dress nice. Everyone be ready by 7.

> Owen: Where are we going?

> Beckett: A surprise.

> Maeve: I don't own anything nice.

> Owen: You would if you stopped getting rid of everything I buy you.

MAEVE SENT a middle finger emoji and I smiled. I'd seen her shoot her alphas the bird several times over the past week, but it seemed almost like their love language.

> Me: Im off early tonight. Wanna go shopping?

THE CONVERSATION BUBBLES started and stopped so many times I could almost picture Maeve typing replies and deleting them. Finally, she texted back–

> Maeve: Fine. Pick me up when ur off work. See everyone at home.

A GROUP TEXT. And I'd been included. Maybe it was childish and a bit desperate, but my heartrate kicked up that I'd been included as though already an official packmate.

I'd told Maeve I was off early but hadn't actually asked Kai. But now, I would beg if need be so I didn't look like an asshole.

"Any chance I can take off a little early today?"

Kai glanced at me, down at his phone, then his attention quickly raised to me. "By that smile, I'll assume that was your omega texting you."

I shook my head. "The pack. Date night. And Maeve needs something to wear according to Beckett."

My boss's body shook as he chuckled. "Take off. There ain't shit going on, not until we either get an assignment, Sophie finds a new building, or those assholes show back up." He waved his hand in the air as though shooing me away.

A smile blooming quickly on my face, I turned off my computer, then shot off a text to Maeve that I was on my way home.

I needed to change out of my black shirt and cargos I wore for work, but I'd showered this morning. It shouldn't take me more than a few minutes tops then I could take my omega shopping. I swore I could already hear her protests over me spending money on her, but at least this time there was a good excuse – I was doing as our alphas wanted.

Our alphas. *My* omega. *My pack.*

Damn. One week and already… I felt like I'd found my home in the two alphas and beautiful omega.

CHAPTER 14

<u>Maeve</u>

I turned side to side, looking at myself in the mirror, then stepped out to get Wilder's opinion.

His eyes widened and his pupils dilated. Obviously, he liked what he saw.

I, on the other hand, felt a bit like a fish out of water. I couldn't remember the last time I'd donned a dress or a skirt. My usual aesthetic could only be referred to as homeless chic. Sure, I bathed daily, brushed my hair and teeth, but my clothes hung off my body and hid my shape, my hair was pulled up in a ponytail or bun more often than not, and I barely owned any makeup, nothing like what I saw in the videos on social media.

"What exactly is considered dressing nice? I mean, what if I just wore some cute jeans and a sweater?"

Wilder chuckled. "I'm pretty sure Beckett wouldn't have mentioned dressing a particular way if he'd only meant to wear our normal clothes."

Normal for him was black on black, like the sexiest super soldier. Normal for my alphas was their business polo and jeans. And since Beck had come out and said dress nice, I could only imagine he was speaking more to me than the others since normal for me was stretch pants or jeans.

We were obviously going somewhere with some form of a dress code. Or, if I knew anything about Beck, he was going out of his way to impress Wilder.

I was pretty sure the beta didn't require the whole wine and dine thing, although I had learned he was more than happy to enjoy a sixty-nine.

My cheeks heated as memories of our time last night flashed through my mind, but I ducked my head before he could catch the blush.

"This one isn't right," I said, turning my back and hurrying back to the dressing room where an armful of dresses and skirts waited for me.

The dress wasn't really that bad, but I needed to put some space between me and Wilder before I started perfuming over the memories and had to drag him into the dressing room with me. Even if we didn't get caught, I was only just getting used to accepting the fact that I could enjoy physical pleasure without fear of being hurt or enslaved.

Guilt slammed into me again as I tugged the dress over my head. At no point had either of my alphas done anything that would have even given me a glimmer of fear over something like that. And I'd deprived them of my body, of any form of intimacy, even the mental or emotional kind.

But I was trying. It didn't come naturally to me. Even before Clay, affection hadn't been something I doled out with ease, nor had I ever been comfortable with being pampered like other omegas. But I was trying to touch my alphas more, trying to refrain from tensing when they tugged me into their arms for a hug or when they brushed their lips over my temple or forehead.

Tonight. Tonight I would try to be…more feminine. Or girly. I might not have had a crap load of makeup, but I owned enough to at least highlight my eyes and gloss to make my lips look plumper and more kissable.

Slick dampened my panties as I wondered whether I should ask Wilder to stop for flavored gloss, something my pack could kiss off at the end of the date. As in, all of them. As in…all of them in the bed with me, all naked, all showering me with attention.

Shit. Was my heat getting close? For as long as I'd used suppressants, it might be nice to let my pack, to let my omega enjoy the week with her alphas and beta.

More slick coated my upper thighs and my body grew warm, my skin a little too tight.

Yep. Definitely moving into my cycle. How much time did I have to decide whether or not to experience this heat naturally?

I couldn't focus on that now. Especially if I didn't want to ruin the dress I was currently trying on.

This one wasn't right, either. It was a little too conservative. Not that I was keen on flashing my ass and cleavage at complete strangers. But I looked more like I should be joining a convent rather than going on a date with my pack.

Without bothering to give Wilder a glimpse, I tugged it over my head, put it back on the hanger, and moved on to the next one.

As the silky fabric slid down my legs, I blinked at my reflection. It flowed easily, not restraining me in any way. But it was tight enough to showcase my small curves, the front dipping low enough to tease at a glimpse of cleavage if I turned the right way. The hem fell to my knees, alleviating the fear that I would show the restaurant my ass if I bent over too far.

All in all, I felt sexy. Which was a mildly unfamiliar sensation. It wasn't something I strived for or normally cared about.

But when I stepped out and Wilder's eyes slowly traveled from my head to my toes and back up, I felt…beautiful. Pretty. Desirable.

"Is this too much?" I asked. My voice sounded deeper, a little husky, almost breathy as his gaze felt like a caress along my body when he did another slow perusal of my body and the dress.

"It's perfect," he said as a beta purr rumbled in his chest. It was softer, not quite as deep as my alpha's, but it was there. He liked what he saw.

Wilder unfolded from the chair and walked toward me until I had to tilt my head back to look into his face. I didn't back away. I never backed away from a perceived threat and I sure wouldn't start with my beta.

My beta. *Mine*. We hadn't made anything official, but he was just as much my beta as Owen and Beck were my alphas.

His eyes were full of heat as he raised a hand and grazed his fingertips over the thin straps of the deep purple dress. I would need a jacket or coat; it was definitely a little too thin and too skimpy for the late October weather.

But since Beckett hadn't said anything about being outside, I had to trust that a little outerwear would suffice when walking to and from the vehicle.

His fingers grazed along my collarbone, over Beckett's mark, then up the side of my neck, leaving gooseflesh in its wake as my sensitive skin reacted. Yep. Definitely getting closer to my heat. Even his soft, gentle touch felt as though it sent waves of pleasure through my body and straight to my core.

A shaky breath escaped my lips as I stared into Wilder's beautiful eyes that were definitely closer to blue now. I'd been right about my earlier suspicion – the shade of my beta's eyes shifted with his emotions. And right now, he was turned on.

I knew the feeling.

"I think this is the one," I said, trying to force myself to step out of his reach, but my feet felt as though they were glued to the floor.

"Definitely the right one," he said, his eyes dipping to my lips a second before raising back up.

I wanted him to kiss me so bad I swore I could already taste his sweetness on my tongue.

His arm slowly snaked out and wrapped around my back, pulling me so close I could feel his hardness pressing against my stomach. And then he did as I'd hoped for and dipped his head until his lips barely caressed against mine.

It was such a sweet kiss, chaste. Yet my body heated to the point I was close to begging him to bend me over in the dressing room.

All it took was the conscious decision to release the control I clung to so tightly and now I felt as though I'd lost all control over my body and, honestly, my heart and mind, as well.

When he pulled back and looked into my eyes, we both gasped for air as though we'd just made out for an hour.

"Definitely the right dress," he said, dropping his arm and taking a step back.

His hand raked through the soft brown hair I'd had my fingers tangled in just last night and mussed it in the sexiest way.

I swore everything my guys did was sexy these days. How had I gone so long without noticing, without succumbing to my physical needs, without succumbing to my deepest desires?

I knew the answer to that – I'd been scared. Scared of being hurt, scared of being rejected, scared of letting someone too far into my heart only to lose them or for them to turn into someone else.

Like Clay. He'd courted me properly, had convinced me he was my Prince Charming. He was the modern-day Dr. Jekyll and Mr. Fucking Hyde.

Beckett and Owen knew the basics, knew that I had willingly moved into Clay's house for a formal courting. But none of my pack knew all the details and I wasn't sure whether I wanted them to know. I didn't want them to see me as that person, that stupid girl who'd thought I needed to be saved by an alpha, who needed someone to take care of me and subsequently had turned into a damsel in distress who required a rescue from complete strangers.

Something I had never told either of my alphas was that there had been two alphas, two men who'd promised me the world. But I'd only ever seen Leon twice after I'd been locked in the basement. I had wondered if he'd left because he couldn't stomach what Clay was doing. But why the hell hadn't he done something to stop his friend? Why hadn't he let me out of the basement or even call in the authorities?

Nope. I wasn't going to let my past, my memories, my nightmares ruin the night Beckett had planned for us. I was going to wear this pretty dress, do something with my hair past simply brushing it or pulling it into a messy bun, and do up my face to look…pretty. Or at least prettier and omega-like.

Huffing a laugh to myself, I quickly turned on my heel and headed back to the dressing room to change into my regular clothes. We needed to find some shoes and something to wear over the dress to stay warm.

Just before pulling the door shut, I glanced up at Wilder to find him watching me, that same hungry look in his eyes.

Yup. Good thing I was buying this dress because I was so close to ruining it due to my raging hormones and libido.

CHAPTER 15

<u>Owen</u>

 ck merely grinned any time any of us questioned him about his plans for the night. The only clue any of us had been given was to dress nice. So, I currently sat on the couch in a charcoal suit, gray shirt, and black tie. Beck was dressed in a similar manner, but he was wearing a white shirt and burgundy tie.

"How long does it take to put on a dress?" I grumbled.

Maeve was the last woman on the planet I would assume would take more than the time required to shower for a date. I hadn't even seen what she'd picked out when Wilder had taken her shopping.

Although, I had absolutely smelled her heightened scent as well as her sweet slick when she'd rushed through the house. Neither of them smelled as though they'd fucked, but she was definitely feeling the effects of arousal. Which, of course, did nothing for the boner I'd sported since finding the beta and omega asleep and naked on the couch, their scents making me feel drunk. And high. And so fucking horny.

Beckett chuckled, crossing his ankle over his knee as he relaxed and waited. Did that mean there wasn't a set time, no reservation? Or had he anticipated the fact at least one of our packmates would cause us to run late?

Honestly, the last person I would have assumed would cause us to run late would be our omega. Then again...our beta was missing, as well. If those two were upstairs bumping uglies while I sat in a stuffy suit with my zipper causing a permanent imprint in my rock hard cock...

A door closed upstairs, and the scent of oranges and sweet cream met my noise before Wilder rounded the corner and descended the stairs. Holy fuck. The beta wore a black button up shirt, black tie, and black slacks, a black jacket draped over his forearm. He'd combed his hair away from his face in a sleek, old Hollywood fashion and I swore I was going to blow my load from his appearance alone.

I could already foresee wrapping my fist around my cock the second I was behind my closed bedroom door.

"Maeve not ready yet?" he asked, glancing up at us from his phone.

I quickly averted my eyes and did as Beck, crossing my ankle over my knee in hopes of hiding my boner.

"Not yet," Beckett said. And I could feel his eyes boring into the side of my head and could practically feel the laugh he was holding in at my reaction to seeing the beta all cleaned up.

A door slammed upstairs and feet softly hit the floor as though she was running. "Sorry! Sorry!" she called out as she carried a pair of heels dangling from her fingertips.

I unfolded my legs and slowly stood, my eyes going wide as they ran along her body from head to toe.

"Holy shit," Beckett breathed out behind me.

A moan escaped my lips before I could swallow it back. Our omega was dressed in a deep purple, silky slip-like dress that moved with ease, yet highlighted her curves. She must have been wearing some kind of strapless bra, because, although her tits were straining against the material, her nipples weren't showcased like they were in her tanks and tees.

As though the dress wasn't tempting enough, her curls had been tamed and looked so soft and shiny. And…was she wearing makeup? Her eyes looked defined and a touch smokey, her lips shimmery and red.

"Fuck me," I blurted out.

"Save that thought for later," she said so nonchalantly I almost believed she meant it. "I'm having a hard time buckling my shoes." She held them up and shook them as though we didn't know what she was talking about.

Beck patted the cushion beside him, then lowered to his knees when she sat down. They looked like Cinderella and her Prince as he settled first one foot then the other on his knee and carefully slid her feet into the strappy numbers, buckling them in place.

He held out a hand and waited until she was steady on her feet before offering the crook of his elbow. "Shall we?"

Even with her heels, she still stood almost a foot shorter than the tall alpha, tilting her head back to look into his face with a smile. "You plan on telling us where we're going any time soon?"

"Nope," he said, popping the *p* with his lips.

Fuck. I was more than sexually frustrated because even Beck was starting to look good to me. Or maybe it was merely the sight of my omega on his arm that appealed to me, the fact she looked more at ease and more relaxed in this setting than she had in…well, since she'd joined our pack.

As much as I wished it was because of me, I was still grateful to whatever beta voodoo Wilder possessed. We just wanted our girl happy.

Beckett guided Maeve to the garage with Wilder and me following closely behind. He settled her in the passenger seat, which would leave me in the backseat with Wilder.

Pulling the seatbelt in place, I did my best to ignore the heat rolling from Wilder or the way his scent mixed with Maeve's in the cab of the SUV.

I had never really entertained the idea of adding anyone else to the pack. I hadn't truly thought of myself as a family man until the day we'd met Maeve and my heart felt as though it had completely shifted, as though a hole I didn't know existed had been filled by her mere presence.

And now Wilder made me feel like the fucking *Grinch*, like my heart had grown three sizes simply to make room for him in my life.

"Can we at least get a hint? I mean, I not only put on a dress, but I'm wearing makeup, for fuck's sake," Maeve said. Her arms were crossed as though she was pouting, but there was a soft smile on her lips and her scent didn't hold a hint of the burnt smell like when she was angry.

"Hmm. A hint. You have to dress nice to enter," Beck replied.

We all groaned in unison at his terrible joke.

After about twenty minutes, our packmate pulled the SUV off the highway and turned into the downtown area before finally parking in a lot full of high-end cars.

Problem was, there were a lot of buildings lining the area, all still open, all still bustling. Still had no idea what exactly the giant alpha had in mind.

He climbed from the driver's seat but stopped. "Don't you dare open that door, omega. This is a date. And you're going to let us dote on you."

"I thought this was a date for Wilder. You're courting *him*, not *me*."

"We are courting him. And it's a date for all of us. And you and Wilder are our dates, meaning you will let me open your damn door." Then he swung his shut with a smirk and rounded the hood.

"I'm not waiting for someone to open my door," Wilder said with a chuckle, pushing from his side.

And yeah...I might have taken a second to check out his ass as he stepped out.

By the time my feet hit the pavement and I rounded the vehicle to join our little party, Maeve was sandwiched between Beck and Wilder, leaving me the odd man out.

Hell, why not just continue the trend since I was the only one Maeve didn't seem interested in furthering any deeper connection than what we'd had through the past eighteen months.

You just want her happy. You just want your pack happy.

It didn't matter how many times I reminded myself of that; I felt a bit rejected and, honestly, lonely. Even when she shared the pack bed with us, even when she let one of us hug her closer, it always felt as though she was tense, as though she was mildly uncomfortable with physical touch.

Or at least she was uncomfortable with *my* touch.

Well, shit. We were on a pack date and here I was feeling sorry for myself. For fuck's sake.

Wilder glanced back at me as I followed and jerked his head. A confused smile quirked up my lips as I put a little pep in my step until I was directly beside him instead of following my pack like a stray puppy.

His fingers grazed against mine and my heartrate kicked up a bit at the innocent touch. I had no idea whether it had been intentional, but it definitely hadn't been unwanted.

Fuck it. Without giving it too much thought or giving myself time to change my mind, I wrapped my fingers around his, then sighed when he turned his hand to twine his fingers through mine.

I waited for some awkward moment, but it felt so natural to feel his warm palm against mine.

Beck pulled us all to a stop outside a building with a sign over the door that read *Plumes et Fouets*. The bouncer was dressed in tight leather pants, a chain shirt, and makeup that looked as though it had been applied by a damn artist.

"Party of four. We have a reservation under the name Pack Taylor," Beck said.

We'd never really given thought to what our pack name would be since it had been three of us for so long. But I supposed if we were going to use a surname, Beckett's was as good as mine. It was definitely easier to spell than mine. Very few people spelled Gutierrez correctly unless I gave it to them letter for letter.

The bouncer checked down the list and nodded, looking up at Beckett with a smile. "Awesome. Let's get you seated." He lifted a hand

and someone made a beeline down the hall and smiled. "Pack Taylor is here."

"Follow me," the small beta said. She was dressed in a similar fashion to the bouncer, except instead of a chain shirt, she wore what could only be described as a corset, the swells of her breasts peeking tantalizingly over the top.

The hall leading from the front door was dimly lit by antique chandeliers overhead. There were sconces here and there with lit taper candles that flickered and danced in the breeze.

A chemical note touched my senses – suppressors were being filtered through the air, camouflaging even my pack's scent who were all within touching distance of me.

Only two people could fit side by side as we followed the hostess, so Maeve clung to Beck's arm while Wilder kept his hand entwined in mine.

"What is this place?" I asked as music began to thump against the dark walls.

Beckett merely smirked at me over his shoulder, his eyes lowering to touch on my hand in Wilder's, before he turned back to follow the hostess.

Plumes et Fouets. I wracked my brain for the few French words I knew and could only translate plumes to feathers. Feathers and…what?

And then everything clicked into place.

The hostess pushed open a cushioned door, the music flooding the hallway, and led us into a room that was only barely brighter than the hall. Tables were situated in semi circles around small, raised stages.

And on those stages…

"Holy fucking shit," Wilder breathed out beside me.

Plumes et Fouets. Feathers and whips. Beckett had made a reservation at a fucking fetish club? What the hell was he thinking? We barely knew Wilder and were trying to win him over, trying to convince him to join the pack. And Maeve had only just began to accept intimacy, first from Beck then from Wilder.

"What are you doing?" I asked Beckett, grabbing his bicep and pulling him to a stop before we moved much further into the room.

"Taking my pack on a date. Dinner and a show." He grinned and pulled his arm free so he could continue following the hostess until she sat us at a table in front of a woman who was currently strapped to a large, wooden X on the stage, an alpha trailing a feather along her exposed flesh. The only parts of her body not visible were her breasts and her sex.

I glanced at Maeve after Beck pulled the chair out for her and found her looking around the room with wide eyes.

"Um...don't think I'm a weirdo...but this is kind of cool," she muttered, turning her attention to the three of us. "But why did we have to dress up?"

Beck nodded his head toward the rest of the room. Every single person in the room was dressed to the nines, some even wearing tuxedoes.

"It's upscale. No touching. No public sex. Dinner and a show," he said with a shrug.

"We could've gone to a movie then gotten fast food," Wilder said with an awkward smile. Even in the dark room, I could see his cheeks were flushed and his pupils were dilated. I assumed mine looked exactly the same.

"Is this okay?" I asked Maeve. "We can go somewhere else."

"It's fine. I had no idea anything like this existed."

"There's more. There are several different shows, including drag and burlesque. I was hoping for the latter, but that's not scheduled until next month," Beck said.

"Can we come back for the others?" Maeve asked.

Beck smiled down at our omega and winked. "Sweetheart, if you'll let us, we'll take you anywhere you want. I'm surprised you let Wilder buy you that dress. Which, by the way, looks fucking amazing on you."

Her cheeks burned bright pink and she ducked her eyes. I wasn't sure I had ever seen our Maeve look so unsure or shy. Angry, yes. Violent, absolutely.

She was out of her comfort zone but was taking it like a champ. In fact, I would go so far as to say she was thriving outside of her comfort zone.

Had we coddled her far too long? Entertained her need to inflict pain and destroy shit to the point that we hadn't allowed her to heal?

And why the fuck hadn't either of us thought to find her a therapist so she could work through what she'd endured while with that Clay fuck?

Another time. All those thoughts, all those worries were for another time. This might have been a completely unorthodox date, but there was no reason we couldn't enjoy ourselves.

I just wished I could smell my pack's scents. Something about the way they watched the scenes playing out around them made me wonder if our omega wasn't already perfuming.

CHAPTER 16

<u>Maeve</u>

 ur plates had been set in front of us, but I was having a hard time taking my eyes from the stage in front of us as well as those around the room.

For some reason, I'd expected to immediately be uncomfortable with so much skin on display. This was some kind of sex club, but not. No one in the room, not even those on the stage, were actually having sex. They were merely playing out various fantasies and fetishes.

As I cut my steak, I jumped at the sound of a crack to our left. Abandoning my meal for a moment, I turned and watched as an alpha who was currently restrained with his hands high over his head groaned while the small beta woman swung some kind of leather strap, like a whip, and smacked his engorged cock.

"Wouldn't that hurt?" I asked Wilder who sat to my left.

I wasn't a prude. And I was far from a virgin. But I would have thought a whip against a man's cock would have been painful. Any time I'd ever seen a man hit down there, even by accident, they'd cupped themselves and doubled over.

"Some people like pain. It turns them on. Sometimes even gets them off."

"Really?" I said with a wrinkle of my nose.

"You've never…spanking? Anything?"

My cheeks flamed hot as Wilder asked me such personal questions. But hell, we were in a sex club, nonchalantly eating dinner while performers simulated sex, inflicted pain with clamps and whips, or even trailed feathers along mostly naked skin. It was all foreplay.

Did that mean these people would later…?

Had I ever been spanked? That's what Wilder had asked me. And now my alphas were watching me closely, as well.

Clearing my throat, I slipped a piece of steak into my mouth and chewed slowly, giving myself time to decide whether I wanted to answer. Because the truth was, while, no, I had never been spanked, I'd always wondered about it, wondered whether I would like it.

Until my alphas, though, I had never trusted anyone enough to intentionally inflict pain on me or control me in any way. Even with Wilder our first time, I'd set the pace, I had climbed onto his lap, I had ridden him so I could maintain full control over the moment.

After swallowing my bite and taking a sip of my wine, I cleared my throat again to stall for at least a few more seconds.

"I'm not great at, uh…I don't like to hand over control." My cheeks had to be tomato red. They were on fire, the heat radiating down my neck and into my chest.

My thighs were damp with slick. This dress might not have been the best idea for this kind of date. Much more of the show or this conversation, and there was a good chance my dress would end up showing exactly how my body was reacting and ruining the beautiful fabric.

It would be so humiliating to walk through this place looking like I'd sat in a puddle. I supposed I could always slip my coat back on before standing in hopes of covering the evidence of my arousal.

The more Wilder watched me expectantly, as though waiting for me to elaborate, the more uncomfortable I grew. Sure, I was trying to open up more to my pack. And yeah, I wanted to let them in, wanted Wilder to get to know me as well as my alphas. But the last thing I wanted to do was dredge up the past when we were sitting in the middle of a fetish club, dressed all nice, and on a pack date.

Glancing up at Owen, who was watching me with narrowed eyes, I did my best to communicate my discomfort without actually saying *hey, could we stop talking about my reluctance to allow a man to control me because of my past abuse?*

I might have held myself at arm's length from my alphas, but they still knew me, knew every facial nuance, could practically tell what I was thinking with nothing more than a glance in my direction.

"Is there a schedule online or something?" Owen asked, leaning forward to catch Beckett's attention.

They had a quick, silent conversation with nothing more than their eyes then Beck nodded.

"Yeah. We can arrange our next date for one of the other shows. What do you think, Maeve? Drag or burlesque?"

"I kind of want to see both," I admitted, sighing with relief when Wilder turned and listened to the alphas instead of focusing on me or pressing for more information.

The performers switched, those on the stage bowing lightly and stepping down to allow the next group to take their place.

I don't know why I thought they would simply stay there the whole night. But with some of the activities taking place, I assumed they would probably get sore or overstimulated. I know I sure as hell would even with the tickling.

We chatted a little more as we finished our meals, then Beck tempted me with dessert. What could I say? How could I say no to a dessert that happened to also be entertainment?

Our waiter set a large tray with a dome in the center of the table once it had been cleared, then lifted the cover. He poured something over the top of a ball of chocolate that had to be at least as big as a globe. The chocolate melted and a plume of smoke or steam bellowed from inside. The waiter then put a flame to the tray and flames erupted in a ring before quickly snuffing as the caramel, whipped cream, and syrup spread mixed with the alcohol that acted as the fuel.

With a wide grin, I clapped my hands and giggled. I would have been completely content with a simple bowl of ice cream or a slice of cake. But this was so much better.

"I should let you take me out more often," I said to Beck. And the look in his eyes sent warmth to my heart and slick to my core.

For so long, I'd avoided allowing my alphas to dote on me, to treat me the way their instincts demanded of them. I might never be comfortable with being smothered with gifts, but I could at least allow them to introduce me to new experiences. Especially when we experienced it as a pack.

As we all lifted our spoons to dive into the communal dessert, a woman was helped onto the stage in front of our table. She was small, nearly my size. It was hard to tell whether she was a beta or omega with the absence of scents, but my guess was the latter if her petite stature and curves were anything to go by.

The woman's dark hair was braided down her back, her body barely covered by anything more than lacy lingerie. No one was naked, but there was definitely the illusion of nudity with the thinner materials or the way the pieces clung to their bodies.

She was beautiful, but it wasn't lost on me that my guys only had eyes for me. Not that I expected them to be blind to beauty. But they only barely graced the new performer with a quick glance before turning back to our conversation and the dessert.

"So what made you want to work with ORE?" I asked before sliding the spoon between my lips.

"My sister was in a situation similar to those we worked with. She was courted by a pack, then we didn't hear from her. Unfortunately, no one got to her in time. But after her death, I was determined to do what I could to make a difference," Wilder said.

"Oh my gosh. I'm so sorry," I said. My heart ached for him.

"Thank you. It's been years since her murder. But I decided since I was a little...I guess you could say bigger than most betas and I'd always been a little on the meaner side, I decided to join the academy."

"I don't think anyone could ever describe you as mean," I said with a teasing smile.

"Oh, I had a temper when I was younger. It got worse after Beth's death. But the academy and a shit ton of therapy helped level me out so I could be a productive member of society rather than turning into one of the assholes we fight against."

"You're a good man," Beckett said as he used his spoon to slice off a piece of the chocolate shell that hadn't melted.

"I appreciate that."

I winked at Wilder when he smiled in my direction. He really was a good man. Sweet and funny and so passionate. He was so similar to Beckett. Owen could be sweet, but he tended to wear his worries and stress like a shield or a cape, always grumbling and broody. Especially when it came to my extracurricular activities. Or maybe *because* of said activities.

As all kinds of thoughts spun through my head, that maybe I could accept that these men cared about me and that I didn't need to punish the world for what happened to me, a loud crack sent ice through my veins and stole the breath from my lungs.

My head slowly tilted back to look at the woman on the stage near our table. She'd been strapped to that same wooden X with her back to us, her long braid tossed over her shoulder. A man in a mask that only covered his nose and eyes stood behind her with a cane. His arm drew back and shot forward again until the long, thin cane smacked the center of her back, leaving a red welt in its place.

My mouth went dry. My heart began to pound a painful cadence in my chest. Adrenaline burned through my veins and I was having a hard time drawing in a full breath.

Oh shit. Was this a panic attack? Was I seriously losing my shit in public, in front of complete strangers, in front of Wilder?

My alphas had seen me at my worse. They'd seen me fall apart. But I hadn't been so lost to my memories in close to a year unless my nightmares could be counted. But watching as my torture was played out as a sexual fantasy not more than a few feet from my face brought everything back, every minute of my time in that basement, every moment of agonizing pain back to the forefront of my mind until I had a hard time deciphering past from present, memory from reality.

Shoving back from the table, the chair beneath me toppled to the ground as the sense of fight or flight built in my chest.

"Oh shit," Owen breathed out. "Take care of the bill," he barked out, rushing to my side, lifting me into his arms, and nearly sprinting through the building and away from the table.

With my arms wrapped around my alpha's neck, I buried my face into his neck and inhaled, groaning with a sob when I couldn't detect his scent with the stupid filtration system.

"Outside. Please," I begged as my eyes burned with the tears that welled then soaked into the fabric of his suit jacket.

"Almost there, baby girl. Hold on," he muttered, pressing a kiss to the top of my head.

My body swayed and jostled, and then fresh air ruffled my hair and gave me the chance to draw his warm herbal scent deep into my lungs.

A rattle started in his chest as he purred, comforting me a touch more. But it would take more than his scent or purr to ease the fear and anxiety that turned my stomach until I felt as though I would lose my dinner and dessert all over the parking lot.

Owen didn't set me on my feet, didn't release his tight hold on me. He repeated soothing words that sounded foreign in my muddled brain and continued to purr as he hugged me close to his chest, his lips brushing over my cheek, my temple, and the top of my head.

Finally, after what felt like an eternity later, Beckett and Wilder joined us. The locks popped and a door was opened. Owen slid into the backseat with me cradled in his lap.

Doors *thunked* closed, the engine came to life, then we were on the move. And the entire time, I kept my face buried in the crook of his neck so I could breathe in the safety and security of my alpha.

The tears began to flow in earnest as a whine pulled from my chest. Owen tensed below me and his purr intensified as his arms tightened around me until I struggled to breathe. Yet... I didn't want him to let up his hold, didn't want him to release me.

As long as I was in his arms, my past couldn't touch me. The alpha was gone. I personally ended his life. I had punished other alphas for their part in victimizing omegas.

So then why couldn't I make my body listen to reason?

Oh. Right. Because, regardless of reality, my body remembered every moment of my time in hell.

CHAPTER 17

<u>Beckett</u>

Fuck. What was I thinking? I should have known better.

But how could I have known one of the performers wanted to be whipped? Oh, and not just whipped, whipped with a fucking cane that left visible marks on her pale flesh.

The look of panic and terror on Maeve's face would stay with me forever. I needed to fix this; I just wasn't sure how.

Owen had taken her to her room the second we'd all walked through the door. I wanted to join them, to wrap my body around hers, to apologize for putting her in a situation like that, but I would give her time. She needed to relax a minute.

A pipe squeaked from down the hall. Owen was running a bath for her. Hopefully, he would climb in with her and continue holding her, easing her pain with his presence and alpha purr.

A knock on my bedroom door startled me. "Yeah?"

Wilder pushed open the door, his brows drawn together, pain and concern evident in his gray eyes.

"What the fuck just happened?"

Maeve had told him a little of her past, had even allowed him to see the raised scars on her back and legs. And, as much as I felt like a dick about it, I was about to give him more details about her past. It really wasn't my secret to share, but if the three of us wanted Wilder to join us, we needed to be honest with him and fully let him in.

"She showed you her scars." He nodded. "She told you about… about her past and all that?"

"She said she was held and tortured and that you two found her while installing a security system."

"Yeah. We'd been hired to install it and found out after finding her chained in the basement that the system was to keep her in because she repeatedly tried to escape. Actually, she had succeeded a few times, but had never gotten far enough to hide or find help."

Fuck. I really hoped Maeve didn't hold all this against me later.

"She was held by an alpha for four years. She'd been…gifted to this asshole by her family. They hadn't exactly been overly loving, either. She was nothing more than a trophy, something they could use to make money or earn favor. There had been two alphas, but Maeve said the other disappeared after a while. She said he never returned, not that she saw. We all assumed he was sickened by his packmate's behavior and took off. Though I'm not fully convinced of that. I always wondered…anyway," I said, waving my hand in the air. "When we found her, she was barely skin and bones and couldn't walk on her own. Owen restrained Clay – his name was Clay Soren–"

"She told me that part," he said, interrupting my story for a brief moment.

"Owen restrained Clay while I released Maeve and carried her upstairs. She struggled, of course. And I let her lower to her feet once I got her up the stairs. She immediately grabbed a butcher knife from the block and lunged at Clay, shoving the blade straight into his chest and through his heart. The fucker was dead before he hit the floor. She stood there and watched the blood form a puddle, even let it glide around her feet."

I inhaled deeply and glanced toward my door as though I could see my omega through the wood.

"It was another struggle to get her to let me carry her out of the house. She could barely hold up her own weight. She was so weak. The clothes she wore…" I let out a shaky breath. "They were filthy and stuck to her body by dried blood. She was covered in injuries, and a few had been infected. We'd had to have her sedated just so we could get her medical treatment. Then, she refused to leave her nest if either of us were in the room. She was like a wild animal the first few months. Honestly, it wasn't until close to a year later that she even let us touch her or sleep in the pack bed with her. And…the morning you came to hang out with her was the first time we'd had sex in almost eighteen months."

"Holy shit," Wilder breathed out. "How the fuck did you hold out that long?"

I chuckled a humorless laugh. "It wasn't easy. But neither of us would have done anything that might have set her back from her healing."

"Is that why she–"

"Hunts alphas? Yeah. I think in her head, she's hunting Clay. Over and over again. She's punishing him."

"She trusts you. She trusts you both," Wilder said.

"Yeah. Took a long time to earn that trust, too."

"Why did she trust me so easily, though?"

"You're not an alpha. In her mind, you're not the enemy. The short time since she met you a whole new side of her has appeared. She seems…fuck, she seems happy. I know we're supposed to be courting you and winning you over, but I'm begging you to stick around. I can't promise she won't have another meltdown like the one she had tonight, but I promise she's worth it. And you and Owen can deny it all you want, but there's obviously something brewing between you two, as well."

His cheeks went pink and he averted his eyes.

"Yeah. That's what I thought." I chuckled and kicked off my shoes.

"Is she...should I go in there? I don't want to overwhelm her, but should I go check on her?"

"Won't hurt. Trust me – if she doesn't want you in there, she'll let you know. Just...I hope you have quick reflexes because she tends to throw shit."

Memories of the first few months made me smile. She'd thrown pillows at us anytime we opened the nest door to leave her food. Not that a pillow would hurt, but she'd graduated to heavier things when she'd finally wandered out of her room and was surprised when one of us stepped in without knocking. I'd received my share of bruises from pieces of furniture or knickknacks flying at me from across the room.

Wilder sucked his lips into his mouth and looked as though he was rubbing them together while deep in thought.

"I am a beta. I'm supposed to be calming and shit," he said after a few moments.

Another chuckle escaped me. "Yeah. You're supposed to be calming and shit. Just follow her lead. Go slowly. Hell, if she's lost enough in her memories, she might not even notice you at first. But don't push her. That won't go well."

I knew that firsthand. I'd tried to do as I always did and push myself on her, convinced my mere presence would help her realize I was the furthest thing from a threat to her or anyone, for that matter.

It took a few more moments for Wilder to nod and turn on his heel, leaving me sitting alone on the side of my bed.

Part of me wanted to strip and join my pack in the bathtub. But Maeve tended to get overwhelmed. And I felt like a complete and total asshole for being the cause of her backslide.

Well, not totally the cause. I should have done a little more research before making the reservation. I don't know why I'd picked something so inherently sexual other than the fact I was hoping to push everyone a little closer, maybe toss a little gasoline on their smoldering libidos. It felt as though everyone was dancing around each other and that wouldn't do, not if we were going to become the type of pack I craved.

Pulling off my socks, I shucked my jacket and tossed it onto the bed beside me. My tie and shirt followed, then finally my pants, leaving me in nothing but my boxer briefs.

It was early enough I wasn't quite ready for bed, but late enough there wasn't much else for me to do. And I had no intention of checking my work email. I had always kept my life and work life separate and refused to even think about our company until official office hours.

As the minutes passed, I found the tension in my shoulders easing. I didn't hear any screams or protests coming from Maeve's room, so that had to mean she'd welcomed Wilder into the room...if she was even coherent enough to know he was there with her.

Kicking back, I laid out on my bed and reached for the TV remote. Streaming movies in bed for the win.

Another knock on the door had me frowning as the door cracked open.

"She's asking for you," Wilder said, a ghost of a smile on his handsome face.

The door didn't have to be completely open for me to know the beta was standing at my door butt ass naked. Probably dripping water on the floor, too.

Oh well. None of that mattered if my omega needed me. Needed *us*. Needed her pack.

Without hesitation, I tossed the remote on the bed and hurried from my room, down the hall, and into Maeve's quarters then her ensuite bathroom.

I could hear Owen's soft murmurs before I pushed open the door. I'd been right about him drawing her a bath. She was huddled against his chest, her arms hugged around herself as she rested her cheek on Owen's broad chest.

When her eyes raised to my face, she released a soft whine, forcing my legs to move faster. My omega needed me. Nothing else mattered.

After shoving my boxers down my legs, I carefully stepped into the deep tub to avoid slipping or shuffling her too much.

She instantly opened one of her arms as though beckoning me closer.

I didn't need to be asked twice.

Owen wore the same stern, serious, concerned expression he always wore when it came to our sweet Maeve. I moved as close as I could without cuddling to her other alpha, then shifted so Wilder could climb in.

She was now engulfed by the bodies of her pack, Owen and I purring for her while all our combined scents eased her a little more. No more whines escaped her, but she looked so small, so fragile, her eyes holding a faraway look as though she was back in that basement, seeing the dark, cold room instead of the enormous bathroom or garden tub she was soaking in.

"We're here, sweetheart," I murmured against her hair, pressing soft kisses to her shoulder, her cheek, anywhere I could reach while being crowded by the other two men.

"I'm sorry," she whispered.

With a frown, I pulled back enough to look into her face to find fresh tears welling in her eyes.

"For what?"

"For freaking out and ruining our date. It was great. I don't want you to think I didn't enjoy it or didn't appreciate it."

"You have nothing to be sorry for." I lowered my head and pressed a gentle kiss to her soft lips. "I should have checked into the scenes before taking you."

"It's been long enough. Why do I still keep freaking out?"

"First of all, you haven't had an attack in a long fucking time," Owen said. "Second, you literally just watched your trauma play out in front of you when you weren't expecting it. Anyone would have reacted the same way."

"Bull shit," she muttered. "I'm supposed to be stronger than that."

"No one expects you to be some emotionless cyborg, Maeve," Wilder said.

She huffed a laugh, but a smile never graced her beautiful face.

"You guys didn't expect me to ruin the night, either. I'm sorry. I… damn it," she said, breathing out the curse under her breath.

"You didn't ruin anything. I had a great time," I said. "Except the last portion. But hey, you got your pack naked in the tub with you. That's a win in my books."

She laughed in earnest this time, a genuine smile stretching her lips and plumping her pale, freckled cheeks. The makeup she'd worn was streaked and smudged below her eyes, making them a little smokier but not taking away from her beauty in the least.

"I know I'm not officially pack, but am I allowed to request a pack bed cuddle?"

Maeve lifted her head and looked at the beta. "You're pack. Officially. If…did I scare you off? Did I ruin everything?"

Tears welled in her eyes again and I had a moment where I wished that Clay fucker was still alive so I could kill him again. Slowly. And painfully. Maybe inflict twice the lashes along his bare flesh that he'd inflicted on her.

"You didn't ruin a damn thing, Maeve. I want nothing more than to be with you. To be with all of you," Wilder said. And I wondered if our omega caught the look he shared with Owen.

CHAPTER 18

<u>Maeve</u>

The four of us soaked until the bubbles began to pop and the water cooled. Even sandwiched between my guys, I'd begun to grow chilly.

So, Owen had lifted me in his arms and held me while Beckett dried me off and Wilder prepared the pack bed. And yeah, I totally took the opportunity to ogle my pack completely naked.

I had truly believed the night would be completely ruined, that my splintered mind would haunt me with memories, that I would stay stuck in the nightmare of my time in that basement.

Until my alphas purred, until my beta's sweet scent soothed my tight muscles, until their strong arms circled me and made me feel secure. Safe.

I wasn't alone. I had three amazing men in my life who cared about me, cared about my wellbeing.

And...I loved them. All three of them. It had taken time to allow my heart to feel that way about my alphas, but Wilder had wiggled his way in pretty much from the first moment we'd spent together, from that first moment our eyes had locked together at the bar, from the first moment his lips had crashed down on mine.

"I can walk," I said when Owen carried me through my room to my bed that would easily fit all of us.

"I'm aware," he replied.

I turned a frown on him, but the crease between my brows instantly smoothed at the sweet smile on his lips.

He wasn't carrying me for my benefit but his own. He needed me close as much as I'd needed him earlier.

"I'm sorry," I repeated.

"Stop apologizing for shit that's out of your control," Beck said.

"I'm sorry for scaring you guys. And for falling apart. I'll try harder."

"For fuck's sake," Owen grumbled with a roll of his pretty hazel eyes. "I get that you don't want to believe us, but we've all told you over and over there isn't a single thing about you we want changed. Do we want you happy and healthy? Absolutely. But there is nothing you can do that would change our feelings for you."

He lowered me onto the bed and took the towel Wilder offered to dry himself off before climbing under the sheets and blankets with us.

"Have you tried therapy?" Wilder offered.

I wrinkled my nose at him. There was something about reliving my history with a stranger, of telling them all my deepest, darkest secrets and fears that made me anxious.

"Don't knock it. I had to go through years of therapy after my sister's murder. It helps. You just have to find the right person. Someone you trust."

I crawled into the bed beside Owen and held the blanket up for Beckett to join me on the other side.

"I trust you guys."

"But we're not trained to help with trauma. You know you can talk to me, to us, about anything. But a licensed therapist can help you put the trauma in the right box so it won't sneak up on you and catch you off guard. Mine helped me work through the rage so I didn't–"

"Set off concussion grenades in the middle of a protest?"

He threw his head back and laughed loudly, his face so sweet with his wide grin. "Exactly."

Then Wilder stood at the side of the bed as though unsure of where he should climb in since my alphas had claimed either side of me.

"Here," Owen grumbled, scooting closer to my side and holding the blanket up for Wilder.

"For fuck's sake. Why don't the two of you just kiss and get it over with?" I blurted out as I got situated under the blanket.

The room went silent and all movement ceased. Looking around, I snorted at the looks on my alphas' and beta's faces.

"What? You don't think I've noticed the heated looks or the fact the two of you were holding hands going into the restaurant? If I can fall in love with three men at the same time, why can't the two of you be in love with two people at the same time? Not that I'm saying you're in love. Yet," I said, muttering the last word softly though I knew they could all hear me.

The mattress shook beneath me. Turning to Beck, my smile widened at his terrible attempt at holding back his chuckles.

"I've been saying pretty much the same thing," he said to me.

"Well?" I said, scooting until I was sitting with my back against the headboard. "Just close your eyes, count to three, and get the awkward first kiss over with."

"Maeve," Owen warned.

"What? Here." I leaned over and kissed Beck, then Owen, then finally grabbed Wilder's face and drew him closer so I could press my lips to his.

"Was that supposed to make this any less cringe worthy? Because I seriously feel like my mom is trying to fix me up on a date right now," Wilder said with an awkward chuckle and flaming red cheeks.

"Wait...did I read things wrong? I'm not trying to make the two of you uncomfortable. I just thought...it seemed like you were attracted to each other. I'm fine with it. I mean, if you're not. Or if you are. You guys want me happy and that's all I want for you."

And it was kind of a turn on to think of my alpha and beta making out. But I didn't voice that part, not wanting to influence their decision or force their hands in anything.

Owen and Wilder glanced at each other. And I could have sworn all the air was sucked out of the room, as though everything was suddenly in slow motion like in those romance movies I sometimes forced my pack to watch when I was in a self-indulgent kind of mood.

I hadn't been wrong. The look they shared…it was the same look I'd seen on their faces when they looked at me, when they saw me naked. The same look I'd seen on Wilder's face before we'd crashed into each other the first day he'd spent at the house with me.

My heart skipped a beat when Owen grabbed Wilder by the back of his neck and jerked him closer, slanting his mouth over my beta's immediately.

Wilder was shocked into stillness for about half a second. Then he melted into the kiss, his arms wrapping around Owen until they were chest to chest.

And my body went up in flames as slick gushed from me and my core fluttered as though desperate for something to fill it. I needed… fuck, I didn't know what I needed.

All I knew was everything south of my bellybutton felt achy and hot and empty.

Before my brain and body had time to catch up to each other, I slid my hand down my body and under the blankets until my fingers slid through my wet folds.

The air grew sweet and heady as my perfume exploded from me and mingled with the signatures of my alphas and my beta. Everyone was feeling the same arousal, though I suspected Beckett was reacting more to me than seeing our two other packmates kissing so deeply they appeared to forget they had an audience.

"Beck," I whimpered as I toyed with my clit then slid my hand down so I could press a finger into my entrance.

"I'm here, sweetheart," he said, leaning forward to press his lips to mine, his tongue pressing into my mouth as his hand smoothed over my hair, my face, down my throat, then finally to my breasts. He massaged one and dipped his head to press kisses along the swell of the other, teasing the pebbled nipple with his tongue before sucking it between his lips.

And I continued to pump my own finger into my pussy yet couldn't find release or relief.

Another whimper tore from my lips. Wilder and Owen pulled apart and snapped their heads toward me and I was tempted to beg them to go back to kissing. The arousal coursing through my system was almost alien. I had pushed away any thoughts or feelings of a physical connection for so long, it felt freeing to give in to my omega needs. Especially after losing myself to my past mere hours ago.

I felt safe. That was exactly what I'd ignored for so long. This was my pack. These were my men. And they had as deep of a need to care for their omega as I had for them to be happy.

"I need…"

Beckett continued lavishing my body with attention. Owen pulled from Wilder and scooted so he could claim my mouth. Wilder crawled to my legs and urged them apart before lowering his face to press wet kisses along my thighs until he reached my core. His tongue was warm as it swiped slowly through my folds.

And then he devoured me like a starved man, the sensation of his mouth on me, of his lips sucking on my clit, his tongue pushing into my entrance, building that need, that fire higher and higher until I thought I would combust.

"We've got you, sweetheart," Beckett said, his breath cooling the places where he'd left open mouth kisses on my breasts and nipples.

And they did. All three used their hands and mouths to pull an orgasm from me so strong I tore my mouth from Owen's and cried out.

Wilder didn't let up, pulling a second one only moments after the first until my legs shook.

"Wilder. Stop," I giggled as everything became overly sensitive.

He pressed a few more kisses, then raised his head. Before he could swipe my slick and release from his lips and chin, Owen yanked him up again, kissing him deeply, savoring in my sweetness on the beta's lips.

"Fuck. You taste so good on his lips," Owen growled, pulling away from Wilder to look down at me with blown pupils and pure, carnal need all over his beautiful face.

I needed more. Two orgasms, and already I needed more.

I was right. It was this day that finally cemented in my heart and mind that I could let go, that I was safe, that no matter what I said or did these men would never hurt me, they would never send me away, they would never leave me.

They were mine. They were mine as much as I was theirs.

My legs scissored together as I tried and failed to create enough friction to ease the growing need between my legs.

"More. Please," I begged, turning pleading eyes to Owen.

"I need you to ask me, baby girl. I need to hear you say the words so I know you're with us," he said, brushing a hand over my hair.

"Take me, please. Fuck me. I need you inside me. I need your knot."

If letting go made me this needy, I couldn't even imagine how desperate I would be if I allowed my next heat to come naturally. Big *if*, though. It had been a long damn time and I wasn't sure I wanted to endure a week of pain and fever.

When Owen settled between my open thighs and notched the head of his thick cock against my entrance, I couldn't help but wonder whether I would be enduring a week of anything but absolute pleasure if I allowed my pack to help me through it, if I allowed my alphas to do what was ingrained in their very molecular makeup, their need to care for their omega in every way possible, their need to breed.

Breeding was off the table, though. I wasn't prepared to even contemplate motherhood. Not until my fractured mind was at least a little more healed. Not until my heart no longer contained so many cracks and breaks.

My body stretched around Owen. My back arched at the blissful invasion, a long moan escaping my lips, nearly mirroring the deeper one that fell from his lips.

How long had it been since I had felt Owen inside of me? How long had it been since I'd allowed myself to become completely lost to the sensations, the pleasure his body gave me?

Too long. Way too fucking long.

His hips started a slow rhythm, his thick length rubbing all the right places deep inside my pussy. Between my constant rushes of slick and my releases, I knew the bedding and mattress below me would be damp.

More. I needed so much more. I didn't know more of what, but my body craved something I couldn't name.

Beckett returned his attention to my breasts, alternating between laving them with his tongue and kissing me deeply, his taste warm on my tongue. Had I ever tasted all of him? Had I ever tasted all of either of my alphas?

And why were all these desires and fantasies coming to my mind when I had a cock balls deep inside of me?

Perhaps I was right when I'd wondered if my heat was closer than I'd assumed. I didn't feel feverish or achy, but my body, my *cunt* felt needy.

"You're so tight," Owen grunted. A muscle jumped in his jaw and the tendons stood out on his neck as though he were holding back.

I'd been with Wilder a few times since he'd temporarily moved into the pack house. After that first morning with Beckett, he'd licked me to release twice. This was the first time in months, maybe longer, that I had felt Owen sliding in and out of me, the first time I felt his skin pressing against mine in such an intimate way. This sure as hell wasn't a cuddle in bed after I freaked out my pack.

This was far better, and I could have kicked my own ass for ignoring my own needs as well as my pack's.

Fuck it. It was time to stop the internal whining, stop dwelling on my regrets, and enjoy my time with my men, enjoy the future we were building together, including adding a beta to the mix.

Speaking of my beta...

He knelt beside Owen as he pumped into me and stared down at where Owen's cock slammed into me as his hips began to thrust harder, shoving his knot against my opening until I was ready to beg for the stretch, the feeling of being locked around my alpha.

Owen turned his head and accepted an open mouth kiss from Wilder. And that was all it took for another explosion to start in my womb and send ripples of pleasure through my limbs.

My voice sounded strange in my own ears as I cried out, whimpers mixing with the scream of release.

When Wilder's fingers reached down and toyed with my clit, sliding along to caress and toy with Owen's knot, another orgasm crashed through me, stealing my breath until I felt as though I would pass out before I felt the stretch and exquisite burn of my alpha locking inside of me.

CHAPTER 19

<u>Wilder</u>

What the hell was I doing? I'd been completely on board with dating Maeve. I didn't care what anyone thought – I was pretty sure it had been love at first sight with her.

But every minute I spent with the pack the more my feelings for Owen were growing. And it was beyond simple attraction. I wasn't even sure what exactly drew me to the surly alpha. He was practically my opposite, so serious and broody. If there was anyone similar in personality to me, it would have been Beckett.

Not that the giant alpha wasn't good looking; I just didn't feel myself pulled toward him, didn't feel that same magnetism I felt toward Maeve and Owen.

According to Maeve, I was officially pack. I supposed I should cut the lease on my apartment and move the rest of my crap in. Although my furniture would look a little out of place here. I hadn't bothered spending money on things like the couch and bed since, until recently, I rarely spent much time at home, always working.

It had been over a week since the last time I'd been called in for duty. And as much as I enjoyed spending time with Maeve and the alphas – *my* alphas – I was antsy. I couldn't remember the last time I'd had so much downtime. I needed to work. I needed to feel as though I was making a difference.

As much as I enjoyed working for Sophie, as much as I liked my coworkers, maybe it was time to return to ORE. The missions tended to be more dangerous, but I had a full schedule with them and didn't feel as though I was sitting on my hands while omegas were constantly at risk.

Shuffling feet drew my attention to the entryway into the kitchen a moment before Maeve appeared. Her red curls were pulled into a bun high on her head, some of the tendrils escaping and framing her face and grazing her neck.

"Good morning," I said with a smile.

She grunted and made her way to the cabinet with the mugs. It wasn't until she'd taken a few sips of coffee before she fully made eye contact with me.

"Did I keep you up last night?"

A frown drew my brows together. We had all stayed up pretty late enjoying each other, but I wouldn't say she was responsible for that. Hell, it had been one of the greatest nights of my life.

"I think we all fell asleep at the same time," I said, grabbing her chair and pulling it closer until our thighs were pressed together.

Her copper-colored brows drew together to mirror my own frown. "You didn't hear…all that?"

Tilting my head to the side, I tried to make sense of what she was asking me.

"I have night terrors," she said, answering my confused expression.

"You had one last night?"

She huffed a laugh but there was no humor to the sound nor a smile on her face. "You're a heavy sleeper."

"Shit. I'm so sorry." She'd had a nightmare and I hadn't heard any of it. I hadn't been there for her.

"Sorry? Why would you be sorry? I would have felt terrible if I'd woken you up. It's bad enough the alphas had to deal with it."

"My job is to be there for you," I said. There was no reason for me to feel like such an asshole. Not like I'd intentionally ignored her.

"To your defense, we kept you up pretty late. You're allowed to be tired."

My face grew hot as my dick swelled in my sweats. All she would have to do was glance down to see what thinking about last night did to my body.

"You alright now, though?"

She shrugged up her narrow shoulders and took another sip. "It's…I don't know. It's kind of weird after a night terror. It's not like a normal nightmare where you have to get your bearings. Night terrors make me feel trapped. Or paralyzed, I guess. It takes the guys forever to wake me up, and then those freaking feelings linger like oil on my skin. Even now I swear I can feel the stickiness. If that makes any sense."

Nodding my head, I reached across the small space and gripped her hand. "It makes total sense. And I'm still sorry I wasn't there for you."

Maeve turned her hand in mine and squeezed, a forced smile on her face. "Actually, I'm kind of glad you didn't witness it. From what Beck has told me, it's awful. And since we finally talked you into joining our pack, I don't want to risk scaring you away."

"Oh please," I said, pressing a kiss to the top of her head as I stood to refill my mug. "I watched you kick an alpha's ass, witnessed you trying to blow people up, and you still haven't scared me away."

"I did *not* try to blow people up. I merely tried to make them leave. Which was a total success, by the way. So…you're welcome. Again."

A chuckle bubbled up in my chest. She was holding to the concept that she'd done us a favor. And, while I couldn't totally argue with her on that point, I was glad she'd been staying home and away from possible felonies or incarceration. I might have been able to talk Kai into letting her alphas pick her up; I wasn't sure how much persuasion I might have with local PD or even higher.

Carrying my refilled mug back to the table, I sat beside her and turned so I was facing her. "I've been thinking about contacting ORE. See if they have any assignments. Or an open spot."

Her wide gold eyes turned to me. "You don't want to work for Omega Change anymore?"

"It's not that. I just…I haven't worked in over a week. I need to do something."

"Now you know how I feel," she said before taking a sip of her coffee.

"What do you mean?"

"I don't have a job. I don't have a car. I'm stuck here every single day unless one of you get me out of the house. I don't have a role other than being the omega to my pack. I don't have a purpose."

Well, shit. I didn't like the thought of her being out in public with so many alphas, especially after what she'd been through before our alphas found her. But when she laid it out like that, it was hard to avoid the fact she had been turned into what she didn't want – an ornament. She was a housewife. She was a reluctant homemaker who had no desire to clean or cook or do any of the domestic things so many omegas appeared to enjoy.

Had those assholes not destroyed the main offices of Omega Change I might have been able to call in a favor with Sophie. I supposed she could still use their services, though. That was part of what Sophie, Joy, and the others did, find safe jobs for omegas and offered escorts to and from their job sites, even providing on site guards when needed.

"Hey, um. So Omega Change offers education or job training as well as job placement. I don't want to step on our alphas' toes, but maybe I could ask Sophie if she could find something that would be a good fit for you."

Her smile slowly stretched across her face. "One, I love that you said *our* instead of just mine."

"Well, you're the one who said I was officially official and all that," I teased.

"Two…hell yes! That would be amazing. If Owen or Beck have any complaints, they can deal with them. I'll just threaten arson or something if they put up too much of a fight."

I tossed my head back and laughed. I knew she was kidding, but I also knew she would absolutely threaten some form of violence if she didn't get her way. The alarm codes had been changed, but that wouldn't stop her from walking right through the door with the damn thing blaring to get what she wanted.

Maeve tilted her mug back and finished off its contents before jumping to her feet and carrying it to the dishwasher. "Okay. Now I'm in a really good mood. I'm going to jump in the shower and wash off the sweat and cum from last night."

A groan tore from me as my dick thumped against my sweats in a plea to be freed at her words.

"If the alphas get up before me, fill them in. And if they have any protests, make sure you tell them about my threat. Or rather my promise. Can you call her today? Do I need to go meet with her?" She was rambling and stopped in the doorway, looking around the room as though in thought. "Shit. Do I have anything that would pass as professional attire for an interview?"

"Maeve," I said through chuckles. "You don't need a suit to talk to Sophie. And it'll probably be over the phone at first, so you don't have to worry about that. Besides, the people who worked at the office before it was destroyed wore what would be considered business casual, so I think you're fine in jeans or whatever."

"Will you contact her? See if she has anything for me? Or if she can help me? I literally have no skills. I've never had a job, but I'm smart and can learn fast. Tell her all that."

I wasn't sure I'd seen her so excited or animated in the short time I'd known her. And I fucking loved it. She might not require gifts, but I would definitely call Sophie the moment she stepped from the kitchen if this was the reaction I would get from her. The smile she wore as she ran from the room did something to my heart.

I loved her. I didn't care how soon it was or whether love at first sight was nothing more than a marketing ploy for romance writers. I loved Maeve in a way I didn't know was possible.

Pulling my phone from my pocket, I pulled up a group text between me, Kai, and Sophie and asked if the latter was willing to work with Maeve to either get her some form of job training or whether she had anything available for my omega.

Sophie: Absolutely. Does she know what she might be interested in doing?

Me: She said she's never had a job but she's willing to learn.

Sophie: Let me do some digging. Maybe set up an appt with her. See what sounds like something she might want to do.

Me: I really appreciate it, boss.

Sophie: Ew. Don't call me that.

WITH A SOFT LAUGH, I tucked my phone back in my pocket and gripped my mug between both hands, reveling in the warmth of the ceramic.

I should have probably donned a shirt before coming downstairs this morning, but, like Maeve, I felt a little sticky after our marathon love fest.

Another huff of laughter escaped me. Owen had kissed me. And fuck yes, I'd loved it. He kissed with a passion I would never have thought he was capable of, a passion that made me wonder whether my feelings for him weren't nearly as strong as they were for Maeve. If they weren't yet, they were definitely getting there. And quickly.

Within a few weeks, I'd met an omega, met her alphas, and found my pack, something I'd started to think would never happen. We were a small pack, but I felt as though I fit in here, like I'd known these people my whole life.

I still couldn't believe they thought they needed to court me. Perhaps I should have teased them and demanded gifts, demanded I be wined and dined and *absolutely* sixty-nined as often as possible. Played hard to get a little.

Heavy steps thumped overhead then down the stairs. By the cadence, I guessed it was Beckett. The big alpha was incapable of being quiet, not with his size. He had to stand somewhere close to six-foot-five or more.

"Morning," he said as he rounded the corner and went straight for the coffee maker.

If I wasn't mistaken, he had a pep in his step. I was curious to see how Owen reacted this morning, especially after our make out session before, during, and after we'd all made love to our omega last night. Or I supposed it could be considered this morning, as well, since we went well into the wee hours.

"Morning. Heads up, Maeve is going to talk to Sophie about getting a job today," I blurted out.

Beck turned with the mug to his lips, his eyes wide and brows raised. Even after he lowered his coffee, he continued to stare at me with the same surprised reaction.

"I take it Owen doesn't know."

"Haven't seen him yet this morning," I said with a shrug.

"He's not going to be on board," Beck warned before taking a seat across the table from me.

"That's what Maeve is worried about. She said she was going to threaten arson if you guys tried to keep her from it." I rested my forearms on the table and leaned forward a little. "She feels like she doesn't have a purpose," I said softly.

"Of course she does," he said. He leaned back in his seat and studied me a moment before turning to look toward the kitchen doorway as though he could see Maeve through the walls and the floor leading to the bedrooms upstairs.

"Other than being our omega?"

When he turned back, he had a thoughtful look on his face and his brows were drawn together. He didn't say anything for a few minutes, simply sipping at his coffee and turning his attention to the sunny patio out back.

"Shit," he muttered.

"Yep. I think if she had something to do other than hang around here all day, she might be less prone to...well, shit, less prone to act out."

"She's not acting out. It's her omega wanting to punish Clay. And since he's dead, she takes it out on any alpha who pisses her off."

I chuckled. I couldn't help myself. After everything she'd gone through, the little redhead was a hellcat and full of so much fire. If she'd been afraid in that bar or in the middle of the alphas at the protest, she sure as fuck didn't show it.

"Owen is going to be a hard sell," Beck said.

"Hard sell for what?" the alpha in question said as he entered the kitchen.

Unlike the rest of us, he didn't immediately go for the coffee, instead pulling out ingredients to make breakfast.

And yep, he had an obvious pep in his step. But he also avoided eye contact with me, even when he glanced at the table.

Fuck. The last thing I wanted was for him to be uncomfortable around me. Whatever I'd thought was growing between us might not go any further than last night. And I would have to be completely fine with that if I wanted to a part of the pack.

"Maeve wants to get a job," Beck said, simply blurting it the way I had.

Owen's shoulders tensed, but he didn't say anything for a few moments as he cracked eggs into a bowl and whisked them.

"A job where?" he asked without turning to look at either of us.

"I called Sophie. She's going to talk to Maeve and see if she wants to go to school, get some kind of job training, or go straight into the workforce," I answered.

It was another few minutes before Owen spoke again. He poured the eggs into a sizzling skillet and slipped some bread into the toaster. Then finally turned to look at me and Beckett.

"Security?" he asked, a spatula clenched in his fist as he crossed his arms over his chest.

He'd showered before coming down, as evidenced by his damp hair. And, unlike Beck and me, had tugged on his clothes. In fact, he was wearing his uniform the two alphas wore when they had clients to see. Which meant the two would be leaving for a few hours for the day. That would give Maeve and I some time together, give her some space to speak to Sophie and figure out some arrangements.

"There's security at any job site utilized by Omega Change. Hell, I could probably even bribe Kai and Sophie into letting me be her personal security."

"You'd get paid to hang out with our omega all day?" Beck teased with a huff of laughter.

"Yep." I popped the *p* at the end and grinned unrepentantly. "Does she not have a driver's license? She mentioned not having a car, but I had no idea whether she could drive or not."

"No license. No birth certificate or any form of identification to get her a license," Owen said before turning back to the stove.

After he scrambled the eggs and plated them, he finally poured his first cup of coffee as the toast popped up.

"Is there a way we can get her some fake identification so she could at least have some form of a state ID?" Beck asked.

"I think she would be overjoyed with a license. And a car of her own."

"That she would use to cause more trouble," Owen grumbled. There was no smile on his face or in his words.

"The question is do we take the risk so our omega is happy, or do we continue to make her feel as though she's a prisoner?" I asked.

Part of me felt odd discussing pack matters, but according to Maeve, I was a full blown packmate. Meaning I had as much say over our lives, over our omega's life, as the alphas did.

"She feels like a prisoner?" Beckett asked. He looked as though I'd punched him in the nuts.

"Wouldn't you? She has no transportation, meaning she can't go anywhere without an uber or one of us driving her. The codes have been changed, so she can't even step outside when no one is home."

"That's for her own protection," Owen said, pointing the spatula at me before dropping it into the sink.

"I understand that. But she's still a prisoner here. She told me this morning she feels like she doesn't have a purpose. She's just...existing, not living."

"She said that?" Beck asked.

"Not the last part. I paraphrased that."

Owen leaned against the counter a moment and stared at me, the first real eye contact he'd made with me since joining us in the kitchen.

Damn, he was attractive. So handsome in a broody kind of way.

"She's going to talk to Sophie?" he finally asked.

"Yeah. I already texted her and Kai. She's supposed to call me back after doing some digging. Then the two can talk and figure something out. I think having something to call her own might actually be good for her. Although, I still think we need to try to talk her into seeking therapy, too."

My hope was that talking to a trained professional might help with her night terrors and panic attacks.

Owen carried the plate of eggs and toast to the table before retrieving butter and jelly, then finally grabbing four plates for the pack.

"As long as there is enough security, I think it's worth a shot," Beckett said.

It was another long five minutes of Owen's silence before he nodded. "Okay. I think I would feel better at least meeting the security on the worksite, though."

"That'll piss her off," Beck said, reaching for the bowl of scrambled eggs.

"I don't care if she's pissed at me as long as she's safe," Owen said.

He finally raised his eyes to my face, leaned over, and pressed a quick kiss to my lips, shocking a gasp out of me. "Thank you for taking care of our girl."

Apparently, he didn't regret last night.

CHAPTER 20

<u>Maeve</u>

"You're going to be talking to her on the phone. It doesn't matter how you look," Wilder teased as I went through my closet.

"I need to look professional," I yelled back.

I had tossed so many outfits onto my bed, but none of them were right. All this time, I'd refused to wear anything more than jeans or stretch pants. And now I was regretting it.

"Maeve," Wilder chuckled from where he lounged on my bed in nothing but a pair of sweats.

Were I not so damn nervous, his relaxed and half-dressed state would have distracted me. After last night, after bouncing back from something that, in the past, would have set me back for days, maybe even weeks, I felt alive. I felt lighter.

These men, my alphas and my beta had helped me fix something that I'd thought was permanently broken.

Now, I was actually scheduled to talk to Sophie about finding a job, a career, a role in my own damn life outside of holding down the couch when my pack was out.

Hell, even when my pack was here, we cuddled or watched TV. Or had sex for hours like we had last night.

After so long, I'd finally let Owen past all my walls. I'd made love to him – or he'd made love to me – and dropped the barriers so Beck could feel me through our bond.

I still didn't have that same kind of bond with Owen, the same mark that I carried from Beck. And, after last night, I wanted it almost as much as I wanted a job.

Okay, maybe I wanted it more. I wanted to feel my pack in my chest, wanted to be able to tiptoe down the threads in my chest to feel their emotions, to carry them in my heart no matter how much distance separated us.

What would he say if I asked for his mark on my body before I started my new job? Or my first day of school? I hadn't decided which I wanted. I'd wait until after talking to Sophie to find out what kind of resources she had available to someone who was practically nonexistent since I didn't have a stitch of paperwork that proved I existed.

Honestly, I didn't want my real name and address listed anywhere. Even with Clay dead, I always had a fear that the other alpha would blame me for his friend's death and come for me, regardless of the fact he'd disappeared after the first few months.

At least I thought he had. I'd never heard his voice through the floor, and he'd never entered the basement. I had always assumed he'd left to find a new life or a new pack.

Peeking my head from the closet, I found Wilder rifling through the stack of fabric piled on my bed, messing up the order. "Stop touching," I ordered. "How hard would it be to change my last name?"

His brows shot up his forehead. "You want to change your last name?"

"Well, I don't have access to any of my personal stuff. I know I could go order a new birth certificate so I could get an ID, but I would rather not…"

"You'd rather no one knew where you were?" he guessed.

"Yeah."

And it wasn't solely Clay's former buddy. I had no desire to ever see a single member of my family again. They'd held no love for me in their hearts, had had no problem handing me over to a monster, so why should I give a shit about them?

"What last name would you want?" he asked, sitting up and smiling when I slapped his hand away from my perfectly stacked pile of clothing. If he messed with them, I'd have to put them back in order before rehanging them.

"I don't know. Owen's? Beck's? Yours? Any but mine."

Wilder tilted his head. "What *is* your last name?"

I waved my hand. "It doesn't matter. I haven't gone by that name in years."

"Is Maeve even your real name?"

My head jerked up as I frowned at him, but he was grinning. "Yes. Maeve is my real name, dork."

Hefting a few hangers, I returned my clothes little by little until they were back in order and smoothed in a line.

"Seriously. You can be naked on this call. She's not going to see you. In fact, I think naked is my favorite outfit."

"You're a bit of a horndog, aren't you?"

Crawling onto the bed, I nipped at his lips, then squealed when he wrapped his arms around me and flipped me onto my back.

"Only with you, beautiful."

He sipped at my lips until my body grew warm and my panties became damp with my slick.

"Sorry to interrupt, but we're heading out for the day. See you two in a few hours," Beckett said.

He crossed the room and bent over the bed to press a kiss to my lips, then shoved Wilder's shoulder. Owen was right behind the big alpha, leaving a kiss on my lips, then, without hesitation, pressing a kiss to Wilder's.

Last night had opened a floodgate of emotions and attraction between two of my packmates and I didn't hate it. In fact, watching their lips lock made me want to beg my alphas to stay home so we could hang out in bed all day, replaying last night's events.

"Good luck with your interview," Beck said.

"It's not really an interview. But thank you," I said, shoving Wilder off and sitting up before I let my body distract me from what I needed to do today.

"Good luck, baby girl," Owen said with a wink.

My surly, bossy alpha was being way more agreeable to my getting a job and leaving the house than I would have thought. Looked like Wilder was good for the entire pack, not just me.

I shifted my weight from one foot to the other as my alphas left my room, glancing back at me once before disappearing around the corner.

Why did them wishing me luck send butterflies flapping in my stomach? There was no reason to be nervous. According to Wilder, Sophie was cool and chill and down to earth. And he'd said this was merely a phone conversation, not an interview. I'd never even been on an interview. If Sophie wanted to meet with me, I might actually have to watch some how-to videos so I didn't make a complete fool of myself.

"You're not the first omega she's dealt with who's never worked before," Wilder said, pushing to a sitting position with his legs thrown over the side. "It's one of the main reasons she started Omega Change, to give your designation a chance to live your own lives and earn independence. I promise you'll love her. She's funny and a bit sarcastic, so don't take a whole lot she says seriously."

His words should have helped, but I was still nervous. This was a huge step for me. Not only would I finally have something that was all mine, but I would be out in the world, among strangers, among alphas. And, no matter what happened while on the job, I couldn't attack an alpha for doing something I thought was shady. That was a guaranteed way of getting fired before I earned my first paycheck.

"What time is it?" I asked before lifting my hand to chew on the skin around my thumbnail.

"You've got about fifteen minutes before she calls."

"Should I at least put on some mascara or something?"

He chuckled a deep, rumbly sound and held his arms out for me. I stepped into them, settling between his spread knees.

"She's not going to see you over the phone, beautiful. Stop stressing. I promise you everything will be totally fine."

Moving closer, I let him envelop me in a hug and rested my head on his shoulder. I was so much shorter than my guys that I barely had to bend forward to let him hold me.

"What if I'm terrible at a job?" I muttered against his bare shoulder.

He was so warm, his body so firm under my hands. But for the first time since that day on the couch, I didn't feel the need to strip him naked and ride him like a rabid cowgirl.

I was scared. No. Not *scared*. Nervous. And worried I would end up either making a fool of myself or ruining my chance of building a life outside of simply being my pack's omega.

"Then Sophie will find you something you're good at. No one expects you to be a savant at your first job, Maeve. I didn't just step into my role at ORE without extensive training. And a lot of therapy."

With a heavy sigh, I pulled away. "You're not going to let that go, are you?"

"I'm not going to pester you about it or try to force you to talk to someone, but I told you it helped me after my sister's murder. Just... think about it. That's all I'm asking."

With a huff, I rolled my eyes and crossed my arms under my breasts. "Fine. I'll think about it. But–" I said, holding up my hand to cut him off before he celebrated. "I'm not making any promises."

My phone rang and my heart began to race. "Oh man," I said, snatching it from the nightstand and quickly searching the room for somewhere to sit.

Not like she would know if I reclined beside Wilder.

"Hello?" I answered after the third ring.

"Hey, Maeve. Good to finally talk to you. Wilder said you're interested in entering the work force."

"I am," I said. Damn it. Why did my voice sound so shaky and breathy? No way she couldn't tell I was a nervous wreck.

"Any idea what interests you? Other than civil unrest?"

My eyes widened a second before I realized she was giggling over the line. Her alpha must have told her it had been me who'd caused the group to depart.

"Thanks for that, by the way. Gave us an opportunity to clean up the office a little and retrieve anything else that survived the attack."

"You're welcome?"

I shrugged when Wilder raised his brows in question.

"Did you finish high school?"

"No. I was pulled out my sophomore year. My parents thought I needed more training on how to be a good omega."

"Assholes," Sophie muttered. "Okay. Not a big deal at all. You're far from the first omega who wasn't able to graduate high school. Nor will you be the last. Are you interested in furthering your education? Getting a GED and possibly taking some college courses?"

I could hear Sophie typing over the line and wondered if she was taking notes, entering me into her system, or possibly even playing a game on her laptop.

"I don't know. I don't even know what I would go to school for or what I want to do other than get a job."

"Do you like to cook? Do you mind getting your hands dirty? Or how about typing or computer skills?"

"Don't like to cook. Definitely don't mind getting my hands dirty." Wilder snorted at that. "I can type and I'm okay on the computer. I don't know how to make spreadsheets or anything like that, but I can research on the internet and stuff like that. Um…I'm also really good with firearms and other weapons. And I'm great at hand-to-hand combat."

"Okay…that is seriously bad ass. Do you realize how fucking amazing it would be if I could hire you as a guard against alphas? I would love to see their faces when one of our designation puts them on their asses." Her voice was softer and I wondered if she was trying to keep someone from hearing our conversation.

"I know that won't really translate into a job in a retail store or whatever, but…yeah. That's pretty much all I'm good at right now. But

I'm smart and hard-working and learn fast," I said, tacking on the last part quickly so she wouldn't think I wasn't interested in literally anything she was willing to send my way.

"Any chance you can come by my house this afternoon? Joy and her pack are making an appearance, too. Joy is my assistant, so between the two of us, we can definitely find something perfect for you."

"Um…hold on a second." Pulling the phone away from my ear, I turned to Wilder. "Could we go to Sophie's? Her assistant is going there, too."

"Absolutely," my beta replied in a heartbeat, his smile turning into a full-blown grin.

"Sophie?"

"Yep. Still here." I'd never met the woman, but I swore I could hear a smile in her voice.

"Wilder said he can bring me over."

There was a beat of silence. "Do you not have a car yet?"

"No car. No driver's license. No ID." Shit. Would this be a deal breaker?

"Okay. First thing on the agenda is mocking up some kind of identification for you. I have a lot of people on my contacts list who hire omegas and pay cash so they don't have to register anything with the government. But I'd rather us be prepared just in case. Do you want to use your given name?"

"No," I said before she fully finished her question.

"Great. Just think of what last name you want on your papers before you get here and we'll get you started. Noon okay?"

"Noon?" I whispered to Wilder, who nodded. "Okay. Noon it is."

"Can't wait to finally meet you. See you in a couple hours. Bye."

"Bye," I said, then tossed my phone onto the bed.

Wilder's smile faltered then fell. A frown caused a crease between his brows. "What's wrong? I thought you would be more excited."

Tears burned the backs of my eyes and I felt like an idiot when I turned to him and said, "I still have nothing to wear."

CHAPTER 21

<u>Maeve</u>

I was bordering on tears from my lack of professional wear. Then Wilder barked out a laugh and carried his phone into the closet where I'd scoured through every single item for the fifteenth time.

On the screen was a pretty blonde holding a toddler. Her face was bereft of makeup, her hair was twisted into a top knot, several tendrils hanging loose as though her ponytail holder couldn't retrain them, and, from what I could see, was wearing a hoodie with an obvious stain from who knew what.

"She said chill out and wear something comfortable. You're not going into some high-rise, corporate office building. We're going to her house for a chat. I told you – Sophie is super laid back. She didn't even wear suits into the office. Joy wore blazers, but usually over graphic tees. Whatever you put on will be perfectly fine."

"What if she finds a job where I do have to wear suits or nicer clothes?" I said, my voice coming out far whinier than I would have liked, and my eyes welled with tears. Why were my damn emotions all over the place today?

"Okay, first of all, do you know when you're heat cycle is coming? Because you've been…a little up and down lately."

"I don't know," I said, swiping my fingers under my eyes to keep the tears from trailing down my cheeks. "Soon."

I'd wondered about that very thing last night when I'd felt damned near insatiable while with my pack.

"Feel better now? She's a mom to a toddler and working from home. She's not expecting you to show up in a power suit. Just throw on some jeans and a sweater."

"What about…this?" I asked, waving a hand around my frizzy curls and probably looking like a crazy woman.

"Brush it. Or pull it back. Or whatever. Again…you saw how Sophie looks today. She's not throwing a pageant at her house. You'll look amazing in whatever you put on. Get dressed so we can get on the road."

"Did you already text the alphas?"

"Yep," he said. "They said good luck again. And told me to tell you to have fun."

Fun? How the hell was this going to be fun? I was minutes away from hyperventilating.

Okay. Breathe. I just need to breathe. Sophie seemed extremely laid back and she'd gone so far as to send a picture of her looking very not office ready. And her assistant was bringing her pack, so it wasn't like this was some kind of formal meeting.

Pulling on a nicer pair of jeans, a sweater that had always made me feel pretty, then a sliding my feet into a pair of mid-heel booties, I hurried into the bathroom and stared at the mess that was my hair. Brush it. Ha! That would only make it worse. But I didn't have enough time to start from scratch to refresh my curls. So, I twisted it back and wrapped a scrunchie around it. After my rat's nest was tamed, I swiped on some mascara and a bit of tinted gloss.

Not quite Wall Street ready, but at least I looked pulled together and polished. After slipping on a pair of silver hoops that Beck had bought me early on when he'd hoped I would be a stereotypical omega who thrived on sparkly and pretty stuff, I turned this way and that and actually approved of the person looking back at me.

"You look beautiful," Wilder said when I grabbed my bag and let him know I was ready.

"You say that no matter what I'm wearing."

He shrugged his shoulders then followed me from my bedroom and down the stairs. "Well, because you are."

I snorted a sound of disbelief, but I appreciated his compliment and support. I hadn't asked yet how the conversation went when he'd alerted my alphas to the fact I was interested in seeking a life outside of the house. Almost two years with Beckett and Owen and I was still stuck within these four walls day in and day.

Especially since Owen put me on lockdown.

"Do you think Owen will give me the new code now?" I asked as we both pulled our seatbelts into place.

"I think as long as you're leaving to go to work and not to burn down any cities or assault anyone, he'll be fine giving you the new code."

"Oh, please. I've never tried to burn down anything." There was no reason to deny committing assault. Wilder only knew about the two occasions where he'd been a witness to my outbursts.

But I had a feeling he wasn't lying or feeding me a bunch of crap when he'd said nothing would cause him to run away or reject me or the pack.

Pack. The four of us were pack. A small one, but a strong one, nonetheless. I knew my guys would protect me as fiercely as I would protect them. Not that any of the three of them needed protection. Two of them were big alphas and my beta carried a gun for a living.

Didn't mean we couldn't watch over each other. Who knew? Maybe there would come a time when one or all of my packmates were outnumbered and I would need to jump in.

"What's so funny?" Wilder asked as he pulled onto a main road that bisected the town.

"Just thinking."

"About?"

No way was I telling him. Honestly, I was merely trying to distract myself. But, even in the short time I'd known Wilder, I already knew exactly what he would say if I told him I was thinking about how I could jump in and throw fists to protect my guys.

"How far away is Sophie's?" I asked instead of answering his question.

I glanced up at him to find him smirking at me with a cocked brow. He knew full well I was dodging and changing the subjects. Thankfully, he let it drop.

"Only about ten or fifteen minutes. Most of ORE and Omega Change live fairly close, although there are some outliers who moved out to the boonies. Country living and all that."

"I've always thought I would like to live in the country. Somewhere isolated. Somewhere I could have a garden and chickens. Maybe even horses."

"Can you ride?" he asked.

I shrugged up my shoulders. "Don't know. Never tried."

"Well, then. I just came up with an awesome date idea. And if the alphas aren't into it, it'll just be you and me riding horses through trails. Romantic, right?"

A grin stretched across my face as my body shook with quiet laughter. Neither Wilder nor I could quite be considered romantic. But that didn't mean we didn't have our own type of romance. And riding a horse beside Wilder with no one around definitely sounded romantic, even in the typical sense.

"Do the alphas know you want to live in the country?" he asked me.

"I'm not saying I want to live in the country. But the idea is appealing. I mean, our house is already pretty isolated. But...I don't know. I've always wanted a pet. My parents would never let me get so much as a hamster growing up. The thought of a dog or cat snuggling with me. Or stepping outside in the morning to my little hobby farm. I don't know. I should probably start with a goldfish to make sure I can keep a living creature alive before going headfirst into cowgirl life."

Wilder barked out a laugh. "I will pay you to put on some short shorts, a plaid shirt, cowboy hat, and boots. Like…name the price."

Whether Wilder was trying to lighten the mood and distract me from my nerves or simply making conversation didn't matter – I felt better. My stomach was no longer turning with anxiety.

Entirely too soon, Wilder pulled down a driveway to a pretty two-story house that looked like it hopped straight out of a magazine. It was quaint and charming and there was so much pretty landscaping. With the temps getting cooler the flowers were nonexistent, but that did nothing to take away from the cottagey charm.

A pretty woman with white-blonde hair stepped out with the most adorable toddler on her hip.

She smiled and waved as Wilder and I stepped from the vehicle.

"It's so great to meet you," Sophie said, making her way to my side and giving me an awkward side hug.

"You, too," I said, trying to pull from her arms without appearing rude. I just wasn't much of a hugger. It was hard enough to let my pack hold me, even as an omega.

Sophie pulled away and narrowed her eyes at me. "You might be the first omega who hates touch."

My head jerked back and my nerves came rushing back. Great. I'd offended her before we'd even stepped inside her house. "What makes you think that?"

"Well, for one thing, you're not clinging to your beta for dear life. And you broke the hug within a half a second. Prior abuse? Past trauma?"

"Uh…" I looked up at Wilder with pleading eyes.

But he didn't placate me, only shrugged and nodded his head toward Sophie.

"She has experience with abuse. And she's literally heard and seen it all. Nothing you can say will shock her."

"Yes. Past trauma. And abuse," I admitted, my voice coming out strained through my quickly closing throat.

"Assholes," she muttered then winced, turning to look at her daughter. "Mommy said a bad word."

"No bad words," the baby said in the cutest voice, the words slurred like she was still figuring out the whole speech thing.

"That's right. No bad words. This is my daughter, Lara."

"She's beautiful," I said. And genuinely meant it. I hadn't thought much about motherhood, but seeing the love on Sophie's face as she looked at her daughter made me wonder if I would be able to avoid the way I'd been raised and actually do right by any child I birthed.

Nah. Not yet. I'd only just started to find my inner strength, only just began to grow comfortable with trusting my alphas and now my beta with the vulnerability of making love to me.

Adding a child to the mix while I was still pretty broken was a recipe for disaster.

"Come on in. Joy and her pack will be here any minute." She turned and led the way up the two concrete stairs and into her house.

It was homey and lived in with tasteful décor and a mixture of pretty furniture and toys littering the floor.

"I would say sorry about the mess, but I can't keep the house clean when she's awake," Sophie said with a laugh.

"Your house is seriously so pretty," I said, looking around. Even the toys gave it a lived in, relaxed feeling and made me want to flop on the couch to watch cartoons with little Lara.

"Thank you. We try. It's kind of a mashup of Kai's and Devyn's furniture and stuff. I didn't have a whole lot when we moved in together, so I had to add my flair when I moved in with two men." She rolled her eyes but there was a smile on her lips and so much love in her eyes.

Did I look like that when I talked about my pack? Could they see what they meant to me when I looked at them? I had built walls around my heart for so long. If they didn't know by anything more than my words, I needed to make sure that changed. I wanted them to feel as cared for as they made me feel.

The two men in question rounded the corner, a handsome beta reaching out to take Lara from Sophie's arms. I assumed the baby belonged to the big alpha shaking hands with Wilder since she had the same dark hair and bright blue eyes as Kai.

"Good to see you again, Maeve," Kai said with a raised brow.

"Oh, that's right. I forgot the two of you met," Sophie said with a wide, shit-eating grin. "Don't listen to my mate. I appreciate your...*help* with making those asshats leave the property."

"Maybe next time talk to Wilder or me before you have any good ideas," Kai said. "We'll leave you ladies to your business." He jerked his head for Wilder to follow him, then the three men disappeared further into the house, taking the baby with them.

The front door opened as Sophie led me into the living room and motioned for me to sit. A woman with shoulder length, blonde hair and a wide, warm smile hurried down the hall followed by two alphas.

"Sorry I'm late," she said. "These two wanted to grab some beer for the BBQ."

I frowned at Sophie. "Is this a party?" I hadn't planned on staying all day, simply meeting the owner and operator of Omega Change to plan for my future.

"Nah. The guys find any excuse to fire up the grill and down some beers. Most of them worked together at some point. Wilder, Kai, and Beau still do."

"Is Beau the scary looking tattooed guy?"

Both omegas barked out a laugh. Joy said, "No. That's my alpha Justus. He was my first mate. And don't let his looks fool you. He's a big ol' teddy bear."

"I heard that," a male voice called from somewhere deeper in the house.

"I didn't whisper it," Joy called back.

A laugh burst from me. I couldn't help it. These omegas were so comfortable with their alphas, their mates. And, yeah, I was comfortable with my pack, but was I nearly as sweet and playful to them as Joy and Sophie were with theirs?

They love me the way I am. I had to remind myself that when I felt the insecurity begin to rise, that stupid voice that echoed in my mind that I wasn't worthy of good alphas, that I didn't deserve a loving pack.

The more I thought about it, the more I realized that voice didn't solely belong to Clay. It often sounded like my mother, as well. This bull shit, these insecurities started long before I was chained up and beaten by that asshole alpha.

But it wasn't true. None of it was true. And now, I wanted nothing more than to leave Sophie's, make my pack all come home, and tell them that I'd had an epiphany.

Not that I would suddenly become some squishy, emotional omega. But at least I was finally starting to see myself the way they did, the way they had all along and tried so hard to show me.

"Alright, now that the party's here, let's get started." Sophie turned her laptop toward me and instructed me to go through a long ass questionnaire.

The problem was…I didn't know the answers to a majority of the questions. I didn't know what I liked to do. I didn't know what I refused to try. I didn't know fuck all about myself because I'd never really been allowed to live a life of my own. My alphas had taken care of me and struggled to help me heal, but even they had kept me under lock and key for almost two years.

Okay, yeah. So it was because I had a tendency to break the law. And the two incidents that Wilder had witnessed was barely a drop in the ocean of bull shit I'd already committed.

But none of that helped the fact I had no idea what I wanted to do to earn my own money.

"What's wrong?" Joy asked, leaning forward from her spot on the couch across from me.

There was zero judgment on her face.

Looking from her to Sophie and back, I sighed. "I don't know how to answer most of this. I really don't know what I like and don't like. The only absolutes are I don't know how to cook and I'm not overly great at computers."

"Oh, Joy! She's been trained in hand-to-hand combat and can use a crap load of weapons," Sophie said, her grin wide and her brows high.

"Okay. That is the most badass thing I've heard in a long time."

"Right?" Sophie said with a giggle.

"Shame it doesn't translate into a job, though," I said, flopping back against the couch.

I probably shouldn't pout in front of my prospective boss, but I was frustrated. And...I was extremely comfortable with both women already. Instead of feeling as though I'd only just met them, they both felt more like lifelong friends.

"We'll find you something, girl. If the first one doesn't work out, we'll find another. I've got quite a list of omega safe jobs. And all of them allow a personal guard if you're not comfortable being alone in public."

I snorted. "Don't tell that to my pack. They'll probably demand all three of them be assigned. Owen and Beck have their own company, have the house entirely secured, but they still stress about me being home alone."

"Because you sneak out and cause havoc," Wilder said from what I presumed was the kitchen.

"Snitch!" I called back, then smiled.

Of my three guys, Wilder was the first to break through the heavily fortified wall around my heart. He'd been easy to play with and joke with and had helped thaw the ice enough for me to let my alphas in, as well.

If I could find a job, a role, a purpose in my own life...I might just be on the way of having the perfect life. Or at least the perfect life for me.

CHAPTER 22

<u>Beckett</u>

"**I** thought we were celebrating," Maeve said with a pout as she watched me push pieces of clothing aside.

"We are celebrating. You need a whole new wardrobe. Then I'm taking you to the salon. Did you want your nails done, too? I just told them to book out a couple hours in case you wanted more than a trim."

"What's wrong with my hair?" she asked, pulling the ponytail over her shoulder and toying with the ends.

"Absolutely nothing. But I want you to feel amazing for your first day."

"Beck...I wear a uniform. I don't need new clothes. And I'll probably pull my hair back every day so I don't get too hot. Therefore, I don't need to go to the salon."

"Have you ever been to a salon?" I asked, raising both brows.

Her pale cheeks blushed a soft pink. "No."

"Then how do you know you won't like it? Even if they just give your ends a trim, it'll give you a little boost. And the shampoo feels amazing."

"Beck?" she asked, stopping me as I moved to another rack. "Do you go to a salon for your haircuts for the pretty girls and the scalp massage?" Her smile slowly stretched across her pretty face as she teased me.

"One – my stylist is a pretty beta *man*. Two – hell yes, I go for the scalp massage. Don't knock it 'til you try it."

"How do they even reach your head? Do they stand on a stool?"

I wasn't that tall compared to other alphas. But standing next to my omega, I must have looked like the giant she called me.

"Fine. No new wardrobe. How about some new undies and bras? Or PJs. Or…lingerie?" I waggled my brows up and down and earned a girly giggle, the sound going straight to my dick.

"Why bother with lingerie when it always ends up in a rumpled ball on the floor anyway?" she replied with a flirty smile.

"Keep it up and I'll find us a dressing room."

"Why? You plan on trying on some of that lingerie you were talking about?"

I had loved Maeve since the moment she came into my life. But from the moment Wilder joined our pack, she had started breaking through her shell and was not just the fiery, sassy woman who had us wrapped around her little finger but was becoming quite the flirt.

"Brat," I said, playfully swatting her on the ass before guiding her to another department of the store.

"Oh. I can actually use a new pair of shoes if I'm going to be on my feet all day."

"Deal," I said, taking her hand in mine and leading her to that department.

I would have rather loaded the cart up with bags of clothes, lacy panties, and see-through bras, maybe even some jewelry for her adorable ears or to drape around her soft neck, but I didn't want to push her and make what was supposed to be a fun outing for the just the two of us into something that pissed her off or stressed her out.

Maeve was showing all the signs of being in preheat, meaning she would either have to put off her first day or end up taking off a week shortly after she started her new job. Since the place was considered safe for omegas, they scheduled accordingly in case one of their employees needed the week off during their cycle.

Her nest had been stocked from the moment she came to stay with us, but, after she'd finally stopped hiding out in there, it was rarely used. Unlike other omegas I'd known throughout my life, she didn't retreat to that space when something upset her. Nope. She just went on a rampage and assaulted alphas or destroyed property.

Biting back the chuckle that bubbled up in my chest, I let her scour the selection of sneakers and walking shoes until she chose a couple pairs in her size to try on.

She sat on a stool and laced a pair up, her ponytail of curls spilling over her shoulder. "What if I'm terrible at my first job and get fired?" she said softly.

"Then Sophie will find you another one. And I don't think you'll be terrible. But since you'll be working with the public, you *will* encounter alphas."

"I know," she said, standing to test the fit and comfort of the shoe. "I can't attack an alpha for pissing me off while on the job. Sophie already warned me. But Wilder will be there."

Of course the beta had volunteered to work as our omega's private security for the first few weeks of her first job. I wasn't sure how much of his presence was for her and how much was for our peace of mind. But I was grateful for his role either way.

"What if they get pissed that I have my beta there?" she asked as she toed off the current pair to try on another.

Lowering until I was balanced on the balls of my feet, I waited until she raised her eyes to my face. "You are not the first omega to have personal security. Wilder and Kai have been on several assignments where they were hired to watch over an omega while she got comfortable in her new position. Sometimes the omega requires full time, ongoing protection. No one will look at you any differently or look down on you. I promise. Sophie only works with the best people.

Even if Wilder wasn't there, the managers are all trained to watch for danger and keep an eye out for their omega employees."

She huffed and sat back against the side of the aisle. "Do you know how stupid it is to have to go through all this shit simply because I was born a specific designation?"

"You're a rare gem. Remember that. You're protected because you're special."

"Not according to those asshole protestors," she said as she crossed her arms.

For someone so petite, she always looked so fierce, always ready for a fight.

"The operative word is *asshole*. They are assholes. And they don't speak for alphas. At no point in my life have I thought of omegas as anything less than special, perfection, a designation to be revered and cherished."

A ghost of a smile quirked up the corners of her lips. "Keep saying shit like that and we *will* end up in a dressing room. You're real close to earning a blow job, Beck."

"You're going to make me blush," I teased. In reality, my dick was so hard I was surprised it didn't poke a hole through my slacks.

She smiled and shoved at my shoulder, nearly knocking me off balance.

"I think these will work," she said as she stood and walked back and forth. "They're comfortable and feel like they have a little spring to them."

"I know you want a job, but I just want…we don't expect you to work. We don't expect you to financially contribute to the household. Any money you make is yours. Cool?"

"I really thought you were about to try to talk me out of working," she said as the crease between her brows smoothed.

"You were going to fight me on it, too, weren't you?"

She boxed the shoes up. I took them from her and nodded at the display.

"Grab a second pair as backup."

"I had every intention of fighting you on it. Especially since Wilder will be there. There's no reason to freak out if our beta will be there every damn day."

I knew she'd begrudgingly agreed to having a full-time guard while she was working but had acquiesced to keep Owen and me at ease. I wasn't completely against her being in the public or having a job. She definitely didn't need to work; our company made enough money that neither Maeve nor Wilder needed to add anything to our income.

But Wilder loved his job. And I had a feeling his job was part of his therapy after losing his sister and not being able to protect her.

Our omega was bored. And, according to Wilder, she felt as though she didn't have a purpose other than merely existing. I could understand that. Since she tended to get herself in trouble any time she left without one of us in tow, she'd been more or less on lock-down. This wasn't the first time Owen had changed the security code to keep her from leaving the house without one of us knowing. And the two times she'd first met Wilder had only been a drop in the well of her many felonious situations. There had been even more that could have resulted in misdemeanor charges.

Maeve had returned home from Sophie's in a great mood. Apparently, the owner of Omega Change was going to help Maeve secure a form of government ID, so she had to choose what last name she wanted on her birth certificate. And yep, I wanted her to choose mine. Though I wouldn't pressure her.

Our omega was in her mid-twenties and had never been taught to drive a car. She had no way to get around without one of us – or Ubers, as she'd done on more than one occasion – and I wondered if it was time to change that.

Then again, since Wilder would be with her every day at work, she could actually ride with the beta. That didn't mean she wouldn't want a form of independence. Whether she drove herself or not, she could at least learn how to drive.

That was a conversation for later. For now, I was still determined to spoil my omega as much as she would allow me. I hadn't bothered cancelling the salon appointment. Even if she didn't want a new style, she could at least let the stylist pamper her a bit. Who knew? She might end up liking it.

Eh. Wishful thinking. Since she was finally breaking out of her shell and allowing us to treat her like our omega, she might end up letting us dote on her a little more. But again…wishful thinking.

"Anything else? Bras? Undies? And the lingerie is still on the table."

"I don't need lingerie, Beck," she said, bumping me with her shoulder as we walked. "Maybe underwear and socks, though."

"I swear shopping with you is like receiving gifts from my grandma."

That sweet tinkling giggle that I was addicted to filled the space between us as she led the way to the women's department.

With all her teasing, she hadn't invited me into the dressing room while she tried on a few different sports bras. What could I say? I was still stuck on the threat of a blow job.

CHAPTER 23

<u>Wilder</u>

*I*t had taken a few days for Sophie to find something for Maeve, but now she was in a uniform that consisted of a black pullover shirt, black slacks, and a black apron, clearing tables and hefting drinks to patrons.

She was officially a bus boy – Girl. Whatever – and an occasional food runner. And I sat in a booth where I could see the entire restaurant, the front door, and the kitchen in order to keep an eye on our omega.

And I was bored shitless. As much as I would love to play on my phone or even read a book, the thought of taking my eyes off Maeve for even a second sent anxiety coursing through my system. In my line of work, it could only take a second for someone to get hurt. What if she was accosted because I was distracted by a video on my phone? What if she needed me and I was engrossed in a book?

Yeah, those were somewhat irrational fears, but not something I could control. My job had taught me vigilance. Since Maeve was my omega, I was even more on edge. The mere possibility of anything happening to the beautiful redhead made me want to wrap her in my arms, drag her to the truck, and rush her back home.

Irrational, yeah. But I was sure the alphas would feel even more strongly about it. Especially Owen. He'd more or less tried to talk Maeve out of going to work, assuring her the three of us made enough to support the pack.

But it wasn't solely about the money for Maeve, and I fully understood that. In the time I was at home waiting to be called back into work, I'd gone stir crazy and felt as though I was simply existing instead of actually living. Our omega deserved the same fucking thing.

She hustled by, barely glancing at me as she carried a tub full of dirty dishes. This was only her third day of work, but she seemed happy, if not completely worn out by the end of her shift.

And she was only working four-hour shifts. Her body would grow used to the work and she would no longer require a catnap when we got back home.

The morning rush was over, so she had a lot of tables to clear. I contemplated jumping in and helping her but knew she would hate that. My girl wanted her independence. If I even *offered* to clear a few tables she would see it as me doubting her abilities, doubting that she could do her job.

I watched as her fiery red hair appeared across the restaurant, then moments later she was at my table. "I'm off. Ready?" she asked.

Her hair was coming loose from the bun she'd carefully placed before her shift, the curly tendrils frizzing in places, others sticking to the sweat along her forehead and temples. And, maybe I was just madly in love, but she was the most beautiful being I'd ever seen in my life. Even now, disheveled and wearing an apron spattered with drying food, smelling a bit like the kitchen, like food and dishwater.

Nothing a hot shower or long bubble bath wouldn't fix. Preferably one of those would be shared with me.

Standing, I joined Maeve and put my hand on the small of her back, guiding her from the restaurant while keeping an eye on our surroundings. Just because she wasn't specifically an at-risk omega didn't mean the perfume rolling from her while she was in preheat wouldn't attract the wrong kind of attention.

I was curious as to how long her preheats generally lasted. I knew she had only allowed the alphas to help her through a couple of her cycles during her time with them, but three weeks of symptoms seemed to be longer than what I'd seen other omegas go through.

If she was cramping or in any form of discomfort, she didn't say a thing. Didn't complain. Hell, she didn't even complain about her swollen feet or her exhaustion from her new job. Simply showered and napped. Then she was back to her sassy, sexy self an hour later, busting our balls and teasing the pack.

Once we were in the truck and on our way home, I glanced at her as she rested her head against the back of her set. "Well? How do you like it?"

"It gets hot," she said.

"That doesn't really answer the question. Do you want Sophie to look for something else?"

She rolled her head to look at me, her russet brows drawing together. "Why would I want something else? Everyone is really nice. And I told my manager I was close to my heat; she said to just text her if I needed the time off. Sophie said the places she worked with were more than willing to work around our cycles, but Sasha just said to text her. On TV, they always make you request time off and could deny that request."

"I'm sure there are some alpha owned businesses that aren't so flexible. But Sophie knows what she's doing and won't work with assholes."

Maeve chuckled softly and turned to watch through the windshield. "One of the waitresses gave me some of her tips. I have cash. In my pocket."

Her statement filled me with joy and a touch of sadness. Something as simple as earning her own money, more than likely no more than twenty dollars, made her feel accomplished. As much as I would love to see her at home with a round belly and in full nesting mode, I loved the sound of happiness in her voice even more.

"Yeah. They tend to tip out their bussers since y'all make their job easier."

"They're all really nice, too. The cook set aside an order of sweet potato fries for me, and I didn't have to pay for them."

A green fog slithered through my stomach. "Is he an alpha?"

I saw her shake her head in my periphery. "No. Only betas and omegas work there."

Okay. A beta fed her. He was simply being nice. So why did I feel the need to return to the restaurant later to vet this guy, to question him, to make sure he wasn't flirting with my girl?

I couldn't go after every single person who found my omega attractive. She was beautiful. Stunning. And even if they fed her or flirted with her, she wouldn't leave me, leave *us*, leave her pack.

Shit. He might have simply been being nice and I was sitting in the driver's seat working up all these scenarios and getting my hackles up for no reason.

A small whimper sounded from beside me, so quiet I wondered if I'd imagined it.

But glancing at my girl, my heart clenched at the sight of her hand over her lower stomach and the furrow of her brows.

"You okay?" I asked.

"Mmhm," she said. But the crease between her brows didn't smooth and she looked paler than normal.

"Are you going into heat?" I asked. Shit. I would have to text the alphas and get them home before they were done with work for the day.

"Preheat," she muttered. But I could hear the pain in her voice.

"You've been saying that for close to a month, beautiful. Did you take a suppressant?" That would explain why she hadn't fully gone into her cycle.

"No. I, uh...I thought I would let my body go through this one naturally. And Sophie said she was worried about long term effects of the suppressants. I don't know if I'm going to keep taking them."

I'd heard Sophie on the phone with doctors when we were still in the office, had heard her lobbying members of congress for further studies. There was a fear that the suppressants could cause infertility or even permanent damage to the reproductive system.

The praise for her decision was on my tongue, but froze in my throat when a long, keening whine tore from her throat.

Reaching over, I pressed the back of my hand to her forehead. "You're burning up. This isn't preheat, beautiful. You're going into heat."

"I just started my job three days ago," she said around another whine.

"And your manager told you it would be no problem to cover you for the week."

I had to shift my weight to the side to pull my phone from my back pocket.

"What are you doing?" she asked.

"Calling the alphas. Time for them to come home."

With a move fast enough to surprise me, she reached over and snatched the phone from my hand, tossing it onto the center console. "They don't need to come home. I'm fine," she said, crossing her arms under her breasts and doing her best to look as though her body wasn't completely rebelling and torturing her.

"Baby, as much as I love the idea of riding through this heat with you, I can't give your body what it needs. The alphas can help with the pain and fever."

"I said I'm fine. It doesn't even hurt that bad."

"Yet," I said, turning to look at her a second before pulling into our driveway. "It doesn't hurt that bad *yet*. Why wait until you're delirious with fever and your uterus is doing its best to terrorize you?"

She didn't argue, but when I reached for my phone again, she grabbed it and shoved it under her leg.

"Do you really think I won't reach under your sweet ass to grab that?" I asked, hoping my tease would at least elicit a smile or giggle.

It received neither.

Pulling the truck into the third spot in the row – my designated spot – I rounded the hood and pulled her door open when she didn't immediately climb out.

She was doubled over, her breath coming in pants. Yep. She was going into heat. We were no longer in the beginning stages. She had maybe an hour before her body would lose herself to her hindbrain. And I would much rather she be in the nest or even the bathtub before that happened.

Not that I would turn her down if she wanted me to bend her over the hood of my truck or even take her right there in the passenger seat.

Unfortunately, anything I did would only lend her temporary relief. Her omega needed a knot to ease the discomfort, the pain and fever that would plague her for anywhere from three days to a damn week.

My phone was still under her leg. And tears welled in her eyes as she clenched her jaw hard enough for a muscle to feather in her narrow jaw.

"Sweetheart. Please. You're killing me. Just let me text them and let them know what's up. I won't tell them to come home, just make sure they don't dawdle after work."

"Dawdle?" she said, a smile on her face while pain was written all over her face.

"Yeah. Dawdle. Or would you prefer dilly dally?"

"You're a dork," she said, pushing me out of the way so she could step down.

Her hand shot out and reached for me as she stumbled, and my head and heart nearly exploded with fucking panic. Was she dizzy? Or had she just tripped over her own feet?

This was my first time ever helping an omega through her heat. My main role would be ensuring she and the alphas were eating and drinking enough through the next few days, but I would also have to give Beck and Owen breaks and tend to my sweet girl, bringing her enough orgasms so her body would let her rest.

I knew she would protest, but I scooped her into my arms, snatching my cell from the seat, kicked the truck door shut, then carried her into the house, up the stairs, and straight to the bedroom.

"Let's get you in the tub. Can you handle a warm bath, or do you want it cooler?"

Her skin felt too hot to the touch for my comfort, but I wouldn't decide what was best for her. She had a voice and I wanted her to use it.

Setting her on her feet, I bent at the knees to look in her face. Her eyes were still glassy, but they looked unfocused and her pupils were blown. Her sweet honey citrus scent was strong as her perfume exploded from her and her tongue darted out to lick her lips.

"Hang in there, beautiful. Can you tell me if you can handle a warm bath? Or do you need it cooler?"

Her hands reached forward and cupped my junk through my pants as she moved closer, tilting her head back as though waiting for my kiss.

Guess I would have to make the decision for her. I'd start it warm, and if her fever climbed, I'd add cooler water. For now, she needed to wash the smells of the restaurant from her skin and hair.

It was way harder to pull her hand away from my hard dick than I would have thought. Especially when she squeezed lightly and began to rub my length through my pants. I had to hold her wrists in my hands and walk backward, guiding her into the bathroom with me.

Once I got her situated, I had every intention of telling the alphas to get their asses home as soon as possible. She could be pissed at me later. The last thing I wanted was for the love of my life to go through the agony of a cycle without the relief only an alpha could give her.

For the first time in a long damn time, I hated my designation. If I'd been born an alpha, she wouldn't have to wait for Beck and Owen to return home.

But that didn't mean I wouldn't do everything in my power to make her as comfortable as possible while we waited.

CHAPTER 24

<u>Owen</u>

Beck had received a text from Wilder to finish up our work and head home. Maeve was not only going into heat, but she was finally willing to let us do as our biology demanded of us and take care of her. Of course, it was a biological need to breed for both omega and alpha, but our bodies didn't seem to care that we had no desire to procreate. At least Maeve didn't.

Beck had received the text. Not me. I don't know why a little sliver of jealousy slithered through my gut that the beta had texted Beckett first, had let him know that our omega needed her alphas. And I wasn't sure whether it was because Wilder texted Beck or because he let Beck know about Maeve instead of me.

Maybe a little bit of both.

"Did you contact the last client?" I asked Beckett as I sped home, ignoring the speed limits and barely slowing at stop signs long enough to ensure I wouldn't crash into some pack heading to the park or some shit.

"Yeah. Gave them a heads up that we wouldn't be able to make it for a week. Gave them the number of someone else in case they were at risk."

Most of our clients simply wanted top of the line systems or backup cameras. But we often served clients with omegas who were at risk or had a house full of pups. We didn't ask questions about their personal life, only made sure they had adequate coverage of their home.

"Do you think we should stop and get her something? New blankets or whatever?" Beck asked.

"She has a nest full of blankets and pillows she's only used once in the last year and a half," I answered. Although I wouldn't mind getting her a heat gift. Not that this was her first heat. And not that she would expect a gift. Hell, our fiery omega would probably reject anything we might buy her.

"What about some fuzzy socks? Or pajamas."

"When is she going to wear the pajamas?" She'd be spending the next few days naked when her body demanded constant attention from us.

"After?" Beck said, turning to glance at me as I turned onto our street.

With a shake of my head, I hit the indicator, then turned onto the paved driveway that would lead to our house.

Would she and Wilder already be in the nest? Would he already be with her, would they be naked and making love?

My dick instantly hardened at the thought of the two people I wanted more than my next breath moaning, sweating, writhing as Wilder brought her to orgasm over and over. I couldn't help but wonder whether I would have the energy to finally act on a few fantasies I'd had about our beta while trying to help Maeve through this heat.

Fuck.

Reaching down, I adjusted my boner and pulled the SUV into the garage, parking beside Beck's vehicle. Wilder's truck was at the end of the row. As I pushed open my door, the sweet and heady scent of Maeve's perfume nearly bowled me over.

"Damn," Beckett muttered, inhaling deeply and blowing it out with a moan. "That's strong as fuck."

Rushing through the door, I was already pulling my shirt over my head as I ran through the house and took the stairs two at a time.

Soft whimpers touched my ears as I neared her bedroom door. I followed the sounds to the bathroom. Wilder held her in his arms in the tub as she straddled his lap, lifting and falling on him as he stared up at her through heavy lids.

The water sloshed, some of it splashing from the tub when her movements became more frantic.

"Is she okay?" Beck asked as he stopped beside me.

"Her fever was really high," Wilder answered, though his eyes stayed on our beautiful omega. "We've been in here since I texted you."

A frown drew my brows together as I lowered to my knees and put my hand in the water. It was barely lukewarm. Which, of course, would be great for her fever, but I had no idea how the hell Wilder could be comfortable.

Then again, it was hard to focus on anything else with Maeve's tight cunt wrapped around your cock. At least I sure as hell couldn't. Now that her pheromones were floating on the air and sending a lust drunk sensation straight to my brain and cock, I was barely able to keep my thoughts straight. I would be lost the moment I was buried inside her tight, wet heat.

"Baby girl?" I asked, moving so we were eye to eye.

Her head turned, but her gaze was unfocused as she stared at me, her hips still rising and falling on Wilder as she rode him.

"You okay?"

"Alpha," she moaned, lunging at me.

I grabbed her before she could fall out of the tub and hit her head on something. Wilder grunted with the abrupt motion. I couldn't imagine having Maeve's movement was comfortable, especially if his cock had been tugged to the side.

"Careful, sweetheart," Beck said, wrapping a towel around her as she tried to climb my body and wrap her legs around my waist. Her back might have been covered with the terry cloth, but the rest of her soaked my bare chest and stomach and the cargo pants I wore to work with the bath water and her sweet-smelling slick.

Wilder was climbing from the tub as I carried our omega from the bathroom, making a beeline for the nest.

Shit. We hadn't prepared, didn't have any easy to eat food or bottled water ready for the next few days. Beck and I would be servicing our sassy girl, so hopefully, Wilder would have enough mental bandwidth to bring food and water periodically.

Especially for our girl. She would be so lost to her hindbrain that she would forgo anything that didn't include release or knots.

"Wilder?" I called out as I gently extricated Maeve's arms and legs from me so I could remove my shoes and shove my pants down my legs.

"He headed to the kitchen. Grabbing water," Beck said.

Damn. For a beta who'd never been a part of a pack, his instincts were impeccable.

"Alpha," Maeve whimpered before a long, needy whine escaped her lips.

"I'm here, baby girl."

Beck appeared in my periphery, his clothes already missing as he knelt beside her and pushed her hair from her face.

"I need you to listen to me, sweetheart," he said, hovering over her so she had to focus on only his face. "We're going to take care of you, but you have to let us know if it becomes too much. And you have to eat or drink when we give you something. Can you do that for us?"

"Alpha, please," she whined.

Maeve hated designations, hated when anyone referred to her simply as omega. But right now, with her body taking over and her hormones in overdrive, all she could focus on was her physical needs, the pain that was wracking her uterus, the fever that burned through her veins, causing a flush to her cheeks, chest, and neck.

"Should we...does she need cool cloths or something?" Beck asked. "She wasn't like this last time."

"It's been a long time. Her hormones are out of control," I said, running my hands up her legs as she scissored them in an effort to find some relief. "We're here, baby girl. We've got you."

I knew what she wanted. She wanted me buried inside of her, wanted my knot locking us together, my seed painting her inner walls. But as I stared at her beautiful pussy shining with slick, I couldn't help myself.

Lying on my stomach, I settled between her thighs and licked a long, slow path through her folds. Her fingers instantly tangled in my hair and pulled me closer as her hips began to rock as though she was trying to fuck herself on my tongue.

Fuck, she tasted so good.

Oranges and sweet cream mixed with the honey and citrus scent as Wilder reentered the nest. He stretched along Maeve's other side, across from Beckett, and my eyes rolled up to catch a full view of his beautiful body and engorged cock, the tip glistening with precum.

If my face wasn't buried in Maeve's delicious cunt, I might have leaned over to lap the drop away, to savor the taste of oranges and cream.

Later. Another time I would finally take Wilder the way I wanted. I would finally allow myself to lose myself in the beta who was becoming as important to me as my omega.

For now, I would focus all my attention on the woman who was moaning nonstop as she continued to fuck my face.

"You need more, sweetheart? Do you want your beta's cock?" Beckett asked.

"Wilder," she whimpered.

Opening my eyes again, I watched as Wilder knelt beside Maeve's face and fed her his cock, slowly pushing past her open lips as Beckett held her head up.

Damn. I hadn't even buried my cock inside of her and already I felt my balls tightening as I fought the urge to come from the scene a few feet from my face.

CHAPTER 25

<u>Wilder</u>

My eyes nearly rolled back in my head as Maeve's tongue circled the head of my cock before she slid her lips over the shaft, taking me deep into her throat. Beckett teased her tits, licking and sucking her nipples into his mouth. Owen's face was buried between her thighs, devouring her like a starved man.

But his eyes were on me. On my cock fucking into Maeve's mouth.

Fuck, I wanted him. I had never found myself so attracted to an alpha. I didn't think I could ever want someone as badly as I'd wanted Maeve. But I wanted Owen. I wanted to feel his mouth on me. I wanted to feel him buried inside of me. I wanted to feel his ass clenching around my dick.

It was so much more than that, though. As surly as the dude was, I saw the gentleness in his eyes any time he was with Maeve. I saw how fiercely he cared for the pack, how much he loved each of us.

Maeve's moans around my cock distracted me from my obsession with both my alpha and my omega and directed all my attention to trying to hold back from spilling down her throat.

I would recoup quickly. We all would. Part of the fun of helping an omega through their heat was the fact our bodies would be primed and ready to go within minutes. The need to breed was strong, the biology driving our every thought and action.

"I need to pull away," I said, running my fingers through her hair. "I'm—"

She reached over and wrapped a hand around my thigh, keeping me close, keeping my cock in her mouth.

"Come in our omega's mouth. Give her what she needs," Beckett said before pressing gentle, wet kisses between her breasts.

Turning my eyes to where Owen's mouth was on Maeve, I knew the moment he pushed her over the edge as she swallowed hard around the head of my cock and moaned a deep, guttural sound, the vibrations pulling a dizzying orgasm from me.

I threw my head back and grunted as my cock jerked, spilling jets into her mouth and down her throat as she continued to moan with her own release.

"Holy fuck," I breathed out, pulling from her mouth slowly when my balls were empty.

The head of my cock released with an audible pop as she kept the suction around me and I had an urge to shove my length right back into the velvety heat of her mouth, to feel her tongue running along the ridge on the underside of my dick.

Dropping back onto my haunches, I bit back a moan as Owen sat up, dragging the back of his hand across his mouth to clean Maeve's slick and release from his chin and lips. I would have much rather kissed him and cleaned the sweetness from his face with my lips and tongue.

"Alpha. Please," Maeve whined.

She'd just had a release and already her body was demanding more. This was one of the perks of having a bigger pack than one like ours. Our girl only had the two alphas to help her. I would do what I could, but her body would need their knots to dispel the worst of her symptoms.

"I'm here, baby girl. I'm going to fuck you, make you come all over my dick, then shove my knot in that tight little pussy of yours. Is that what you want?"

"Yes. Please."

Fuck me. Her pleas to have Owen fill her sent blood rushing to my dick and made me hard all over again.

"Fuck our omega. Give her what she needs," Beckett said, kneeling on the other side of her head and offering her his cock.

He grunted softly when she took his length into her mouth in one quick move instead of easing her lips around him.

"Holy shit, omega. You're going to make me go blind."

Owen stiffened and watched for any reaction from Maeve. When she either didn't notice Beck's use of her designation or didn't care, he went back to pumping into her, the muscles in his ass and back bunching and releasing.

Owen truly was a beautiful specimen of masculinity.

Fuck it.

Moving closer, I gripped his face in my hands and slanted my mouth over his as he thrust hard and fast into Maeve. His tongue instantly pushed past the seam of my lips to deepen the kiss. His warm, calloused hand wrapped around the shaft of my cock and I swore I was fucking lost. Lost to sensation. Lost to the moment.

Not lost. In love. Fuck, I was in love. I was in love with two people, with one of my alphas and my omega.

But I sure as hell wouldn't say it. Not now, anyway. Maybe when my pack wasn't ruled by their hindbrain, when their hormones weren't raging and my omega's emotions weren't riding a rollercoaster.

Owen's hand left me, his lips tore from mine, and he leaned over Maeve, pushing her knees until they were nearly touching her chest.

"You doing okay, baby girl?" he asked her, slowing his pace a moment as he stared into her eyes.

"Knot. Please, alpha. I need your knot."

Concern touched my heart. Not only did she repeatedly use their designation, but she was almost non-coherent as she babbled nonsense between moans and begged each of us to touch her, to fuck her, begged her alpha to knot her.

I knew this was the first heat she'd shared with Beck and Owen in over a year. A lot of that concern came from the fact she'd used suppressants for so long – her heat might be stronger, her needs stronger, the duration of her cycle longer.

As much as I would love nothing more than to stay locked in this room, bringing her pleasure for hours on end, after a few days, all four of us would become exhausted.

Shit. I needed to contact Sophie or the restaurant to let them know Maeve wouldn't be able to work her next few shifts.

When Maeve swallowed Beck's cock again while raising her hips as though chasing Owen's cock and knot, all rational thought left my brain.

Instead of slamming into her, Owen slowly pushed forward, his knot stretching her tight entrance, until he was fully seated inside of her.

She screamed around Beck, sending him into his own orgasm. His fingers tangled in her red curls as he threw his head back and grunted, his abs tightening as he spilled down her throat the way I had moments ago.

"Fuck. You're so tight, baby girl," Owen said through clenched teeth.

He continued to pump into her in shallow thrusts until he dropped on top of Maeve, holding his weight on his elbows, and barked out her name as he filled her with his seed.

I'd already gotten off once and already I was ready to go again. Maybe it was a good thing I hadn't been born alpha; there was a damn good chance I would be insatiable with someone like Maeve.

Beckett pulled himself from Maeve's mouth, bending to press a kiss to her forehead before dropping onto his back. Owen was still locked inside of her, so he rolled until she was straddled over him, her legs on either side of his hips, and ran his fingers gently up and down her spine. Her scars were on full display and all I saw was the marks of a fucking survivor.

Unfortunately, that put both of them on full display for me. Since it appeared we might have gotten her through the first wave and she might be able to get some rest, I grabbed one of the dozens of blankets folded against the wall and draped it over their bodies.

"I brought some bottles of waters. Either of you want one?"

Owen nodded. Beckett held up a hand.

With a chuckle, I grabbed one for them each, cracking the seal and twisting off the cap before handing the first one to Owen. Beckett could open his own; he didn't have our omega using him as a mattress.

"I'm going to go grab some munchies, something easy to eat between waves. Any requests?"

"Make sure to get her some fruit and some kind of carbs," Beckett said after taking a deep swig of his water.

Without bothering to pull on any clothes – what was the point when I'd have to get naked again the moment Maeve woke back up – I left the nest and headed through the house. At least outside of her quarters, the air was clearer, which meant my head was clearer. At least for now.

Rifling through the cabinets, I grabbed a few bags of chips and pretzels and tossed them onto the counter. Then I searched the fridge for fruit that I could cut up into small bites since there was no way in hell any of us would be able to get her to take the time to eat a real meal. We would end up having to force slices of strawberries or apples past her lips to keep her energy up.

Washing and cutting up a variety as quickly as I could without losing a tip of one of my fingers, I piled it all into a big bowl, tucked the bags under my arms, and carried everything back up to my waiting pack.

Maeve's perfume was like a fucking aphrodisiac as I climbed the stairs, the scent calling to my dick and making me want to drop everything and rush back to my omega, to bury my cock inside of her, to fill her the way Owen had.

I assumed – and hoped – that she was on some form of birth control since none of us had bothered to purchase any condoms. Since she'd used suppressants for so long, I could only assume she would have taken the same precautions against an unplanned pregnancy.

As I stepped through the door into the nest, my heart began to race behind my ribs. Maeve was once again awake and was sitting up, slowly riding Owen while Beckett pumped his cock into her mouth.

She should have had more downtime, more time for her body to rest between rounds when her body would crave her alphas.

A few bags of chips and some fruit might not be enough if she continued at this rate for days on end. Hell, the alphas would need a lot more, too. But I really didn't want to leave them long enough to cook a full meal.

"Anyone opposed to me calling in a grocery or food order?"

"No," Beckett said, but his head was lowered as he watched Maeve's head bob along his length.

Neither Beck nor I had been inside of her yet. But I sure as fuck wasn't complaining. I'd never come so hard with nothing but a blowjob. She'd practically sucked my soul through the head of my cock.

"No, you're not opposed?"

"Order the fucking food," Owen barked. Damn, even as a beta, that sound made every cell in my body want to obey. I wasn't sure I'd heard him use his bark on anyone in the short time I'd known him.

Instead of asking for requests, I once more hurried from the room in search of my phone. It was still in the pocket of my jeans that I'd left in the bathroom when I'd run a bath for Maeve, then joined her when she continuously rubbed herself against me, her hand cupping my junk and tugging at my belt.

Tugging my phone free, I pulled up a local grocery store that did home delivery and decided against it. Unless I wanted to cook, that wasn't an option. Even making a frozen pizza would take me out of the nest for longer than I would prefer.

Fast food delivery it was. Even if I had to put everything in the fridge and microwave it as needed, it would still take far less time.

Eighty-three dollars later, the order was put in with an arrival time of forty minutes. That would give me plenty of time to either coax some water into my omega or maybe even play with my pack a little before the doorbell rang.

Jogging back to the room, I groaned. Maeve was now on her hands and knees, Owen pumping into her mouth while Beckett took her from behind. It was like every time I left the room, I returned to another fantasy come to life.

"You're doing such a great job taking your alphas," Beckett praised her with a purr, gripping her hips in his gigantic hands.

Her movements were no longer frantic, her head bobbing slowly and sensually on Owen's length.

"So beautiful," Owen cooed, reaching down to thread his fingers through her hair.

"Food's coming," I said softly, moving further into the room so I could kneel beside my omega, beside my alphas. I would be here in case Maeve needed me. In case my alphas needed me to provide them with water or to give them a break with our sexy as sin omega.

No one responded to my statement. Beckett's thrusts grew faster, harder, until it was obvious he was struggling to hold back.

"Knot our omega," Owen said. "Give her what she needs."

The two would be locked together, as well, but he could roll them to their sides and spoon her while she rested. Or at least I hoped that she would actually rest longer than the few minutes like last time.

"I can't hold out much longer," Beckett ground out.

Owen pulled his cock from Maeve's mouth and lowered until he was eye level with her. "Do you want your alpha's knot, baby girl?"

"Please. I need it. Bite, Owen. I need your bite."

My eyes widened the same time as Owen's. She was too lost to her hindbrain. As much as I knew Owen would love to leave his mark on her, there was no way he would give in, especially if there was a chance she would regret it when her cycle ended.

But when Owen lowered his head, his hands gently pushing her hair away from the shoulder not scarred by Beckett's bite, I wondered if I was wrong.

"Fuck," Beck grunted, pushing forward until Maeve's pussy swallowed his knot. He thrust in shallow moves a few times before stilling, his hands making slow paths along her ass cheeks and up her back. "She'll be pissed later," he warned, but there was no energy to his words.

Owen's mouth opened and he left a wet kiss on her shoulder, pressing his teeth against her flesh only hard enough to leave indentions but not break the skin.

Maeve moaned and shuddered as her orgasm mixed with the sensation of her alpha's mouth on her shoulder.

When Owen finally pulled his mouth from her, she fell forward, nearly tugging Beckett on top of her.

"Shit," Beck said, catching himself on his hands.

"She's asleep," Owen said, moving the hair from her face as Beck rolled them onto their sides to a more comfortable position.

"Thank fuck," Beck said. "I can't believe I'm going to say this, but I'm already worn out."

"We need another alpha," I said, earning glares from both men. With a chuckle, I held up my hands and pushed to my feet.

It was time to get dressed. Tending to an omega in heat wasn't uncommon, but no delivery driver wanted to see some stranger's schlong flopping in the wind.

CHAPTER 26

<u>Maeve</u>

$\mathcal{E}$very inch of my body was sore, my stomach grumbled with hunger, and my mouth felt like I'd swallowed cotton.

Yet slick still dampened my thighs and arousal made me dizzy.

Turning my head, I found Owen on my left, Beck on my right, and Wilder had my feet resting on his stomach. All three were out cold.

The cramps were starting up again. I'd started to have longer periods of time where I could rest, sleep, and had even eaten some fruit that Owen had used his bark to force me to consume. Wilder was constantly holding a water bottle to my lips, urging me to drink.

My brain was totally on board with eating, drinking, and sleeping.

My body? It was like I was a woman possessed and couldn't control my own fucking actions.

Four days had passed. At least I thought it had been four days. Time was elusive, the minutes and hours rolling into each other in the dimly lit nest. The windows were covered, blocking out the offensive sunshine. The nest smelled heavily of my pack and sex – not exactly an unpleasant smell in my opinion. The signatures and hormones of my pack merely increased my need and made my body stay constantly primed.

Or was that simply my heat that made me want someone to be inside of me, touching me at all times?

I wasn't a snuggly omega. Never had been. I wasn't a woman who felt touch starved if one of my pack wasn't holding me in some fashion.

Now? I huffed a silent laugh. If my pack were to leave this room, if they were to even roll far enough that they were no longer skin to skin with me...I might just break down in tears.

I'd avoided going through my heat naturally for over a year. But I couldn't remember my past cycles feeling so erratic and unpredictable.

Scissoring my legs, I tried to find relief to the building pressure without waking any of my pack. They needed rest as much as I did. Of course I knew they would have zero problem if I were to simply climb on top of them and ride them while they laid back and enjoyed themselves, but all three looked exhausted. Even asleep, there were dark smears under their eyes.

The cramping grew more intense until I bit the inside of my cheek to keep from whimpering and waking everyone.

Fuck it.

Slowly, I slid a hand down my body until my fingers slid through my folds. Rubbing at my swollen clit, I squeezed my eyes shut and bit my bottom lip. An orgasm would ease the worst of the cramping, but it wouldn't chase this wave away. Only one thing could do that – a knot from my one of my alphas.

Abandoning my clit, I attempted to push a finger into my center, then added a second. The sound of my slick, my release, and my pack's cum made a sexy yet somewhat embarrassing squelching sound as I pumped into myself, trying to find the right rhythm.

The pain had subsided a tad but was far from gone. I needed more. I needed my pack. I needed my beta and my alphas.

Biting my lip until I worried I'd break the tender skin, I used my other hand to rub my clit while fingering myself. The first tingles of an orgasm began to build and I hoped it would be enough to get just a little more sleep. I felt as though I'd been dragged through the mud, run over by a truck, then trampled by a stamped of wildebeests.

I was so ready for this to be over. At this point, I wasn't sure whether I cared about the long-term effects of suppressants, as long as I didn't have to go through this again.

Although...there was a good chance this heat was so intense *because* I'd taken the suppressants for so long, because I'd ignored my body, because I'd forced my hormones to stay at bay.

Tears began to form in my eyes as the release rippled through me, but the pain didn't subside enough to feel remotely comfortable enough to even make my way to the shower or try for a few more minutes of sleep.

A whimper built in my throat, and I tried to swallow it back, but it escaped through my lips.

My alphas immediately sat up. Wilder's head jerked up and his narrowed eyes looked in my direction as he blinked a few times.

"Maeve?" he said, his voice scratchy with sleep.

"Help," I whined as I continued to pump my fingers into my core in search of relief.

Everyone immediately snapped into action as though they weren't out to the world just moments ago.

"We're here, sweetheart," Beck said as he rolled closer and pulled me over his body until my legs straddled his hips and the tip of his already hard cock teased my entrance.

His hand reached between us and notched himself against my hole, then gripped my hips and pulled me down until his knot nudged against me. The instant he filled me, the pain began to subside.

But it wasn't gone. I needed more. I just...I didn't know exactly what I needed other than my pack, their knots, release from the pain.

"More. Please," I begged. My legs barely held me up as I rode Beckett. He held my hips, supporting my weight, and thrust up into me from below.

"Baby girl, we can give you more, but I don't want to hurt you."

"Please." My voice sounded alien to my own damn ears.

A finger trailed between my ass cheeks then toyed with my back door. The sensation was unfamiliar being as I'd never even been tempted to have anyone back there.

But right now? I felt empty, even with Beck's long, thick cock filling me.

The finger slowly dipped inside of my ass and I moaned. For some reason, I had thought there would be pain. It was simply different... yet so good.

"Yes. More, please," I said, as that finger slid in further.

"You're so beautiful," Wilder said, kneeling beside me. He pushed my tangled hair from my face and claimed my mouth with nothing short of possession, his tongue dancing with mine as though savoring the taste.

There was more pressure added to my ass. Moments later, the blunt, flared head of Owen's cock was pressed against my tight hole and his lips touched my ear. "If it's too much, say so. We would never hurt you, baby girl. I love you. We love you."

I pulled from Wilder's lips. "I love you," I said as tears welled in my eyes. I was no longer completely lost to the hormones, my brain no longer fuzzy. But my body was still in control, still demanding so much from my pack.

As Owen pushed forward until he was fully seated in my ass, he pressed the softest kisses to my shoulder...the shoulder that was still missing my second alpha's mark.

"Fuck me," Beck said from below me.

"I thought I already was," I teased.

When he chuckled, his cock twitched inside of me, pulling a moan from Owen at my back.

"Are you okay?" Owen said, his breath warming the places where he'd kissed.

"Yes," I breathed out, wiggling my hips to urge one of them to move.

Beck's hands were on my thighs, Owen's on my hips. And then

they formed a rhythm, one pulling out while the other pumped inside so I was never left empty.

"Wilder," I said as tears rolled down my cheeks. I wasn't even fully sure why I was crying.

"I'm here, beautiful." He pressed a kiss to my cheek, kissing the tear away. "Tell me what you need."

"You. I need you. I need all of you. More. Please. I need more. I want you in my mouth."

His cock twitched at my words and a tiny drop of precum dripped from the tip. Licking my lips, I leaned down when he shuffled forward so I could reach him without him having to straddle Beckett's face.

Shit. Why did the thought of Wilder's balls so close to my alpha's mouth send a ripple of arousal and pleasure coursing through me? There was nothing sexual or romantic between the two, yet I wanted to find a way to connect the four of us in every way possible.

Wilder tasted as sweet as he smelled, especially when another bead of precum touched my tongue. I could drown in his oranges and sweet cream, live on nothing but him. Not true. I needed my alphas, their hands on me, their taste on my tongue.

His hands were gentle as they tangled in my hair, urging me further, faster as his hips pumped forward until the head of his cock hit the back of my throat and gagged me. Relaxing as much as possible, I let my omega take over and simply enjoyed everything my pack was giving me and took from them selfishly.

Who was I kidding? They might have been as worn out as I was, but they were getting as much pleasure from my body as I was from theirs.

"You're taking your pack so well, baby girl. You look so perfect with your alphas filling you and your beta's cock in your mouth."

Owen's words tipped me over the edge I'd been teetering on until I cried out around Wilder's thick length. His fingers tightened in my hair and he grunted as his hot cum hit the back of my throat. Swallowing as quickly as possible, I savored the taste coating my tongue, my throat, my mouth.

"Fuck," Beckett groaned. "I'm about to blow."

"Fill our omega. Give her what she needs," Owen demanded as he continued to take my ass in a cadence that was on the pleasurable side of pain.

Until today, I'd had no idea how good it could feel to have them both filling me at once, to feel both their cocks in my ass and pussy while my beta took my mouth.

Beckett slammed his hips up, his knot breaching my walls and locking behind my pubic bone, coming with my name on his lips, the sound nearly a curse.

The fullness and the cum coating my inner walls sent me spiraling into another release before the aftershocks of the first had fully died down.

"Fuck, baby girl. You're milking my cock with your tight little ass."

He lasted only a few seconds later, his dick jerking as he shot his load in my ass, but never pushed his knot into me. I wasn't sure how that would feel…but yeah, I was definitely curious as to whether that would send me spiraling again.

The second Owen pulled from me, I collapsed onto Beckett's chest, my breathing as rapid as his, our heartbeats racing as though trying to match the other.

"It's over," I muttered against his hard pec, the sprinkling of course hair there tickling my lips.

"What?" Beck asked, pushing my hair that I was sure resembled a horror villain's away from my face.

"I think my heat is over." For the first time since I'd left work, there wasn't a single touch of pain. My skin no longer felt as though it was on fire while being entirely too tight.

I simply felt sated. Exhausted. Starving and thirsty.

"That was intense," Wilder said as he flopped onto his back, his arm draped over his eyes. "Is it always that intense?"

"I don't know. I don't think so," I said, pressing a soft kiss to Beck's chest just because I wanted to.

I had an urge to bite down on the thick muscle, to sink my teeth into his warm scented flesh.

"As soon as my knot deflates, I vote a pack soak in the tub and a shit load of Chinese food," Beck's voice rumbled through his chest, pulling a sigh from me.

Only weeks ago, I had finally realized I was safe enough to show my alphas and my beta how I felt. But I never for a second thought I would feel so…well, girly. A giggle built in my chest until Beck raised his head from the cushioned floor to look at me with a smirk and a raised brow.

"Feel like letting us in on the joke?"

"I feel good. Like…I mean, the sex was amazing. The heat sucked – the pain, I mean. But…I don't have the urge to stab anyone."

"Well…that's good. Last thing I need is you stabbing someone while my cock is locked inside your perfect cunt."

Lifting up a little, I slapped his chest but couldn't erase the grin. I was on an endorphin high, and I was pretty sure there wasn't a damn thing that could ruin it.

"A bath and Chinese food sounds awesome," I said, dropping my head back to his chest and giving his nipple a playful nibble.

"Keep that up and we might have to put off our plans for later," Beck teased, swatting my ass.

"I'll order the food and run a bath. Bubbles?" Wilder asked.

"Bubbles. Oil. Salts. The works."

As much as I was ready to get back to normal life, to get back to my job, I wanted to relish these moments with my pack, my newfound sense of peace, for as long as possible.

Except something was missing.

Sitting up and earning a groan from Beck, I looked at Owen over my shoulder. "I need something from you."

"Anything, baby girl. You know I would do anything for you."

"I need your mark. I need your bite."

He tilted his head and frowned. "Is this you or your hormones?"

"It's me. It's time. I'm sorry…I should have let you mark me a long time ago. I'm yours, Owen, as much as you're mine. I want the world to know I belong to all three of you."

The sweetest smile lit up his normally broody face before he leaned forward and latched onto my shoulder, the sting stirring a new wave of arousal and causing slick to coat Beckett's cock, his knot, even his waist.

This cycle had sucked...but this moment was pure perfection.

CHAPTER 27

<u>Maeve</u>

"Would you mind taking these out to table six?" Becca asked as she balanced a tray of drinks in one hand, a tray of plates in the other.

With a chuckle, I reached forward. "Which one?"

"Uh…the drinks. I'm about to lose my balance."

With both hands, I grabbed the swaying tray from her and carried them to the table. I hadn't quite gotten the hang of balancing a full tray on one hand the way the waitresses did, but it wasn't often I needed to. I tended to clear the tables more often than delivering anything to the diners.

The dining room was full for the lunch rush and the staff was buzzing around like crazy. I took pride in the fact I had the tables cleared the moment the former diners made it to the front door. I wanted to make sure I was useful, that my manager saw me as an asset in hopes that she might one day train me to wait tables. The tips would be amazing.

I'd been back to work for a month and had opened my own banking account with the fake ID Sophie had made for me under the name Maeve Bratton. That had pleased my beta, but I knew the alphas were jealous. I'd figured it was a good compromise so there was no bickering between Owen and Beck as to who was officially the pack lead. There was no pack lead – we were all equal in our house, including Wilder and me.

I was still trying to talk the alphas into letting me learn to drive and get my own car. But for now, I agreed to allow Wilder to not only drive me in every shift, but to sit at a table near the back of the room so he could act as my personal guard.

Honestly, I thought his presence was no longer needed. Since my heat, I hadn't felt an ounce of that old rage, that old sense of the need for vengeance.

In fact, I felt good. Happy.

And even contemplated bringing up one day adding to our pack whether through another alpha or beta...or even carrying a child by one of my guys. I didn't care who impregnated me; I knew that child would be loved by the entire pack.

I carried the marks of both my alphas, we had all been sleeping together in my bed every night, and I had even graciously accepted a gift from Beck two nights ago. Not that I would ever demand gifts or pampering, but the thick, fuzzy socks were more than welcome with the nights growing cooler.

Life was amazing. Why the hell had I hung on to the anger and hate for so long when I could have been this happy the whole time?

Perhaps it had taken Wilder to open my eyes to what was right in front of me, to show me the loving alphas who'd put their own happiness on the back burner simply to make sure I was okay. After all, they'd not only saved my life, but had helped me cover a murder instead of turning me over to the authorities.

Time and time again, they'd made sure I wasn't arrested, made sure I was safe, had suffered from the lack of any intimacy because they didn't want to pressure me.

I loved them. I loved all three of them. So much.

Glancing at Wilder as I passed after delivering the drinks, I winked at him and gave him what I hoped as a flirtatious smile that held a promise of what I planned for when we got home.

That was another new development – I had become absolutely obsessed with being with my pack, with feeling their hands on me. And not only in a sexual manner – I'd found I loved being held by them, to feel their fingers lightly raking through my hair or the soft caresses along my arms, shoulders, or back every time they were close.

His crooked smile sent butterflies flapping in my belly.

There were three tables that needed to be cleared for the families waiting to be seated. Grabbing my bucket, I loaded the dishes and began cleaning the surface, checking under the table for any trash and pocketing any cash tips to hand over to the waitress. Becca was one of my favorites and not just because she always gave me a large chunk of cash at the end of my shifts. The beta was so sweet and really funny. She was also absolutely gorgeous, and I'd caught Wilder watching her more than once.

The first time had made me a little jealous. Now? Adding to our pack was a good thing. And I had zero opposition to another woman joining us if she made any of my guys happy, just like my alphas excepted Wilder simply because he made me happy.

As I rounded the corner, setting the heavy tub on an empty table to clear and sanitize it, a familiar voice touched my ears. It took me a moment to place it until I turned my head and spotted two men sitting at a booth.

"Maeve?"

Holy shit. No way. Of all the places in the world, Clay and his friend, Leon, sat staring up at me. The look on Clay's face was nothing short of murderous.

How was this possible? I'd stabbed him. I'd watched him die. My alphas had disposed of his body, cleaned up the scene, and made sure there was no evidence of my time in that house.

My mouth opened and closed as words failed to form and my throat felt as though it was closing.

"This is Callum, Clay's brother," Leon said, an unsure smile on his face.

"*Twin* brother," Callum said, a sneer pulling his lips back to reveal straight, white teeth.

Just like his brother, he was devastatingly handsome yet held a darkness in his eyes that hinted at future pain.

"How…what are you doing here?" Leon asked.

He slowly scooted from his seat and stood in front of him, forcing me to crane my neck to look into his face.

My heart began to pound in my chest as my focus bounced from Leon to Callum and back. Was Leon a threat? He'd been there when Clay had tortured me, even if he'd left instead of participating. He hadn't helped me. He hadn't stopped his friend.

And Callum looked at me as though he would love to snap my neck with his bare hands.

Threat. They were both a threat.

Wilder was here. He wouldn't let them hurt me. And the place was crowded. Surely, neither of them would be stupid enough to try anything with so many witnesses.

"That's not my brother's mark," Callum said from where he sat glaring at me.

Reaching up with shaky hands, I adjusted my shirt to cover the scar left by Owen a month ago.

"How are you carrying another's mark when my brother was your alpha?" Callum even sounded like Clay and so many memories, fears, and rage came rushing back, pushing away all the warm fuzzies I'd discovered with my pack.

My hand covered the mark as I started to back away. I wanted to look for Wilder, to signal him, but I was terrified to tear my eyes from the enemy in front of me.

Leon reached for me. I backed up until my ass hit the table behind me, the dishes rattling with the impact.

"Where's my brother, omega?" Callum asked, climbing to his feet until they were both looming over me.

Where Callum looked deadly, Leon looked confused. But that

didn't make him any less of a threat. Clay had once looked at me as though I was the most precious thing in his life...until he got me home and away from any onlookers.

"Dead," I gritted out, refusing to allow this man to intimidate me. I had to remember everything I'd learned from my alphas, remember there was no way I would allow this alpha or anyone to hurt me or drag me from this place, drag me away from my pack.

"Did you kill him?" Leon asked. They were both keeping their voices low, but it sounded as though they were screaming with the way my senses were hypersensitive as adrenaline began to burn through my veins.

People were starting to notice our little meeting, heads turning in our direction as they whispered to each other. That didn't seem to matter to Leon as he reached for me.

My instincts kicked in without a single thought. Reaching behind me, my fingers closed around metal. I didn't even care what it was – I'd been taught to use anything and everything as a weapon.

The moment Leon's hands closed around my upper arm, I thrust my hand forward, burying a steak knife in his side.

Blood coated my hand and spread along his shirt. A woman screamed. Dishes hit the floor and shattered as people began to panic.

And all I could focus on was the fact that Callum was now reaching for me, his lips peeled back from his teeth and pure hatred bright in his eyes.

This was it. This was when I either killed two men in front of so many witnesses and ended up in permanent custody, or I would be taken from the men I loved more than anything in the world.

Either way, I would lose my pack.

Or rather, they would lose me. And I couldn't see a way out of the situation without a worst case ending.

CHAPTER 28

<u>Wilder</u>

 ecca passed my table again, pouring more coffee into my mug with a wink. She was hot. Where Maeve was beautiful, stunning, and had the appearance of being a sweet girl next door while hiding a bad ass inside, Becca wore dark eye makeup, had piercings along the shells of both ears, even one in her nose.

Yet, she was sweet and cheery. They each looked the opposite of their personalities.

The beta also smelled like absolute heaven, a mixture of nutmeg and ginger, reminding me so much of pumpkin pie or other fall treats.

Where Maeve had long, flaming red curls and a petite, curvy body, Becca's hair was dyed a dark purple and was cut to her chin. She was around five feet six or seven inches tall and thin, though her ass was round and her tits were full.

I had no right to be fantasizing about the beta when I was already head over heels in love with my omega and one of my alphas. Not that Owen and I had done anything more than make out a little. No feelings had been discussed; no declarations of love had been made. I was terrified to tell him how I felt for fear his feelings didn't extend beyond sexual attraction.

But...Maeve had teased about adding to the pack. It couldn't hurt to have two betas in the mix, although an alpha would be better when Maeve had her next cycle. It had taken the three of us days to recover from servicing her, of bringing her to climax over and over for almost five fucking days.

As I watched the seductive sway of Becca's hips, a scream tore through the air.

I was on my feet, my neck swiveling as I sought my omega. Whether that sound came for her or not, I needed to know where she was in case this was a true emergency.

Fuck. It wasn't a scream from Maeve, but she was definitely in the middle of the chaos. A man stood over her, his face a mask of rage, while another was doubled over, his back to me.

Shoving through the fleeing crowd, I rushed forward and knocked the first man away, putting my body between the men and Maeve. It took a moment to realize the man was doubled over because there was a handle of a knife protruding from his side, blood staining his button up shirt and the splotch growing rapidly.

My hand reached behind me, trying to find Maeve. But she darted away and lunged at the injured guy, another knife in her hand. "Maeve! Fuck! Stop!"

Her hand and arm were slicked with crimson. She'd stabbed him? Why? What the fuck had happened in the few minutes since she'd left my sight to clear another table?

Wrapping my arm around her waist, I lifted her from the ground and turned so my back was to the bleeding man. "What the fuck is going on?"

"Clay!" she screamed, the sound far too close to a feral cry.

"Clay's dead, Maeve. That's not Clay."

"She fucking killed him," a man growled from behind me.

Releasing my hold on her, I kept her at my back and whirled to look at the man I'd plowed into who was now on his feet. From what I could tell, there were no injuries on him. But that might have only been because I'd intervened before she could thrust the second knife into his chest.

"That bitch killed my fucking brother."

Holy shit. Was this asshole Clay Soren's brother? Why would she think he was Clay? Or had I misunderstood what she was trying to tell me through her rattled mind?

I had to get her out of here. The police would definitely have been called. They would arrest her immediately for attacking a patron. Not just attacking him – she'd fucking stabbed him with a steak knife from her bus tub full of dirty dishes.

Sirens were in the distance. Minutes. I had minutes to get Maeve out of here without this fucker glaring at us stopping us or hurting her. No fucking way would I let him anywhere near my omega. From the look on his face, I had zero doubt he was as sick and twisted as his fucked up brother. He would do far worse to Maeve if given the chance.

"She has an alpha. *Had.* The bitch killed my brother. I have every right to turn her over or claim her as my own."

"Fuck you," Maeve growled, the knife still clutched in her bloody hand.

"She has a pack. The police are on their way. We'll all be arrested. I suggest you leave now before I alert the police that I intercepted two alphas assaulting a claimed and bonded omega. As a former member of Omega Rescue and Extraction, I'm pretty sure they'll believe my word over yours, asshole."

The fucker glared at me before turning that look on Maeve. "Your choice, bitch. Either join my pack willingly, or we'll kill yours and take you anyway. And I promise you, life won't be easy if I have to come looking for you."

He snagged the bleeding man by the arm and dragged him outside, partially holding his weight when the guy Maeve stabbed staggered.

"We need to go. Now." Seconds. The cops would be here in seconds. If we were lucky. We needed to do our best to blend in with the panicking crowd and pray no one fingered her as the assailant.

Once I had her buckled in my truck and was on the way, I lifted my phone and hit Owen's number. It took three rings before he answered.

"Had a problem at the restaurant. Head home. Now!"

I ended the call without anymore explanation. For now, I had to focus on reeling my omega back in. She had a faraway look in her eyes as though she wasn't mentally sitting beside me. The knife was still clutched in her hand, her exposed skin coated in drying blood.

She needed to shower and change clothes. She needed her pack. She needed her alphas.

And we all needed answers as to what the fuck had just happened, how that fucker had found her, and why she'd stabbed the first guy.

Had he attacked her? Tried to drag her away? And how was he related to the first alpha who'd nearly broken her mind and spirit?

"Maeve?"

When she didn't answer, I glanced at her. She stared straight ahead, her eyes wide, her chest rising and falling too rapidly.

"Maeve, you're safe. You're okay. We're going home. Your alphas are going to be there. Everything is okay."

Still, she said nothing. The way she sat statue still, her blinks and breaths the only evidence she was alive…

It terrified me.

Her already pale skin was ashen, her freckles stark against her pallor. Her lips were parted, but she said nothing, but she did twitch when I reached across the cab to lay a hand on her thigh, squeezing lightly in hopes my touch would ground her and snap her out of whatever trance she'd fallen into.

At least we weren't too far from the house. I had no idea where the alphas were working or whether they would be able to drop and run, but I sure as fuck hoped they would be home soon. I would do everything I could for my omega, but an alpha's purr was something I couldn't do for her.

Shit. That might not even be enough. Her skin was clammy as I took her hand and attempted to pry the knife from her clenched fist, but she jerked away from me and released a sound far too close to a growl.

Feral. She was far too close to going feral. We had to drag her back, remind her of the peace she'd found, remind her she had a safe and happy life with a pack who loved her more than anything in the world, that we would do everything to protect her...even if it meant sacrificing our own lives.

After what felt like a fucking eternity, I pulled onto the driveway and hit the remote to send the garage door rumbling open. I'd made sure the entire drive we weren't followed after that asshole's threat.

She'd killed his brother. That's what he had said. Meaning that fucker was Clay's brother. He demanded she join his pack as retribution for killing Clay.

Over my dead fucking body. I knew our alphas would feel the exact same way. And since I happened to have a butt load of contacts with various omega protection agencies, I would call in every favor I had to make sure no one could get anywhere near her.

Once the truck was parked, the garage door was closed, and I'd rounded the hood to open the passenger door, Maeve still hadn't moved, still hadn't spoken a word.

As slowly as I could and ensuring my hands were in her view at all times, I reached over her to release her seatbelt, then slipped my arms under her knees and behind her back so I could cradle her close to my chest and carry her inside.

She might not have been willing to release the death grip on that damn knife, but I had to at least get the blood cleaned off her skin. I had to get the evidence of the attack off her flesh, regardless of the fact there were sure to be numerous witnesses to what she'd done in the middle of the restaurant.

Fuck. That would more than likely end in her termination. Sophie might not be willing to help her find another job since she'd stabbed someone on her shift. This whole situation was beyond fucked up at this point.

With Maeve cradled in my arms, it was difficult to unlock and push the door open, but I managed it after a few tries. I didn't bother removing my shoes before hurrying through the house, up the stairs, and straight to her ensuite bathroom. Just a month ago, we'd all enjoyed a hot bubble bath after being locked in the nest for days, our muscles soaking up the oils and salts as they healed.

"I'm going to set you down, beautiful. Can you stand?"

She didn't say anything, didn't react at all, and I wondered if I should just hold her and wait for the alphas.

Fuck it.

Carrying her into the glass enclosure of the shower, I started the spray while we were both fully clothed. At least some of the blood would rinse away and maybe the water would help her snap out of this.

The tile was cool against my back as I slid down the side and sat, letting the water soak us both.

A tremble worked through Maeve's body and then she began shaking as though she was cold. Yet the water was warm enough.

Shock. My omega was going into shock.

"Wilder?!" Owen's voice boomed through the house as steps thundered against the floor.

"Up here!" I called back.

The alphas charged into the bathroom seconds later, halting a moment as their wide eyes took in the scene.

"What the fuck happened?" Beck asked, tugging his shirt over his head before shoving his cargo pants down his legs.

Owen stripped as well, tossing his clothing in a pile on the floor.

"I'm not sure. I was…fuck. I was distracted." No reason to tell them by what at the moment. "I heard a woman scream. Found her standing in front of two men with a knife in her hand. She'd stabbed one of them. Left the steak knife in his side. The other fucker said he was Clay's brother. Said he would come for her. That she was Clay's omega which gave him the right to claim her since she'd killed his brother."

Maeve's trembling grew stronger.

"Turn the hot water up a little." I didn't think it was cold, but I was running on adrenaline.

Beck cranked the hot water spigot as he stepped in with us. He pulled Maeve from my arms and settled her on his lap, giving me the chance to remove my wet clothes. We would have a mess to clean up later. But that was later. I didn't give a fuck about anything but Maeve right now.

"I need to call Kai. Or...fuck. Someone with ORE. We need to cover this before it hits the light of day," I said, kicking my clothes away from the entrance of the shower.

"Any cops show up?" Owen asked as he knelt in front of Maeve and attempted to pry the knife from her hand.

He had about as much luck as I had in the truck.

"I heard the sirens, but I got her out of there before they showed up. And the men left, too, with their parting threat. Said if she didn't come willingly, they'd just kill us and take her anyway."

"Fucking assholes," Owen grumbled. "Maeve, let go of the knife, baby girl." Her eyes didn't so much as turn in his direction. With a deep sigh, Owen leaned closer and used his bark. "Release the knife now."

She stiffened, but her fingers finally opened enough for him to confiscate her makeshift weapon and pass it to me.

"Should we dispose of it?" he asked.

"Let me make some phone calls to people I trust first."

Carrying the knife through the house, I fought an onslaught of emotions as my heart felt as though it was shattering and rage burned like lava in my veins.

No one would touch my fucking pack. No one would come near my omega. I would shoot down anyone who tried, even if it meant *I* would be the one who ended up in prison.

CHAPTER 29

<u>Beckett</u>

Owen had successfully removed the knife from her hand and the two of us were able to remove her clothes and get her washed up. There wasn't a single drop of blood anywhere on her body. We'd even made sure there wasn't any evidence under her short nails.

But she still wasn't talking. She wouldn't even make eye contact with us when we talked to her.

Our girl was in shock. She was reliving the hell she'd been through before we'd found her and all it had taken was running across Clay's brother. Of all the places in town, in the fucking state, how had he ended up at Maeve's restaurant? And who was the second guy with him, the one who'd been stabbed?

We couldn't get a single answer until Maeve was ready.

Wilder's voice rumbled through the walls as Owen and I dried and dressed Maeve in something I hoped would be cozy and comforting, including the fuzzy socks I'd bought her as my own version of a heat gift. I knew she didn't care about that kind of shit, but *I* did, and it made me feel squishy when I saw them on her feet.

Owen carried her to the nest that had been cleaned after our time in there and laid her on the cushioned floor. He rolled her to her side and spooned himself behind her, a rumbling purr immediately vibrating from his chest as he draped an arm over her waist.

Neither Owen nor I had bothered to get dressed after we'd helped her, but this wasn't about sex. I was pretty sure there wasn't a damn thing on the planet that could make my dick hard when my omega was suffering so badly.

Stretching out on her other side, I scooted as close as I could until her face was tucked under my chin and rested my hand on her hip, purring for her so she could feel us from both sides.

I had no idea how long it would take to bring her back. I had no idea if we *could* bring her back this time. She hadn't been physically hurt, but her mind had splintered during the events of the day. I'd seen with my own eyes how difficult mental and emotional wounds could be to heal.

Sometimes, they never did.

About an hour later, Wilder quietly stepped into the room, crouching down and balancing on the balls of his feet. He'd pulled on a pair of sweats and a t-shirt.

He tilted his head and looked down at Maeve. "How long has she been asleep?" he whispered.

"Not sure. He asleep?" I asked about Owen.

"No," Owen answered.

We'd both purred nonstop for her since the moment we'd laid down. Now that she was asleep, we could probably stop, but I feared the moment we ceased, she would wake again. She needed to rest. And hopefully when she woke up, she would be able to fill us in on what the fuck had transpired from the time she'd clocked in, to the moment she'd stabbed that guy.

She'd told us there had been two alphas when her family had gifted her to Clay. Had he been the other? She'd also told us the second man had never hurt her, that he'd eventually left. Or at least she believed he had since she'd never seen him or heard his voice overhead after a few weeks of her imprisonment.

"Kai and Sophie are on their way. Joy and her pack, too. The girls want to be with Maeve and the alphas want to talk strategy. We're not going to leave her alone for a moment until we figure out what the fuck happened, who the fuck the second guy was, and how much of a threat Clay's brother really is to our omega."

And to us. But Wilder seemed about as concerned with their threats of harm against us as I was…not at all.

As gently and carefully as I could so as not to wake my girl, I rolled away and pushed to my feet. I would need to cover my junk if we were getting company.

"We got to get dressed. Stay here and I'll switch with you until it's time to wake her," I whispered to Owen.

"Shouldn't we give her time to prepare for a house full of people?" Wilder asked.

Looking down at the beautiful woman who'd gone through far more than any one woman should have to, I considered his question. She'd probably be pissed if we waited until six people piled into the house. She'd be groggy and crabby.

"Yeah. You're right. But you should probably do it. She's less likely to attack you."

"Since I'm a beta," Wilder said, saying the part I left out.

"Bingo," I said, jerking my head for Owen to pull away from Maeve so he could pull on some pants. Wilder didn't tell us how much time we had, and I'd rather not greet two omegas and some alphas with my dick and balls cupped in my hands.

We each had our own bedrooms, but over the past month or so, all four of us had slept in Maeve's bed together since it was more than big enough for all of us. Plus, it was easier to snuggle and fool around without having to wander from one room to the next.

I was tempted to tug on some sweats, but the moment anything woke up my dick, everyone in the room would spot the outline of my boner. So jeans it was along with a sweatshirt I'd had since college. The damn thing was threadbare but soft as fuck and my favorite.

Owen stepped into the hallway the same time as me, but he'd slipped his feet into some boots while I'd kept my feet bare. I had no intention of leaving this house anytime in the near future. Therefore, there was no point in cramping my big feet into shoes.

Wilder met us in the hallway, anger and fear in his gray eyes.

"She's awake but she's refusing to leave her nest. I even told her we were getting company. Although that might be why she doesn't want to come out."

"Did you tell her it was just Sophie and Joy?" Owen asked.

Wilder nodded. "Yeah. At least I got her to actually speak. That scared the shit out of me. I'd never seen her so..."

She'd been worse when we'd found her. She'd refused to leave the nest, would attack us if we attempted to come anywhere near her. It had taken weeks before she'd said a single word to either me or Owen. Another few weeks before she trusted us enough to lounge in the living room instead of holing up in her quarters.

She'd also grown so much stronger in the almost two years since we'd become pack. She'd learned to release her rage through other means, even if those means were often illegal or scary.

We all stood in the middle of the hall as though unsure of what to do next. I knew we all felt the same need to rush to the nest, to check on her, to see what we could do to get her through this.

But we also knew that was the exact opposite of what she needed. Maeve was a force all her own. She would work through this, then bounce back like a wrecking ball. My biggest concern was whether she would return to her old ways and start seeking alphas to attack. As magnificent as she was in full vigilante mode, she was also so small and fragile, and I didn't want to risk her getting caught and locked up.

The motion sensor alerted us to an arrival. Wilder headed down first to welcome his friends into the house, Owen and me on his tail.

Sophie and her assistant Joy looked subdued yet determined. The men at their backs looked downright pissed.

"Where is she?" Sophie asked.

"She's going to think you're mad at her," I warned as I guided the two omegas upstairs.

"Why the hell would I be mad?"

"Because you got her that job and she stabbed someone."

"Uh, not mad at all. I just wish she'd stabbed the asshole who'd threatened her, too."

I huffed out a surprised laugh then opened the bedroom door and pointed to the nest entrance. I would leave the women to it. They might have a much better chance of calming her down since neither of them were a threat to her as members of her own designation.

Or...she could become possessive over two omegas entering her nest while she was in such a volatile state of mind.

When they opened the door and stepped inside with zero protests or anything flying through the air, I pulled the bedroom door closed and headed downstairs to speak with the group of alphas and our beta about how the fuck we were going to cover up what happened and keep our omega safe from that douche bag.

"The manager wants to speak with her alphas. She sounded more concerned about Maeve than what happened," Kai said as I entered the living room.

"Have any charges been filed against her?" Owen asked.

"Not that I've seen," Kai said, turning to the other alphas.

"Nope. Nothing has come across the wire that I've seen," one of Joy's alphas, Beau, answered.

Beau and Kai worked with Wilder. Grant was a lawyer and could come in handy if anything did arise, though I would hate to take advantage of someone I barely knew. I wasn't sure what the fourth alpha did, only that he looked as though he wanted to kill someone with his bare hands. Where the lawyer was dressed in slacks and a button-down shirt, Justus was dressed in black jeans that looked as though he'd worn them for a decade, and a black t-shirt covered with a black leather jacket. The parts of his neck and hands that were visible were covered in tattoos, and piercings decorated both ears and there was a hoop through one of his nostrils. The two couldn't be more opposite.

The pack's beta was quiet and I couldn't get a read on him as his attention bounced from one person to the other while we all spoke.

"Do we know anything about the man she stabbed?" Kai asked.

"The only thing I could figure out was the other asshole was the brother of the alpha who held her prisoner and tortured her," Wilder said and was met with a chorus of growls.

These were all good men, good alphas. And betas, of course. Unfortunately, there was a large population of our designation who thought they still lived in medieval times and felt as though omegas were nothing more than property.

"We need to know if she knew the other guy and why the hell she stabbed him. You didn't see what happened?" Kai asked Wilder.

The beta's cheeks blushed pink and he averted his eyes a moment. "I was distracted."

Everyone's eyes were on him, and my brows drew together. "What the fuck could you be distracted by in a restaurant?"

"Becca," Maeve's voice said as she rounded the corner and entered the room with Joy and Sophie flanking her on either side as though her personal security. "He was distracted by my coworker, Becca. She's a gorgeous beta. They're crushing on each other, and she could be a good addition to the pack."

My frown didn't smooth as I watched her shuffle through the room and claim a couch with the omegas settling on either side of her like living shields. She didn't sit beside any of us, didn't cuddle into the side of any member of her pack.

And for some reason, her bringing up adding this Becca woman felt off, as though she was acting as though she'd found her replacement.

"Are you okay to talk about what happened?" Kai asked. "We don't want you to feel pressured, but I need to know what kind of situation we might be up against."

"He was one of my first alphas. He left after a few weeks. That was the first time I'd seen him since. The other, Callum, was Clay's twin brother. In his head, I belong to his pack since I killed his brother, my alpha."

"He wasn't your fucking alpha. Not only did you not carry his mark, but he was a fucking sadist. An abusive piece of shit," Owen growled out. A muscle twitched in his jaw as he clenched his teeth, the fury bright in his eyes.

"That's not how he sees it."

"He threatened us if she doesn't go to him willingly," Wilder said to the room, and was met with yet another chorus of growls.

"Do you think this fucker is a credible threat? Do you need security?" Kai asked.

Maeve's nostrils flared as she curled her feet under her and crossed her arms over her chest. It was both a sign of defiance and a defense mechanism, as though she was guarding herself from the conversation or possibly the thought of being taken and abused again.

"He's a threat," Maeve said, her eyes unfocused as she stared at the wall across the room.

I hated the distance between us. I hated that she was retreating from us again. I hated that she'd had to face a monster from her past. Even if the fucker hadn't been the one to hurt her, it sounded like he was no different than his brother.

"What's the other guy's name?" Kai asked. He'd brought a notebook and was jotting down notes.

None of the men here currently worked for ORE any longer, but the three Omega Change guards still had contacts with their former employer as well as local law enforcement.

"Leon Jacobson. Don't know his birth date or anything like that, so don't bother asking. All I know is he was there when my parents delivered me to their house. He brought me food a few times, I heard them arguing a lot when I was locked in the basement. Then, after two or three weeks..." She frowned and blinked a few times. "I guess it was two or three weeks, I'm not sure because the basement windows were blacked out. Anyway, he disappeared. He never came back downstairs, and I never heard his voice again."

My heart thundered in my chest at the memory of how we'd found her, how emaciated and filthy she was. There'd been a bucket for her to use as a toilet, a blanket on the floor where she slept. That was it. She'd been treated worse than a stray dog.

"He's the one you stabbed?" Owen asked.

Maeve's head jerked up and down in a rapid nod. "I...I don't know why. They stood up. He reached for me and I freaked out. So I stabbed him. I was going to stab Callum, too, but Wilder stopped me."

I sucked my lips into my mouth to hide the smile when she shot the beta a glare as though he'd done something wrong by keeping her from committing murder in the middle of the restaurant.

"Tell me exactly what the brother said," Kai said, his pen poised over the paper.

"Why don't we take a break," Sophie said. And it wasn't a question as much as a strong suggestion. "Has everyone already had dinner? I could order some pizzas or something. Maybe have a few beers and chill out."

She raised a brow at Kai. He sighed and set the pen and notebook on the coffee table in front of him.

"Will you eat?" Sophie asked Maeve.

It took a second before my omega turned to look at her and nodded. "Yeah. I am kind of hungry."

She was still behaving much the way she had before Wilder had come along, but I was just happy she was no longer catatonic or demanding everyone stay away from her. The fact that she rebounded so quickly was a testament to how much she'd healed through our time together.

"Perfect. How about you boys go play somewhere else. I'll order a bunch of pizzas. Do you already have beer or soda or anything?" Sophie asked, pulling her phone free and tapping on the screen.

"Yes, and yes," I answered.

"Shoo. Go do something else," Sophie said, waving a hand before returning her attention to the app on her phone.

Kai smiled and pushed to his feet. "You got a man cave or anything?"

"Did we just get kicked out of our own living room?" Owen grumbled as he led the men through the kitchen where we all stopped for beer before stepping out onto the back patio.

The tiny omega could kick us out of our own space all she wanted as long as she kept helping Maeve.

CHAPTER 30

<u>Maeve</u>

My body felt like there were bees buzzing under my skin and adrenaline continued to burn its way through my veins. But at least I'd snapped out of the living nightmare I'd been stuck in after coming face to face with my torturer's fucking twin.

For a moment, when my eyes had settled on Callum, I'd feared the last year and a half had been nothing more than a dream, that Clay still had me chained in the basement, that I was still being starved and beaten on a daily basis.

It didn't help that Leon had been there. Just the sound of his voice had awakened my fight or flight. Obviously, I went with fight. I couldn't foresee a day when I would ever again allow a man to mistreat me, never again would I become a victim. Not without a fucking fight.

"Do you want to talk about it anymore while the guys are out of ear shot?" Sophie asked.

"I don't want to even think about it," I said, hugging myself tighter.

"Mind if I help myself to your fridge?" Joy asked.

"Of course not. Will you grab me a beer?"

"Me, too," Sophie said as the blonde omega crossed the room.

It had been a long time since I'd simply hung out with other women. Actually, other than at work, I couldn't remember ever just relaxing and chatting with someone of the same sex, and especially not fellow omegas. For once, I was with others who understood the challenges of my designation.

I had no idea whether Joy knew anything about abuse, and I sure as hell had no intention of asking. Being as I had no desire to discuss my past – or even today's events – I wouldn't expect her to spill all her deepest, darkest secrets.

Joy handed out the bottles and took a seat on my other side. As much as I generally would detest such nearness when I was in this kind of mood, something about them crowding me was kind of comforting. Like they were lending me their strength.

I knew I should talk to my pack, let them hold me, let them do whatever their alphas demanded with their omega in distress, but for now, I needed the connection with the two omegas.

"I'm sorry," I said after we'd popped the caps from our beers and settled against the couch.

Both Joy and Sophie turned to look at me.

"For what?" Sophie asked.

I turned to look into her face and found nothing but confusion. No judgement. No anger.

"You got me that job and I fucked it up."

"You defended yourself against someone who once abused you," Joy said from my other side.

"Technically, Leon never laid a finger on me. And being as the only thing he did was reach for my arm, I don't think the police will see it as self-defense. They'll call it attempted murder. Or at least aggravated assault."

"First of all, I'm sure others besides Wilder heard the threats the brother was throwing your way," Sophie said, holding up a finger.

"Second," she said as she lifted another finger, "I highly doubt either of them will report what happened being as the Leon fucker didn't do a damn thing to keep Clay from beating the crap out of you. There's a reason we have not guilty by reason of insanity. Starving and all forms of abuse would make anyone insane. You did nothing wrong and I'm not mad. There's nothing to apologize for."

Sophie's light brows were pulled together as she spoke. She was absolutely angry, but not at me. She was angry *for* me.

She narrowed her eyes at me. "Beckett warned me you would think I was mad. I spoke to the manager; she said you still have a job there and a beta woman said she witnessed a majority of it and was willing to speak up for you."

"That had to be Becca. She has the hots for Wilder." And my beta was obviously attracted to her, as well.

"You don't sound jealous," Joy said with a chuckle.

"Why would I be? They have to share me with each other. Why should I demand their attention was solely on me?"

I didn't bother mentioning the fact something big was growing between Wilder and Owen, as well. It was no one else's business, especially since neither had done anything more than hold hands in public. Anything else they had done had either been while with me… or I wasn't aware of it and they were doing it behind locked doors.

Damn it. Just the thought of the two fooling around in secret warmed my body. But that was far better than the anxiety jitters. Perhaps instead of simply snuggling with my pack tonight I would get lost in their touch to distract me from what my head and heart were trying to convince me of.

"Either way, you've got a whole team on your side. We won't let anything happen. I can promise you those boys are out there discussing security details."

"I'm not going to stop working if I'm not fired," I said. Although I couldn't help but wonder how the other staff would feel about me walking back through the door or whether any of the customers who'd been there had gotten a good enough look at my face when all hell had broken loose.

Would they protest my presence while they were dining? Or had I succeeded in losing the restaurant business?

"Listen," Sophie said, turning so one her knees was bent on the couch and she could face me. "You're not fired, but if you're not comfortable going back there just say the word. I'll find you something else. I have plenty other jobs that I think would be a good fit. Especially with all the good things your manager and coworkers had to say about you."

That surprised me. I really only spoke with Becca when it came to anything more than asking if I'd carry something to or from a table for them. No one was rude to me, but I wouldn't exactly say I'd made any friends.

Until the pack, I'd never truly known how it felt to be loved or cared about for anything more than my designation. And those people didn't care about *me*, only what I could bring them.

"He's not going to stop," I blurted after a few moments of silence.

"Who's not going to stop what?" Joy asked.

"Clay's brother. He *will* hunt me down. And if I don't go with him, he *will* hurt my pack."

Sophie huffed out a laugh. "Trust me when I say there's no way in hell any single member of your pack – or either of ours – will allow anyone to touch you," she said, gesturing to herself and Joy. "And as far as them coming for your alphas and beta, they don't exactly seem as though they're weaklings. They can take care of themselves. And Wilder is one of the best trained guards I've ever met. Kai and Beau pointed out the various sensors and cameras on your property, so not like anyone can sneak up on you while you're sleeping or whatever."

"But they can easily show up while I'm at work. And Wilder is a bad ass–"

"As are you–" Joy said with a smile.

"But even he can't take on multiple assailants at once without opening fire in public. Pretty sure that kind of thing would be looked down on by the police and the public in general. The last thing I would ever want to do is endanger your business."

Sophie waved my comment away. "Let me worry about my

company. You worry about staying safe while we find a way to get this asshole either locked up or forced to keep his distance. I'm not sure a restraining order would do much of anything since it's just a piece of paper, but it's a start."

"Which means I'll have to go to court and see him and his pack."

"Any idea how many are in the brother's pack?" Joy asked.

My neck was getting tired from looking back and forth between them.

Standing, I moved to a chair that was positioned close enough I still felt their support but was easier on my neck when we were all three talking.

"I never met Callum. I wouldn't have even known Clay had a twin had Callum not shown up today." I shivered. "It was surreal. Like…like Clay had come back to life to haunt me. Or like the past year and a half had been a dream or hallucination I'd conjured in my mind." I was struggling to force my voice through my closing throat as the anxiety came creeping back in and my fingertips and toes grew numb.

"Maeve," Sophie said, reaching forward and placing a gentle hand on my knee. "Breathe, honey. What can I do?"

"What?" I asked as her voice sounded far away. I could feel the warmth of her hand, but she sounded like she was talking through a cup or like she was too far away.

I was vaguely aware of Joy standing and passing me. Moments later, arms were around me and I was lifted and set on someone's lap. A deep vibration rattled against my chest, settling my mind enough to remember to breathe.

"I've got you, baby girl. You're safe."

How many times had Owen and Beckett done this very thing through the years? I wouldn't let them near me at first. But then, I'd wake up to them holding me, purring for me when a nightmare forced a scream from my throat and the memories threatened to destroy my mind.

I was safe. I was home with my pack. I had my alphas, my beta. And I had friends.

None of these people would allow Callum or his pack to come for me. And I sure as fuck wouldn't let anyone touch a hair on any of their heads. I wasn't that same girl that was hand delivered to Callum by my family. I wasn't that same girl who'd hidden away in the nest, terrified to be anywhere near my alphas.

Joy was right – I was a bad ass. My alphas had made sure I could protect myself no matter what. Hell, I'd stabbed Leon because I'd seen him as a threat. I hadn't broken down into a blubbering mess, hadn't cried out for Wilder. I had grabbed the closest thing I could and thrust it into his side.

I hadn't killed him, but I'd only meant to keep him from reaching for me. I knew exactly where to stab or cut if I'd wanted to end his life right there at my job.

Inhaling deeply through my nose, I blew it out slowly through my mouth. Owen's arms were around me but not so tight I felt restrained. They knew I always needed an exit, especially when I spiraled. My pack knew exactly what I needed without me having to say a word. Now that I carried both alpha's marks, I needed to be sure I didn't keep the bond closed. They would have known something was off today had I not kept the damn links closed.

"I'm okay."

His lips were warm as he pressed them against my cheek. "Maybe I'm not done holding you," he said, his breath warm against my ear.

"You two are adorable," Joy said.

"Ew. Yuck," I teased, turning to wrinkle my nose at my surly alpha.

He wasn't truly surly; he just wasn't as laid back or playful as Beckett. He always acted as though it was his job to carry the load of the pack on his shoulders. Something that had always caused guilt to eat at me. There was no reason he should constantly be on edge because of his omega.

Owen huffed a soft laugh and kissed me on the tip of my nose. The motion sensors dinged. Owen pulled his phone from his pocket and checked the camera, relaxing at the pizza company logo on the side of the car slowing as it neared the house.

"Food's here," he said, gently lifting me to drop me back on the couch from a high enough distance that I bounced on the cushion. He leaned over and smiled. "I just wanted to see your boobs jiggle," he whispered against my lips before heading for the front door.

Yep. I liked the sexual distraction. I would have to remember that any time those old ghosts returned and threatened to drag me under again.

Or maybe I could do as Wilder suggested and seek help with a therapist who specialized in the kind of abuse I'd endured. I didn't relish the idea of talking to strangers, but Wilder promised it would help me like it had helped him.

That was a thought for another day.

For now, we would all eat, drink some beer, and I would tell the guys everything I could to help them form some kind of plan to keep me – and my pack – safe from Callum Soren.

CHAPTER 31

Maeve

I might have been completely against the plans the guys had come up with, but even I couldn't argue with their logic. Being as I'd had no idea that Clay had a brother, it would be far too easy for one of his pack to follow me or even attempt to snatch me away and none of us would have a clue there was a threat present.

At least my manager hadn't raised a single argument when Sophie alerted her to the possibility of three or more of her hired guards present during each of my shifts. In fact, she had sounded somewhat excited over the prospect of increased safety for her omega and even female beta employees.

This was the third day I'd been back since the incident – I refused to refer to it as the attempted murder – and not a single employee looked at me as though they were afraid. In fact, I'd received a tight ass hug from Becca on our first shift together. She'd been worried when the diners had gone crazy then she couldn't find me anywhere. She'd worried I'd been hurt or kidnapped.

I knew I was right about my feeling she would be a good addition to our pack. Just because I wasn't sexually attracted to her didn't mean she wouldn't be perfect for Wilder. Even Owen and Beckett.

If word had gotten out about what had happened, it sure hadn't hurt business. We were as busy as ever. The waitresses were zooming around the room taking and delivering orders while I dropped off drinks at tables between clearing empty plates and wiping everything down for the next diner.

Life was back to normal. As long as I ignored Wilder in one corner, Beau in another, and a very intimidating looking alpha named Andre who was apparently with ORE and not one of Sophie's hired guards. He was volunteering his time as a favor to Wilder for the help he'd given their omega from the very beginning.

"Any of those boys single?" Becca murmured to me as she passed me to the kitchen.

"All in packs." I glanced at Wilder then back at her. "But Wilder is really sweet."

"And he's your beta."

"And I have two alphas, too."

Becca stopped and frowned at me. "Are you seriously playing matchmaker with a member of your pack?"

Shrugging up my shoulders, I emptied my tub and smiled at her. Honestly…I was concerned all the guys' efforts would fail. They might lose me. If Becca were part of the pack, they would still have someone to hold, someone they could care for, even if she wasn't an omega.

If my alphas or beta knew I was mentally replacing myself in their lives, they would throw a fit. Hell, it might very well be the first time one of them bent me over their knees and blistered my ass.

Couldn't blame them. If I caught wind that a single one of them contemplated sacrificing themselves for me, I would punch them right in the throat. Bull shit. I'd junk punch them and feel zero remorse.

Forcing a laugh, I shook my head. "I mean, we're not exactly the jealous types. And the two of you are into each other. Want me to give him your number?"

Her light brown skin blushed a pretty pink a second before she raised her hands and covered her face.

"Don't you dare," she whispered, peeking at me through a gap in her fingers. "Am I blushing? My face is so hot."

"You are absolutely blushing," I said, giggling as I stepped away to check for trash or any empty plates.

There were only about fifteen minutes of my shift left, but I wanted to make sure I was earning every penny I made. Especially since my manager had been unbelievably understanding over what had happened.

"Hey Sasha? Anything else you want me to do before I clock out? I feel like I'm milking the clock."

My boss turned a confused frown on me. "I'm pretty sure you don't know the real definition of that. Did you even take a break today?"

I shrugged up my shoulders. "No. But we were busy."

"Girl. Go home."

"Want me to at least take the trash out first?"

Sasha thew her head back and laughed loudly. "Not a chance. Unless you want those big alphas following right behind you. We've got it. See you Tuesday."

I was off this weekend. And Sophie and Joy had invited themselves and their packs over for a cookout. Not that I minded. It was kind of nice to have friends. *Girl*friends.

Maybe I should invite Becca.

Hell. Why not? Even if she and Wilder did nothing more than flirt when they were at the restaurant, it couldn't hurt to have another friend.

"Hey," I said as I gathered my belongings. "We're having some people over for a cookout. Wanna come?" I asked her as she typed in an order.

Her finger stilled over the button and she turned a look on me. "I swear, girl, if this is some attempt to get Wilder and me–"

"No," I said, waving both hands as another giggle built in my chest. "That's not what this is. I mean, if something happens...whatever.

Cool. But two of my friends are coming over with their packs. And, um…they're my first two friends. I just thought…you know. We get along…"

She threw an arm over my shoulder. "Aw! You love me! You want me as your friend."

"I'm blushing now, aren't I?"

"Paybacks are a bitch. Text me the address." She grabbed my phone and entered her number before handing it back. "Send me the time and if you want me to bring anything. Although, my family usually just asks me to bring plates and cups. I think that's their nice way of saying I can't cook." Her nose wrinkled and made me chuckle again.

"The guys are cooking. According to Sophie, we're letting them do the work while we relax for once." Not that I ever cooked for my pack. I sucked at it, lost my patience, and usually ended up burning or over salting something.

Waving over my shoulder, I clocked out and found Wilder waiting for me. The other guys were waiting by the door, their attention bouncing everywhere, scouring the parking lot, watching the people in the restaurant, even paying attention to the cars coming and going.

"Ready?" he asked.

I knew all three of them were packing firearms, but they were all concealed under their clothing. I was sure if they'd been given a choice, they would have sat there with rifles resting in their laps. I figured it was a pretty damn good compromise.

"Yep. Oh, and I invited Becca over Saturday," I said as nonchalantly as I could.

And yep, my sexy beta looked interested.

"Let us go first," Beau said.

"Yep. I was already given the lecture by you guys, my pack, Kai, and even Sophie."

As much as I wanted to remind everyone I was trained in so many forms of self-defense and various weapons, I wasn't currently carrying anything more than a small bag that held my forged ID and my brand new debit card, along with a few things like lip balm and scent blockers.

Until ORE or even the local police were able to locate Callum and we could put some kind of permanent security in place, I would simply have to get used to having a shadow at all times.

At least one of my shadows happened to hold my heart in his hands.

I nearly stumbled over my own feet at the realization of how much I actually loved Wilder. I had known him just over a month, but already, he was as embedded in my very being as my alphas.

Beckett, Owen, and Wilder...they were my life. They'd given me a life. They'd given me peace and helped me find my own way in the world, even if I happened to require a guard. But I wasn't the first nor would I be the last omega who required on duty security while in public.

They were my life, and I'd started wondering if it wouldn't be better to simply walk right up to Callum and let him take me to avoid any risk to my pack.

But they would never let me go without a fight. I knew that just like I knew the fucking sky was blue. My pack, my alphas and beta... the three greatest loves of my life would never stand by and allow some piece of shit hurt me the way Clay had.

No matter how many times I went back and forth in my head, there was no way I could ever do anything to hurt them. And that included offering myself on a silver platter. They would come looking for me. And if Clay's twin was half as disgusting as he was, there was a chance Callum and his pack would be waiting for them. They could kill one or all of my mates.

Nope. Having an armed guard until further notice was definitely a better option.

"Should we stop by the store on our way home?" I asked.

A short tap of the horn sounded behind us as Beau and Andre turned onto another road and headed back to ORE headquarters for Andre's vehicle.

"For what?" Wilder asked, glancing at me.

There was the slightest hint of a smile on his beautiful face. Even after everything that had happened, even after witnessing my complete and total meltdown, he still looked relaxed and content. Not once had he brought up my catatonic state nor had he looked at me as though he saw me differently.

Then again, the day we'd first locked eyes I'd taken an alpha down with a well-aimed kick and punch. The second time, I'd set off a concussion grenade and caused mass panic. I supposed he, of all people, would be far less surprised by my antics since it wasn't like he'd ever known me as a mentally healthy woman.

"We could. We've got two days, though," he said with a grin. "Or did you just want some more private time with me?" He winked in my direction, and I rolled my eyes.

I was pretty sure my matching grin let him know I was far from irritated by his incessant flirting.

"If I wanted private time with you, I would just wait until we got back home, drag you into my bedroom, and lock the door."

"Promises, promises," he said.

He glanced in the rearview mirror a second before clicking on the blinker to the highway then tensed. "Shit," he bit out.

"What?"

I looked into his face to find him splitting his attention between the road ahead of him and the mirror.

Turning in my seat, I strained against the seatbelt to get a glimpse of what had him turning on his phone and dialing a number.

"Yeah," Andre's gruff voice filled the cab.

"Incoming. Company on my ass. I'm going to need backup," he said, my flirty beta gone, and, in his place, my sexy bodyguard appeared.

"Six minutes out," Andre said as the sound of an engine roaring filled my ears.

The SUV behind us was getting closer entirely too quickly. Wilder's foot was pressed to the floorboard, but his truck apparently couldn't outrun whoever the hell was chasing us.

I wasn't sure who ended the call first, but there were no longer sounds from the other guys coming from the speakers.

My eyes widened as the SUV darted forward. They were going to hit us.

"Turn around. Sit back against your seat, keep your feet on the floor," Wilder ordered.

I obeyed without a second thought. If anyone knew anything about this kind of shit, it would be my warrior beta.

It took every ounce of control to refrain from tensing for impact. That would only hurt me worse when my muscles were strained.

But I did squeeze my eyes shut and opened the bond to my alphas, sending every bit of love I felt for them down the threads. I had no doubt who was behind us. And if they either took me away or killed me today, I didn't want either of my original heroes to ever doubt what they meant to me.

I felt their panic light up our bond. And as much as I wanted to slam the connection closed, I continued to push my feelings for them through, over and over letting them feel how important they were to me, letting them know how grateful I was for them, for the day they found me, for their patience.

While waiting for the SUV to slam into the bumper of the car, a scream tore from my throat when something slammed into us from the rear driver's side.

My lids flew up and I watched as the world spun around us. No. *We* were spinning. They'd hit the fender and sent us into a three-sixty spin, the tires squealing as they failed to make purchase with the asphalt.

"Fuck!" Wilder yelled as we stopped.

Gunfire popped and glass shattered. "Seatbelt off. Get your ass on the floorboard, head down, and stay there!" he bellowed as bullets whizzed through the windshield.

That had to mean we'd come to a stop facing the wrong direction. Not just because we were no longer facing the way home, but now we were directly in the line of fire.

Why the hell were they shooting at us? If the end goal was to take me as some kind of slave as retribution for my killing Clay, what good would I do them if I was dead?

Perhaps they figured taking my life would be as good a payment. And, honestly, I would much rather be dead than go through even a minute of what I'd gone through before.

Clapping my hands over my ears, I watched as Wilder grabbed a rifle from the backseat and shoved his door open, taking aim and firing.

"Give me a fucking gun!" I yelled over all the noise.

But he didn't so much as glance in my direction, his sole focus on the enemy firing nonstop rounds at us.

Even with my hands covering my ears, the shots hitting the car and glass sounded like explosions and the truck shook with each hit.

Stay behind the engine. That was what my alphas had always told me if I were to ever find myself in a live shooter situation, to find a vehicle and stay behind the engine. That was the safest place. As long as no one was able to make their way around to either side, I should be safe until the cavalry arrived.

Six minutes. Could we survive for six fucking minutes? I couldn't tell how many shooters were firing at us, but there were definitely more than one. And only Wilder.

With my head low, I looked around the cab in hopes of finding the handgun he kept hidden under his shirt when we were in public. Nowhere to be found. And I sure as hell wasn't brave enough to crawl from my spot to pat him down.

But I hated sitting here with no way to protect myself. This was exactly why I'd begged to carry my own gun, even if I kept it in my purse. We didn't have to tell Sasha or my coworkers I was carrying – I would have kept the damn thing concealed.

All I could do was watch Wilder, his eyes focused on the enemy ahead of his, his jaw set in a determined line, his muscles tensed as he kept his body as hidden behind the door as possible.

The door wasn't bulletproof. And his legs were exposed from the knees down as were his head and shoulders.

There had to be something more I could do than cower on the floorboard.

Taking the chance, I reached up and grabbed Wilder's phone.

Hitting the last number he'd called, I waited for someone on the other line pick up.

"Come on!" I screamed at the rings.

"Two minutes out," Andre's gruff voice said from the speakers, barely audible over the rapid and excessive rounds being fired back and forth.

"Hurry!" I screamed. "They pitted the truck. They're shooting at us!"

"Where's Wilder?" he asked, raising his voice enough I could hear him.

"He's right…he's behind the door shooting at them. He's…NO!" Wilder jerked twice as blood exploded from his shoulder and the right side of his head. And then he went down. "He's hit! Wilder's hit!"

Scrambling over the seats, I ignored whatever Andre was saying and peered down at my beta. He wasn't moving. His eyes were closed. I thought I saw his chest still rising and falling but couldn't be sure without getting out.

Oh, fuck no. They shot my beta! And they were still firing as though trying to ensure he was dead.

Reaching down, I grabbed Wilder's rifle, having to practically pry it from his fingers, then swung the muzzle toward the shooters and began to pull the trigger over and over.

Eventually, I would run out of ammunition. Then, we were both fucked. As terrified as I was of being taken or killed, I was even more afraid that the moment I was no longer able to add cover fire, they would simply walk right over and put a bullet in Wilder's brain. From what I saw during my brief inspection of his injuries, the head wound looked somewhat superficial. Or at least it didn't look as though it had penetrated his skull or brain.

Please let him be okay. Please let him live.

If I were to drop the gun and step out with my hands up, would they ignore Wilder? I didn't want to be taken, but I had zero doubts my pack and new friends would do everything to get me back, even if they had to burn the world down around them to find me.

CHAPTER 32

<u>Owen</u>

"Fuck!" I bellowed, slamming my fist against the dash hard enough to crack the thick plastic.

"Stay calm, brother. We'll find her."

We were currently on our way to the hospital. All we knew was that Wilder had been shot and Maeve was missing by the time backup arrived on scene. The beta's truck was riddled with bullet holes.

We were given no details on Wilder's condition and that was part of what was fucking me up – too many unknowns.

The only absolute was we knew who was responsible for the attack. We just had no clue where they were located or where they would have taken our omega.

Or if she was even still alive.

My heart ached. Beckett and I had felt the moment she'd thrown the bond wide open. We'd sensed her panic, but we'd also sensed a rush of love. If had felt far too much like a goodbye.

"Do you feel her at all?" I asked, speaking through clenched teeth as the urge to either cry or punch something again warred with each other.

"Nothing. But that's not exactly abnormal."

Even the usual lighthearted giant of an alpha was subdued, quiet. I should have marked Wilder, too. At least then, we would have felt him through the bond, would have known whether he was conscious.

Or dead.

No. Kai would have told us if our beta had been killed.

Currently, the head Omega Change guard was meeting with ORE and the local police to form a search party. I had no doubt Joy's pack would help, as would Wilder's buddy's pack. We didn't get details, but apparently, Wilder had helped save and protect Andre's omega in the beginning and had stayed friends with the pack. And all four of the alphas were still members of ORE.

While Beckett and I were more than adept with firearms, we didn't have the access to the databases like ORE and the police.

All we could do was sit on our fucking hands and wait. But the moment her location was found, I would demand I be in the frontline. I would personally put a bullet in the head of anyone who took part of injuring our beta and abducting our beautiful omega.

They were both ours. They were mine. And I sure as fuck wouldn't sit by and allow any fucker who touched what was mine go unpunished.

The trip to the hospital felt like it took hours when it was no more than thirty or thirty-five minutes. Beckett dropped me off at the door and tossed the keys to the valet, jogging to catch up with me as I ran to the front desk to find out where Wilder was located.

"Wilder Bratton is in the ICU. Room twelve," the older woman behind the squat desk told us.

She glanced up, down, then did a double take, recoiling slightly at the look on our faces.

I didn't bother smiling at her or doing anything to put her at ease, just sprinted past her toward the elevators to the third floor.

"The ICU?" I growled out.

If he'd merely been hit in the shoulder, I could understand surgery.

But he would have been put in a regular room for monitoring. And no matter how hard I tried to keep all the worst-case scenarios out of my head on the way up, I failed miserably.

At this hour, there weren't many people milling around in the halls, no visitors checking on their loved ones. I didn't slow my stride, even when someone called after me that visiting hours were over. They could kiss my ass if they thought for one second they would keep me from my beta.

Why the fuck hadn't I told him how I felt about him? Why the hell had I held myself back every time I wanted to pull him into my arms, every time I wanted to taste his lips, every time I wanted to make love to him?

My feet skid to a stop at the entry of his room. He hadn't been simply shot in the shoulder. While there was obvious bandaging across his upper torso as though he'd taken a hit somewhere around there, there was also a thick bandage wrapped around his head.

An oxygen tube was up his nose, another that I had no idea of its purpose was in his mouth and presumably down his throat. A sucking, whooshing noise came from a machine to his right.

"No," I barely pushed out as I made my way on rubbery legs to his side.

That machine was breathing for him. He'd been shot multiple times, one of those times in the head.

Wilder was…

My beautiful beta was on fucking life support.

Beckett moved around me to the other side, careful not to jostle any of the dozen wires and cords.

"What the fuck happened?" he growled out as though Wilder could sit up and answer him.

He reached down and hit the call button, turning toward the door and waiting until a small beta nurse stepped through.

"What the fuck happened?" he repeated the question to her.

The woman's voice sounded far away, as though hearing her in a dream, as she rattled off the injuries, the surgeries, and his prognosis.

I heard her say fifty/fifty. She was giving my beta a fifty percent chance of survival. And I couldn't accept that.

Soft steps heralded the nurse's departure, leaving only Beckett and me with Wilder and that fucking whooshing sound of the respirator keeping him alive.

I needed to break something. I needed to destroy something.

I needed to punish someone.

I needed my fucking omega.

Tears burned the backs of my eyes, but I refused to let them escape. Crying wouldn't help Wilder, and it wouldn't help find Maeve.

Fuck. What was happening to her? What were they doing to her? And was there a chance we could help her through this all over again?

The last question was an easy answer – our girl was strong and would bounce back. But I would demand she do as Wilder suggested and find a professional to help her through it this time.

Not that we wouldn't be there for her as much or as little as she needed. I would hold her and purr for her every moment we were together if it brought her even the slightest comfort and peace.

We couldn't just stay here and stare at Wilder in hopes he would open his eyes. Even if he woke up right now, he had a long road ahead of him. Brain injuries were no joke.

Wait… "What did the nurse say? Any brain damage?"

"You were standing right there," Beckett said, his eyes on Wilder.

"I wasn't listening."

"Fifty percent chance of survival. No brain damage, but he lost a shit load of blood and suffered a skull fracture from the round that hit him. If he wakes up–"

"*When*, asshole," I said, cutting him off and refusing to believe there was any other possibility.

"When he wakes up, he could possibly require another surgery on his shoulder and will require a butt load of physical therapy if he wants to hold a rifle again."

My fingers curled into fists as rage and fear burned my stomach and made a red hue color my vision.

Turning on my heel, I stormed from the room, down the hall, and shoved the doors of the department open with more force than was necessary, startling three nurses who were heading my way.

"Sorry," I muttered, barely brushing a glance in their direction.

Heavy footfalls rushed behind me until Beckett's long legs were keeping pace with me.

"Where the fuck are you going?" he asked.

"We can't sit here and do nothing."

"Kai and the others are looking for her."

"And what? We're supposed to stand over Wilder's bed and pray he opens his eyes? We're not doing either of them any good if we sit here and feel sorry for ourselves. We can fucking help. There has to be something we can do to find our omega. It was our responsibility to protect her and we failed."

We failed them both. Wilder wasn't some weak beta. He was a trained soldier. But a pack protects each other. And two of our pack-mates were either hurt or missing.

Anyone who might have been in the hall as we stormed forward quickly moved, their eyes wide as they took us in. Although they could have simply been moving out of Beckett's way, fearing his giant ass would knock them over.

Beckett handed a ticket to the valet; we stood silently side by side, waiting for the vehicle to finally stop in front of us. I had no idea where to go, or where we would start. But there had to be something we could do, some way we could help find our omega.

Clay. Maeve's former alpha, rather her former captor, owned various properties before his death. I had no idea whether his assets had been liquidated or his properties had been sold, but that might be a starting point. The chances of his twin brother simply taking her to what would have been the first place I would look was slim, but I had to keep my mind busy or I would end up losing my shit and beating the piss out of the first person to cross me.

"Shit," I muttered, shoving my hand in both back pockets. "I think I left my phone at home."

Beckett pulled his from the holder on the dash and passed it over. "Hope you have the numbers memorized."

I didn't need to. We both had Kai's number in our phones since our omega was working for his mate's company.

"How is he?" Kai said as a greeting.

"On fucking life support. They're giving him a fifty percent chance of survival." I had to clear my throat when my voice broke on the last word. It took two more tries to get the rest out. "Head injury, but no brain damage. If…when he wakes up, there will be a possibility of another surgery on his shoulder to repair any damage and a long road of physical therapy if he wants to continue acting as a guard of any form."

"Fuck," Kai muttered. "Where are you now?"

"Heading home. I need to do some digging. The fucker who held her when we found her owned multiple properties. I want to see if any of them are either still in his name or were transferred to his brother."

"Good fucking thinking. My contacts at ORE tried to ping her cell but it was left in the truck. She wasn't able to take it with her."

Instead of cursing or punching the dash again, I nodded even though I knew Kai couldn't see me.

"Anything else?" Beckett asked.

"We've got several sets of eyes scouring stoplight cameras in hopes of catching a glimpse of a heavily damaged SUV. That's all Andre and Beau were able to tell us. They saw a black SUV speeding away."

"Why the fuck didn't they give chase?" I said far too loudly as my anger began to boil over.

Either Kai was used to dealing with emotional packs or had the patience of a fucking saint because he kept his voice level. "Your beta was bleeding out in the middle of the street. They knew we would find a way to track Maeve. They needed to make sure they got Wilder medical treatment. Triage, brother."

"Any of the fuckers left behind?" Beckett asked.

I frowned at him, trying to make his words make sense.

"Wilder took out two. They were DOA and taken away in a bus. But by the number of bullet holes in the truck, he was far outnumbered." Kai went silent a few moments. "I'll let Andre and his pack know the update on Wilder. Contact me the moment you find anything. And feel free to come to headquarters if you go crazy in the house without them."

And then he ended the call.

Crazy in the house without them. Beckett and I were heading to our pack house without two of our mates. If we didn't get them back…if Wilder and Maeve died…

A quick flash of the house burning to the ground flashed through my mind before I had a chance to push it away. But there would be no way I could ever stay in that house again if I didn't have my mates, if their scents gradually faded until every hint of their presence vanished forever.

CHAPTER 33

<u>Maeve</u>

Turning my head to the side, I spit blood out of my mouth then returned my glare to the asshole in front of me, never relaxing my stance.

"You really think you're a tough little thing," one of Callum's pack-mates said. Fuck. What was his name? Aaron? Eric?

Didn't matter. I'd seen the two dead bodies lying on the ground when I'd run out of ammo and they'd dragged me away from the truck and Wilder.

Wilder. My heart squeezed painfully in my chest, but I had to force any fear or sorrow away. He had to survive. He had to. There was no other option. Because I would get out of here, whether on my own or with the help of my pack and our friends.

"Fucked you up pretty badly," I taunted.

Aaron or Eric or whoever he was had an obviously broken nose and a bruise was swelling on his right cheek. I'd attempted to kick him in the nuts, but he'd successfully blocked my leg and punched me in the mouth. I was pretty sure I had at least two loose teeth, but I would deal with that later.

I hadn't noticed until I'd been restrained in the backseat of their SUV that I'd received several cuts from the broken windows and windshield when these assholes had been shooting at me. They all still oozed blood, but nothing that would require stitches. Although I would probably end up with a few scars to add to those on my back.

If I survived.

That was my sole purpose at the moment. Keep these guys from raping me and staying alive.

Callum chuckled darkly and shook his head. "My brother was right about you. You're going to be so much fun to break."

He pushed from the wall and stalked toward me as though I was prey. Did he expect me to cower? To beg for mercy?

He'd be waiting a while.

When he was within touching distance of me, I lifted my fists and prepared to block any blow he threw my way. So far, I'd fared pretty well against his packmate. But Callum was as big as his twin, standing a couple inches above six feet and heavily muscled. His arms and chest strained against his shirt as though he bought the wrong size or wanted to show off his body.

Nothing like my guys. Owen and Beckett were both big, both broad and strong and muscular. But they didn't need to put on a show to earn respect; they silently earned it.

By now, they would be using whatever systems they could to track me. They would have called our friends to tap into the resources used by ORE and the police. They would find me.

Keep their dicks away and stay alive. I had been repeating the same mantra since the moment the rifle had clicked with an empty magazine.

Focusing on my periphery while keeping my attention on his eyes, I watched for the slightest twitch of his muscles to predict his moves. I could block just about anything, but that didn't mean I could out muscle him. One good hit and I would be at their mercy.

Not that I wouldn't continue fighting. He could kiss my ass if he thought I would lie on the ground and cry. I wouldn't ball into the fetal position, wouldn't beg him to stop. I would find any weak spot to try to regain the upper hand.

I supposed since this was my first go around with Callum, I would technically be finding and keeping the upper hand.

He darted forward and I instantly tensed. But the bastard didn't reach for me or swing a fist, just laughed and shook his head.

"Yeah. You're real tough," he said.

Slowly, he began to circle around me, but I couldn't turn fully to follow him, not with his buddy still standing there. It would be too easy for one of them to grab me from behind.

So, instead, I made sure I moved so they were each on either side of me, staring straight ahead to keep them right on the edges of my sight.

My plan had sounded great. It had worked wonders when I'd sparred with Beckett and Owen until they decided it was too risky and they feared actually injuring me.

"It's like a cat playing with a mouse," Callum said, earning a laugh from his buddy.

"Only two of you left, huh? And you big bad alphas think you can tame me? Your dumbass brother already tried that. Spoiler alert – it didn't work."

A muscle ticked in Callum's jaw as he ground his teeth. "Two of us here. You still have a few more of your new packmates to meet. Don't worry – after we're done, not only will you be begging for more, but you'll forget all about those dipshits who thought they could keep you safe."

Shit. More? How many more? And I really didn't like the subtle meaning behind his threats. If he or any of the others thought for one second I would lie there and spread my legs, they had a big ol' surprise coming. I would use my teeth, my hands, anything I could to rip off any and every appendage they tried to force on me.

Aaron – I would just go with that name instead of thinking of him as asshole number two – moved on my left. I flicked my eyes in that direction, keeping him in my line of sight.

Which, of course, was a big fucking mistake.

Something hit me in the back of the head and knocked me off balance. I was almost running to keep on my feet and slammed my hands against a desk to keep from falling over. I didn't go down, but now my thoughts were sluggish, and my vision had black dots floating on the edges.

Shit.

Stay alive. Stay conscious. I was honestly terrified of what might happen if I was knocked out. Would they take the opportunity to mark me when I couldn't fight back? Would they use my body to slake their disgusting needs?

"Aw. What's wrong? Not as tough as you thought?" Callum said with another of those stupid chuckles.

"Do you realize how much you sound like a teen movie bully?" I said, rolling my neck on my shoulders as though that would shake my brain back into working a little faster.

"Bitch," Callum said, stalking toward me.

It looked as though he was done toying with me.

I swung the moment he was close enough, hoping making the first move would be enough to catch him off guard.

I wasn't nearly fast enough.

He threw up an arm, blocking my punch so my knuckles barely grazed the side of his head, his other arm shooting out, hand wrapping around my throat and squeezing tight enough to cut off my air supply.

As hard as I tried to keep my wits, my hands and arms flailed as I tried to pry his hand away from my throat. My feet left the ground. Shit. This asshole was literally holding me in the air by nothing more than my throat, and the longer we stayed like this, the spottier my vision grew and the fuzzier my brain. My thoughts were coming slower, that analytical part of my brain that helped me plan for these kinds of situations was all but silent.

No matter how hard I fought it, panic began to settle in as my heartbeat began to slow.

If he didn't release me, I would die within minutes.

Before I could pass out, he opened his hands and let me fall to the ground like a sack of potatoes.

When I should have been jumping back to my feet and preparing to fight, my body instead focused on drawing oxygen back into my deprived lungs. He'd squeezed hard enough that my neck, my esophagus ached. Even my knees hurt from hitting the ground from a couple feet up.

I had to believe my pack would find me before it was too late. I just needed to buy them some time, hold Callum and his asshole packmates off until the cavalry arrived.

They had to. They had to find me. I would do everything in my power to escape, but already I was outmuscled. My head still throbbed from the sucker punch...or hit. I wasn't sure whether Callum had used his fist or something else.

Searing pain shot through my scalp as Callum wrapped his hand in my hair and yanked me to my feet.

Oh, hell no.

Kicking as hard as I could, I smiled with satisfaction when I made contact with his knee and he dropped nearly as hard as I had with a deep grunt of pain. Hopefully, I broke something.

While he rocked on the ground cradling his knee and his buddy was shocked into doing nothing more than staring with his mouth hanging open, I decided this was as good an opportunity as any.

Ignoring every ounce of pain zipping through my nerve endings, I sprinted for the door of the office and yanked it open. The place was big, but there would be more than one exit. All I had to do was find one door that led outside and I would run as hard and fast as I could while screaming at the top of my lungs in hopes of garnering attention from the neighbors. The last thing those fuckers would want was an audience.

Solid plan. And, honestly, the only thing I could come up with without a weapon that could help me take down multiple attackers.

The hallway veered off into three directions. Artwork lined the walls, but I couldn't have told you what they depicted – I had zero intention of slowing down to admire shit with heavy steps thundering behind me as one of the alphas gave chase.

There were so many doors. As I turned a corner, grabbing the edge to keep from losing my balance, I spotted a living room full of windows. I was in the main area of the house. Main area meant front or back doors.

"Fucking bitch!" Callum roared from further back in the house. No way was he the one giving chase. I knew damn well I'd done enough damage he would be limping for a few days, maybe even weeks.

He deserved far worse than that. It appeared he wasn't only twins with Clay in looks – they were both sick, sadistic fuckers who felt as though omegas were nothing more than property, that we were to be owned and treated however they felt was acceptable.

So close. I was so close to freedom. As soon as I was able to get to a phone, I would call my pack, tell them exactly where to send the police, then I would sit in the front row during their trial to make sure they saw my face when they were sent to prison.

As my head was wrenched back so hard my feet flew out from beneath me and I hit the ground hard enough to knock the wind from my lungs…I realized I hadn't been fast enough.

CHAPTER 34

<u>Beckett</u>

Owen and I had scoured through every possible connection to Clay Soren we could find. Problem was, not everything was public. Hopefully, the members of ORE and the police had been able to find something more concrete, somewhere to start looking.

Thus far, we'd only found empty property and a few buildings and houses that had been sold on the courthouse steps when he stopped making payments. Because, you know, he was dead.

Since there was no body to be found – thanks to Owen and me – it had taken a while before the powers that be could actually do anything. But when any communication went unanswered…

Problem was, there were still other places that were listed under his name, but we couldn't dig any deeper to discover whether or not they had been included in the public sale, nor did those that were sold show the names of who had bought it. As far as we knew, his twin could have been the one to step up and take over.

"Can we tap into camera feeds? There's got to be a way to hack into that shit," I suggested, leaning back and staring at my laptop as frustration built, warring with the fear over both our omega and the fact the hospital hadn't given our beta a very good prognosis.

It had been obvious from the first moment that Owen had feelings for Wilder and vice versa. But neither had acted on it any further than a little necking when we were tending to Maeve during her heat. Fucking fools.

This moment in time was exactly why I tried to make sure those I loved knew it every time we talked. There might not be another chance to tell them. If we lost Wilder, Owen would live the rest of his life with the realization he'd never told the beta how deeply he felt for him.

And if we all lost Maeve...

Nope. Wasn't going to even entertain that fucking thought. I had to keep my wits and I couldn't do that if I fell apart.

Especially since Owen had already broken a few glasses, cleared his desk twice in fits of rage, and punched a hole in our shared office wall.

"Only if we knew which cameras to hack. How the fuck are we supposed to hack into every single security camera without spending the next fucking year doing it?"

Holding up my hands, I inhaled deeply and mentally counted to ten rather than lunge to my feet and toss him across the room. I felt the same fucking fear he did; that didn't mean we should take this shit out on each other. And it sure as hell wouldn't help us find her any faster.

"I'm just brainstorming, asshole."

Owen stopped pacing and dropped heavily into the chair behind his desk, his head dropping back. He stared up at the ceiling and, even from where I sat, I could see the tears shimmering. I'd already cried it out in the bathroom. Not something I would ever admit to him or anyone else, though.

I still couldn't believe they were able to get to her, that they had been able to track her without Wilder and our friends noting anything out of the ordinary.

But being as we had no clue how many people were in this Callum asshole's pack nor what any of them looked like, they could have been sitting right in the diner, looking Maeve in the eye as she passed, and no one would have been any wiser.

Fucking Wilder. If he didn't make it, Maeve would blame herself. She would spiral to a point neither Owen nor I would be able to help her.

If he did survive, he would blame himself for her being taken.

It was neither of their faults. The fault laid solely on Callum and his fuckwad buddies. And, honestly, the fault laid with every single alpha who was fighting against omegas living lives like everyone else, fighting against their freedom, against them being able to do something as simple as go to work without being harassed.

An image of Maeve kicking ass while she was being held flashed through my mind and made my lips twitch. She wouldn't allow herself to be some damsel in distress. Even as petite as she was, both of us had made sure she could fight.

But how long could she possibly hold out? Whether she could fight or not, she was one woman against an unknown number of alphas who would be double her size.

When my phone rang, I nearly tossed it across the room in my fumbling attempt to answer it.

"Speaker," Owen barked, pushing to his feet to stand inches from me.

"Kai?"

"We got her," he said without preamble. "We know where she's being held."

"What...how...fuck it. I don't care how. Where? We want to be there," Owen said, his eyes wide, a vein bulging in his forehead.

"We're on our way now." The two of us were already on our feet and running for the SUV as he rambled off an address.

"Any idea of how many we're coming up against?"

"Eleven. Or there *were* eleven. After Wilder, there could be nine alphas in residence," Kai said. The sound of an engine was loud over the line as though whoever was driving had their gas pedal pressed all the way to the floor.

Glancing at Owen, I turned and ran back into my room, grabbing my personal firearm and a rifle. Just because there would be armed guards didn't mean I wanted to go into an unknown situation with nothing but my dick in my hand.

Owen was in the driver's seat. I would rather have driven with his current state of mind, but he was already pulling out of the garage as I yanked the passenger door open and jumped in.

"Put the address in the GPS," he ordered.

"We're on our way. We'll meet you there," I said.

"I'm sure we'll beat you. Do not rush in there without back up if you happen to get there first."

Owen snorted, but I agreed and ended the call.

There was no way anyone would be able to hold Owen back from bursting through the door to where Maeve was being held, but we wouldn't be a lick of good to our omega if we were mowed down by a barrage of bullets by nine fucking alphas. *If* they were all there.

Nine alphas and our tiny omega. If any of them touched her...

She had been beat and tortured and starved for almost four years because she fought Clay any time he tried to touch her, any time he tried to get between her legs.

What was the chance she could fight nine fucking grown men?

Yep. A lot of mother fuckers would die today, starting with Callum Soren.

She'd stabbed someone at the restaurant. Was he part of this new pack? Had he been behind her abduction? And would he punish her for what she'd done?

Too many fucking questions and I was starting to feel entirely too unhinged. My alpha had never been overly possessive, but right now, I felt a feral sensation creeping into my brain until I had a hard time on focusing on anything but vengeance.

Then, once I had Maeve in my arms, I wouldn't let her out of my sight for days...fuck, maybe even weeks.

Glancing at the map on the screen attached to the dash, I dropped my head back against the seat. Seven minutes out.

"Do you have anything else in here?" I asked, popping the magazine of my sidearm to check the number of bullets before slamming it back into place and pulling the slide to chamber a round.

"Just my Glock. In the glove compartment," Owen answered.

I pulled it free and did the same routine, checking to ensure there were plenty of rounds for what could transpire when we arrived at the address Kai had sent us. I didn't bother with the rifle; I kept that thing locked and loaded at all times, my last line of defense should anyone get past the cameras, alarms, and into our house in an attempt to harm any of my packmates.

Three minutes out.

I would have yelled at Owen to drive faster, but he was already exceeding a hundred miles an hour. If we lost control and wrecked, we would be no good to Maeve *or* Wilder.

Several SUVs and trucks came into view, all congregated near the address where the GPS indicated.

Kai stepped in front of our vehicle and held up a hand, his rifle hanging from the strap around his neck.

The men standing at ready were armed for bear, looks of rage and determination on their faces. I recognized a few of them, but the rest were complete strangers. They were here for my omega. They were here for Maeve.

And I was more grateful for their presence than I could ever put into words.

Owen didn't bother killing the engine before throwing open his door and rushing to where Kai waited. I was right on his heels.

"Surveillance hasn't caught sight of her, but there have been a few alphas coming and going. Current count is six. But I sent some men out to track down the others. Any stragglers could send someone else seeking revenge on your mate." Kai was speaking like the leader he was, but the muscle jumping in his cheek belied the calm demeanor.

"What are we waiting for? Let's get in there and get Maeve!" Owen said.

I tucked my sidearm into the back of my pants and readied my rifle. No fucking way would I wait out here while this group when inside. I was going for my girl. And I knew damn well Owen wouldn't wait on the sidelines, either.

Kai opened his mouth but froze when static preceded a voice over the walkie talkie on his hip.

"Control. We have a commotion," a disjointed male voice said.

"Define commotion."

"Looks like the omega is combatting one…negative – two males. Repeat – omega is combatting two males."

"Fuck," Owen growled out, and began to jog in the direction of the house.

No one tried to stop him. Bodies jumped out of my way as I barreled my giant ass through, following on his heels. All Owen had was his Glock. I had two weapons.

But we had over a dozen heavily armed guards currently sprinting behind us, ready to join the fight.

She was fighting. Because they'd attacked her? Because they'd tried to touch her? Because she'd tried to escape?

I had to push any and all thoughts and speculations from my mind and keep the mission in focus. Get inside, fuck up or kill those who'd been a part of taking her away from us, then take my bad ass omega home.

And maybe lock her up for the next year no matter how loudly she protested or how much she fought me on it. I couldn't stand of another asshole taking her, hurting her, or, worse, killing her.

The house came into view. There were no outer lights to herald our arrival, but there were several shining from inside, highlighting rooms not covered by curtains.

And yep, our girl was definitely fighting. I couldn't see her face or body in detail from my position, but I saw her holding her own against two alphas close to Owen's size.

When she threw a punch and one of them actually rocked backward, a surge of pride filled my chest.

That moment lasted less than a second when I watched in what felt like slow motion as she was taken down with a hit from behind. One of the cowards used something, something the size of a vase or decorative statue, and smacked the back of her skull.

Probably a good idea since she looked as though she was doing quite a bit of damage.

Kai sprinted past us and used his shoulder as a battering ram, crashing through the front door and making an entrance for the rest of us.

We filed in, our guns raised, and converged on the cocksuckers who'd taken Maeve, who'd assaulted her.

She was on the ground, her hand was pressed to the back of her head, her eyes unfocused. Her face was swollen and bruised and there was dried blood spattering her face, neck, arms, hands, and clothes.

A red hue tinted my vision as my alpha grew feral at the sight of my omega so battered.

Every single fucker in this house would die.

CHAPTER 35

<u>Maeve</u>

Black dots danced in my vision and my ears felt like they were full of cotton. No matter how hard I willed my legs to push me back to standing, my brain wouldn't cooperate.

Noise. So much noise. Yelling. Gunshots. The scent of gunpowder and blood tickled my nose.

And then there was a familiar face right in front of me. Instinctually, I threw my hands up, prepared to fight, prepared to hold these assholes off as long as possible. I would take the beatings. Bruises and cuts would heal, regardless of any new scars I might carry later.

But if I stopped fighting and they entered my body…

I was positive that wasn't something my newly healed heart or mind would come back from.

"Baby girl, look at me," Owen said.

I was looking at him…wasn't I? Everything seemed to be spinning around me, the motion behind him like I was watching a movie in slow motion.

"Owen?" I asked. Was I hallucinating? I'd been hit in the head so many times through the years, had even suffered concussions, but I couldn't remember ever hallucinating.

"Yeah, baby girl. We're here."

I lifted my head and looked around the room. The men who'd attacked me were either dead on the floor or kneeling with their hands cuffed behind them. There were so many men in black clothes or police uniforms filling the room.

And Beckett was being held back by three men.

"Beck," I said, trying to push to my feet. No way would I sit here and let someone hurt my mate.

"He's okay. They're not hurting him," Owen said, trying to keep me on the floor.

"Stop! Leave him alone," I yelled. Or thought I yelled. Everything sounded hollow and far away.

"They're not hurting him, Maeve. Listen to me. You need to calm down so he'll calm down. He's gone feral."

Feral. *I* was feral. Beckett wasn't feral.

My stomach turned as nausea sent bile into my throat. Leaning to the side, I wretched, but nothing came up. I hadn't eaten or drank anything in hours. There was nothing for my body to dispel.

Owen's hand rubbed soothing circles on my back. Beckett was roaring something unintelligible.

"Let him loose. He needs to touch her to calm down," Owen said.

Swiping the back of my hand across my mouth, I turned as the three men stepped away from my giant alpha and winced when it looked like he would plow right into me.

But he stopped within inches, dropping to his knees, and scooping me into his arms. It hurt. His touch hurt. Then again, everything hurt.

His body was warm and vibrated with a growl laced purr as he carried me from the room, Owen's hand stroking over my head as he walked beside us.

My face burrowed into the crook of Beck's neck. I inhaled deeply, drawing his warm ink and old book smell deep into my lungs.

They'd come for me. I knew they would. They'd found me.

"Wilder?" I asked, peering over Beck's shoulder in search of my beautiful beta. He would have blended in with those clad in black.

But neither Owen nor Beckett answered me.

Memories came rushing back. The bullets spraying the SUV. Glass shattering around us.

Blood. Wilder had been hit. He'd been hit in the shoulder...and the head.

"No," I cried out, hugging Beckett's neck so tight I was sure I cut off his air supply. "He can't be dead."

"He's not dead, baby girl. As soon as you get checked out at the hospital, I promise to take you to see him."

He wasn't dead. But he'd been hurt enough that he wasn't here. And how the hell was he okay if he'd taken a bullet to the head? I thought he'd still been breathing when they'd dragged me away, but that didn't mean he wasn't brain dead or, in the least, brain damaged.

Tears filled my eyes and trailed down my cheeks, soaking Beckett's shirt.

My sweet Wilder. The man who'd shown me that I could allow myself to show love and to be loved. The man who'd helped me learn to let my alphas in.

The tears wouldn't stop, and my throat felt clogged with emotion as I tried to reel them in. My body jostled and rocked as Beck carried me down the driveway to where dozens of vehicles were parked, then scooted into the backseat with me still cradled in his arms.

Owen took the front seat and immediately put the SUV in gear, speeding away from my temporary prison.

I didn't want to see a doctor – I wanted to see my beta. I wanted to see Wilder with my own two eyes. I needed to know he was okay, that they weren't placating me, lying to me to keep me from falling apart.

As every moment of the day flooded my mind, my thoughts grew slower, my lids grew heavy, and I was struggling to stay awake.

I rocked forward and the sound of the vehicle being thrown in park made me open my eyes. But Beckett didn't climb from the backseat, even when Owen jumped from the front seat and ran off.

Lifting my head, I tried to look around, but the world still looked as though it was spinning so fast I had to cling to Beck to keep from being thrown off.

Moments later, the back door was yanked open and men and women in scrubs appeared.

"Sir? We need you to let us take her," a beta said, reaching for me.

The deepest, scariest growl I had ever heard rumbled from Beck's chest.

"He's gone feral," Owen said as explanation.

The bodies parted and Owen appeared. "Climb out, brother. We need to get her checked out. You can carry her, but we got to get her inside."

I had never seen Beckett lose his cool. My gentle giant was exactly that – gentle. He was even tempered and playful.

But when I looked up into his face, I almost didn't recognize the man snarling at our packmate as Owen tried to reach for me.

"Beckett," Owen barked. "Either let them take her or carry her inside. Our omega needs help. You're hurting her."

No, he wasn't. He was holding me tightly, but the pain singeing my nerves had nothing to do with my big alpha.

Apparently, the words were meant to snap Beckett out of his state because he finally scooted from the middle of the seat and stood with me still clutched tightly to his chest.

The nurses and doctors followed closely behind until Beck finally deposited me onto a gurney and allowed them to wheel me into a room where I could be checked over.

"This cut will need stitches," someone said.

"Signs of a concussion," the doctor said as he shone a pen light into each of my eyes and making me feel as though I was being hit in the head with a damn sledgehammer. "Order a CT," he said to someone.

My eyes were on Beck and Owen, terrified to look away as though the moment I blinked too long, they would disappear and all this would be a dream, that I would still be back in that house with those alphas taunting me and challenging me to fights. Callum didn't join, not with his shattered knee. Yep. I was pretty fucking proud of that.

The other hadn't been injured nearly as much. My energy had

quickly waned the longer I battled them, the longer I kept them from getting their hands on me.

They thought they could break me. Callum had delighted in the thought they could train me to be what they wanted out of an omega, their image of a good omega.

They were so fucking wrong. And now, most of them were dead.

Scrubs continued to fill my view as my cuts were cleaned and checked out, orders were given, an IV was inserted into the crook of my elbow.

An hour later, my impatience grew. This was all taking too long. I wanted to see Wilder. My alphas promised I could see him as soon as I got checked out. I hadn't been to radiology yet, but I knew that could very well take hours for them to finally wheel me down.

"I want to see my beta," I said when one of the nurses moved toward me with a needle. They were going to stitch me right here in the room with my alphas watching over us.

"I told you – as soon as they've taken care of you, I'll personally wheel you up to see him."

"Where is he?" I asked. "What floor? What room?"

One of the nurses glanced at Owen but returned her attention to the cut she was tending to on my scalp. I'd felt the sting of the local she'd injected into my skin, but only barely felt the tug of the needle and thread sewing me back together.

"I want to see him now!" I said, putting as much force into my words as possible.

Owen nudged a beta nurse out of the way, earning a frown from the man. "One of your tantrums isn't going to work right now," he said, his voice barely above a whisper. "You don't realize how injured you are. And your other alpha is far too close to snapping and going insane on the people around you. I'm begging you to be patient and stay calm."

This was such a change. Beckett was always the one to use his calm demeanor to bring me down while Owen barked orders at me.

But it was Owen, this time, trying to keep two of his packmates under control.

Turning to look at Beck, my heart hurt. His eyes shimmered with unshed tears, but his jaw was clenched so tightly I wouldn't be surprised if he cracked a molar...or two.

Owen stood over me, watching me, waiting for my reply or reaction. After a deep breath, I nodded. "Fine. But as soon as we're done here, I want to see Wilder," I whispered back.

"I promise."

He still hadn't told me anything more than Wilder was alive. The fact he wouldn't reveal any more details than that sent ice cold fear through my veins. But he was alive. That was the most important part. I loved him enough that I knew I would take him in whatever condition, as long as I still had him in my life.

CHAPTER 36

<u>Maeve</u>

Wilder laid on a bed, wires and tubes connected to him in various places. I was warned before we entered the room that he was on some form of life support, but the nurse alerted us that he'd been removed from the respirator and was breathing on his own.

While that little tidbit eased the fear and pain as Owen rolled my wheelchair into the room, the sight of him bandaged, eyes closed, oxygen in his nose and IV connected to the crook of his elbow made my heart hurt.

More than hurt. My heart felt like it was shattering at the sight. He'd gotten shot because of me. Not because of me, but for me. He'd endangered his life for his omega.

He had to survive. Owen warned me that the nurses and doctors had originally given him only a fifty percent chance of survival without lifelong issues.

But I refused to believe he would be anything but perfect when he woke up. And he would. He had to.

And honestly, I didn't care whether there was any permanent damage. He would always be my Wilder. He would always be one of my greatest loves. He would remain my mate, remain a member of our pack.

Swatting Owen's and Beck's hands away as I stood from the stupid wheelchair the staff demanded I use to move around the hospital, I stood and lined my body along Wilder's the best I could without jostling any equipment or hurting him in any way. I needed to be close to him, to feel his body heat, to rest my head on his chest and hear his heart beating with my own damn ears.

His chest rose and fell with each of his slow breaths, but he didn't move. Tears welled and rolled down my temple to soak into my hair and his hospital gown. Owen pulled a chair up to the other side and rested his big hand on Wilder's. Tears shimmered in his eyes, as well.

I knew why they hadn't told me how gravely he'd been injured, understood they were trying to keep me busy when Beck was so close to going feral over my abduction and assault and Wilder's nearly fatal injuries.

That didn't mean I wouldn't yell at them later.

For now, though, we needed each other.

Stretching an arm back, I waited for Beck to take my hand. I wished we were in a pack room so the three of us could be together, so we could all be in bed with Wilder.

But this wasn't a normal stay. He was literally on the verge of life and death. And all we could do was wait. Wait for him to open his eyes, to see whether he recognized his pack, to see whether we would have *our* Wilder back.

The sounds of chair legs scraping against tile came a second before I felt Beck resting his head on my hip. This was as close as we could get as a pack. For now.

No matter what the hell the doctors said, I refused to believe Wilder wouldn't heal from this. He would heal, he would be fine, he would fight to return to us like he'd helped me do after my most recent meltdown.

"I didn't shut down," I muttered against Wilder's chest.

Owen frowned at me. "What?"

Turning my eyes to his face, I gave him a ghost of a smile. "I didn't shut down after what happened. I fought. I beat some ass and fought to be with you. They didn't win."

A tear dropped from Owen's lashes to land on the sheets wrapped around our beta.

"You did good, baby girl."

AT SOME POINT, the exhaustion from the day had forced my mind and body to shut down. I welcomed the darkness when my eyes slid closed and sleep dragged me under. Luckily for everyone involved, it was a dreamless state. It would have been really fucked up if I'd woken up swinging on poor Wilder in his state.

An arm was wrapped around my shoulders, fingers toying with my hair. Blinking against the bright light of the room, I glanced at Owen to find him asleep, his head resting on the side of the bed, Wilder's left arm clutched in his.

Beckett's head was heavy on my hip and a light snore pulled from his lips.

Wait…my alphas were both asleep.

Jerking my head up, I stared wide eyed into Wilder's smiling face.

"Do you know who I am?"

"Is that a trick question?" he asked, his voice hoarse and scratchy from lack of use.

"Please," I begged as fresh tears welled in my eyes and my throat felt as though it would close with emotion. "What's my name? What's your name? Do you know them?" I said, pointing at Owen then Beckett.

"Maeve. Wilder. Owen and Beckett." His brows drew together. "Did you think I'd have amnesia?"

"You were shot in the fucking head, Wilder. They said…" I cleared my throat when my voice cracked. "They said you could have brain damage. They only gave you a fifty percent chance of surviving and said you could have issues if you did wake up."

"No brain damage. I would know your beautiful face anywhere."

He lifted his free hand to wipe away the tears.

"Do you remember what happened?"

"Well, yeah. I mean…shit's kind of fuzzy, but I remember it. I remember the shootout. I even remember you grabbing my rifle like Rambo and standing over me."

I didn't remember seeing his eyes open after he'd fallen, but for some reason, the fact he'd still been somewhat conscious at that time made me feel a touch better.

"Are you okay?" he asked, touching one of the stitched cuts along my hairline.

I made a dismissive sound. "I didn't get shot in the head. I'm fine."

"You look like you went a few rounds with Mike Tyson."

When we were all home, maybe then I would give him details of what happened while I'd waited for my pack and our friends to find me. For now, we needed a doctor to get their ass in here to make sure he really was okay, then maybe get moved to a pack room so we could be together more comfortably.

"I'm fine," I said, pulling his hand away from where he was tracing the various injuries with his fingertips.

"Wilder?" Owen's deep voice asked in a barely there whisper.

Wilder rolled his head on the pillow to smile down at our alpha. "Yeah."

Owen lunged to his feet, leaned over our beta, and slanted his lips over Wilder's. He didn't deepen the kiss, but he didn't immediately pull away, either.

"Fuck. I thought…I love you, Wilder. I should have told you that. I fucking love you," Owen said as tears coursed down his cheeks.

Wilder's hand raised to cup the side of Owen's neck. "I love you, too, alpha."

"Awww. That only took almost two months," I teased. *Of course* I had to make a joke. Otherwise, I would end up a blubbering mess after first wondering whether I would ever see Wilder's beautiful gray eyes looking into mine, then seeing the absolute love and affection in Owen's eyes.

Beckett stirred. His hand reached over my body and patted Wilder on the chest. "Welcome back, brother."

Owen snorted, but pulled back and scrubbed his tears away roughly with both hands.

"Hate to be the bearer of bad news, but they said if you woke up, you'd end up needing some more surgeries on your shoulder. And physical therapy," Beck said.

"You couldn't wait for that shit?" Owen grumbled.

Like someone flipped a switch, they'd returned to their roles of giant teddy bear and gruff alpha. The world was right again.

"Hit the button. A doctor needs to get in here and check him out so we can move to a bigger room," I said. Now that he was awake, I planned to have one of the alphas go home for a few changes of clothing so we wouldn't have to leave Wilder's side until it was time for us all to go home.

Together.

I knew it. I knew my beta wouldn't leave me. I knew he would return to us.

And Owen had finally spoken his fucking mind. Not like Beck and I couldn't tell how deeply he felt for Wilder. But both men had been so damn stubborn and, apparently, neither wanted to be the first to declare their feelings for the other.

Men.

CHAPTER 37

<u>Maeve</u>

Wilder had been moved to a pack room where the two of us were able to heal without the pressures of the outside world. While my healing took way less time, poor Wilder hadn't been given the green light to go home for over a month.

In the year since that day, he'd gone through two more reconstructive surgeries on his shoulder to repair some torn tendons and muscles. And he was more than itching to get back to work. Much to his chagrin, Kai refused to allow him to so much as don the uniform until he received a release letter directly from the doctors.

Part of me had wanted to return to the restaurant, but…I was scared. I hated admitting that, but the therapist I'd begun to see shortly after Wilder had been released said it was actually healthy to not only admit those things to myself, but to let my pack know when my anxiety was growing over any situation.

So…Wilder and I tended to have a lot of alone time, something we enjoyed thoroughly.

The alphas had returned to work when Wilder was allowed to come home, but they rushed through their jobs and then rushed back home. It was like none of us wanted to be apart any longer than necessary.

I laid on my side with Beckett wrapped around me and watched with nothing short of love blooming in my chest as Wilder and Owen made love. They hadn't wasted another minute since the moment he woke up in the ICU. I swore they told each other they loved each other any time they were in the same room.

Watching their relationship bloom had opened up this strange part in my heart, a part I wasn't aware existed. At first, I thought maybe it was the desire to add another member to our pack. But it was more than that. I had actually begun to contemplate motherhood. The concept of not only carrying one of my pack's children but being a good mother was no longer so terrifying.

Again, that realization came from the love and patience from my pack along with the gentle reassurances from my therapist. She reminded me time and time again that we did not have to follow in our parents' footsteps, that just because my parents had tossed me out like last night's dinner didn't mean I would be anything less than a loving, doting mother.

Callum was currently being held without bail and waiting to stand trial for my abduction and assault. Leon...turned out he'd simply been at the wrong place at the wrong time and let my alphas know he not only held no ill will toward me but he had no intention of filing any form of charges against me for stabbing him.

Oh, and I had even begun to enjoy all the touching and snuggling. And not just from my pack. Wilder and Becca hadn't pursued anything further, but she and I had stayed friends after I resigned from the restaurant. She often visited and I now looked forward to her warm hugs.

I still wasn't big on frilly gifts, though. That was why on the official one-year anniversary of the day Wilder and I had made love, he'd gifted me with a cat. Not that Sir Fluffy Butt Stinky Pants wasn't soft. But he definitely wasn't frilly and tended to only tolerate me.

This pack had rescued me not only from a shit situation, but from myself. They had shown me love I wasn't aware existed. They accepted me for exactly who I was and even celebrated my quirks by taking me on dates to the shooting range or back to *Plumes et Fouet* for the burlesque and drag shows. We never attended on the nights of the fetish shows. Just because I was healing didn't mean I wanted to risk another meltdown in public.

One was enough humiliation to last me a lifetime.

"I love you," Owen muttered against Wilder's lips as he pumped his hips, his hand cupping the beta's cheek before kissing him gently.

For such a burly alpha, Owen was always so sweet and gentle when he made love to either of us. It might be selfish, but I was glad I currently only had to share them with each other. I had Beck's full attention, but sometimes, I liked when all three focused fully on me, touching and teasing me to so many releases.

For so long, I had kept my men at arm's length, treated my alphas more like roommates. I might have missed out on almost two years of the greatest love I had ever known, but never again would I take for granted that, while I might not be your typical omega, I had three men who loved me with every beat of their heart.

And now...I was ready to share that love with someone else.

I would wait until Owen and Wilder finished, wait until we were one big puppy pile, and then...I planned to ask my pack if they would be willing to try for our first child together during my next heat.

IF YOU LOVED Maeve's story of discovering her inner strength, finding her beta, and building a family, I would love if you could take the time to leave a review on your favorite site.

Wait! Have you joined the party yet? Oops...I meant the newsletter! Keep up to date on releases, cover reveals, and giveaways. You can join here!